Michael Frost

Presents

Bedtime Stories

Individual Works

a Malice from This	© 2010	The Music of My Life	© 2010
The Attic	© 2010	My Angel Across the Way	© 2003
The Boogeyman Returneth	© 2002	Reflections in a Place Called Nihility	© 2010
The Brooch	© 2010	The Room Down the Hall	© 2013
Demago	© 1994	The Rose Petal	© 2010
Denouncing the Looking Glass	© 2010	Theo Waited	© 2010
Flakes, The Snowman	© 1996	Though the Heavens Fall	© 2013
The Folly of Murder	© 2009	Victor McSneed	© 1997
Forgiveness	© 2010	When Madness Calls	© 2010
Happy Springs	© 2010	Whimsy-Whimsy	© 2010
I Have What You Need	© 2007	Real Monsters	© 2010

This, and all stories within, are works of fiction. Names, characters, businesses, places, events, locales, and incidents are either the products of the author's imagination or used in a fictitious manner. Any resemblance to actual persons, living or dead, actual events or places is purely coincidental [You should be grateful].

ISBN: 978-1-959715-06-1

Library of Congress Control Number: **2022948558**

Published by **Belen Books, LLC**
St. Petersburg, FL | Winter Park, FL | Chicago, IL USA
www.BelenBooksPublishing.com

Edited by Beverly R. Waalewyn
Cover by Belen Media Group

10 9 8 7 6 5 4 3 2

Printed Worldwide

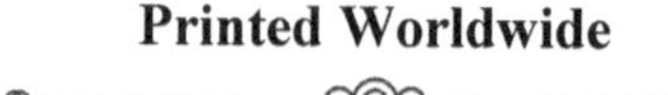

FOR MOM & DAD

"Hold onto the reins of youth, son! Grab 'em, and never let 'em go, for if you do, you'll grow up, and then you'll change, and sometimes, you'll become something you've never dreamed possible!

"You just might become that monster under the bed, and I wouldn't recognize you at all."

—The Incredible Bouncing Bunny, "Backo"

Table of Contents

HAPPY
SPRINGS

Happy Springs

-1-

Sheriff Annette 'Annie' Johnson caught her breath before moving inside the cramped space of the trailer home, and although she covered up her action with the ruse of a passive shrug and an everyday sigh, she was a complete mess inside. Homicides were always an ugly business no matter how clean the scene appeared, and as of so far, *'clean'* was very far away…

For events like this to go down on the same day that her period began was the very topper of her morning, and for her cycle, stress just acted on her already present misery by doubling the intensity of the cramps. Twice the stress, twice the waking hell.

Without letting on to what she was doing, she calmly withdrew a hand from her service pants pocket, pinching two Midol and an 800-milligram ibuprofen tablet between her fingers. She switched hands with her travel mug and deposited the pills beneath the rim. Staring towards the trailer door, she pretended to take a long, thoughtful sip, though she merely allowed the lukewarm coffee to touch her upper lip before guiding the tablets into her mouth.

Another sigh followed after she swallowed them down. Shrugging once more, she silently reassured the two deputies huddled nearby that none of it bothered her in the slightest.

"Well, gentlemen," she nodded towards them, adjusting the round brim of her brown campaign hat so that it dipped heavily on her brow. "Shall we?"

She stepped from the front of her cruiser with the two deputies reluctantly trailing behind, each one in their own right recounting why they ever became law enforcement officers. This had been their second call that day—both apparent homicides without a shimmer of doubt—and it wasn't even noon in their sleepy, picturesque township that no one outside of it even knew its name.

-2-

"Balls of steel, that woman," sounded a rough, huffing voice, and Lyle Portman, the mobile-park attendant, looked up blankly towards Chet Holster, the town doctor and coroner who was busy chugging down on a bottle of Happy Springs water.

Chet had gotten the call just around the same time Lyle had phoned the Sheriff, and in situations of death, sometimes the doc made it to the scene first, but that all depended on who was doing the calling.

"Huh?" Lyle rasped, his stomach empty of all its contents, which now lay splattered in the entranceway of the distant trailer home… and on its steps… on the front of his shirt… as well as in the patchy grass in front of it.

He didn't look well at all.

"The Sheriff," he nodded in the direction as Annie and her boys entered the trailer home, which another deputy was busy encircling with yellow warning tape. He swished the last mouthful around, then swallowed, finishing up with a long sigh. "Man, that's some damn good water. You look like you could use some. Hold on."

Chet turned and reached through his rear window, opening a small cooler he kept back there to hold insulin, insect wipes, saline tubes for cleaning wounds, and his corned beef sandwich, and pulled out two frosted-blue tinted bottles. Returning, he handed one to Lyle, who nodded appreciatively.

"Thanks."

"No problem," the doc smiled and leaned back against his car. "Now, what were we talking about?"

"The Sheriff's balls," Lyle mumbled and shrugged, opening the bottle and drinking it nearly empty. "You're right; it is good."

"Told ya." The doc nodded, folding his arms while he waited. "But yes, she has a set on her stronger than brass… more like titanium. I have some equipment back at my office made of it. Light as a feather, but stronger than steel it is."

"But she is a *'she,'* Doc," Lyle shuddered as the cold water settled in against his tender insides, questioning the sphincter down there at the top of the stomach and whether it should let loose again. He took another swallow, giving it the what-for, and grimaced, relieved that the stomach didn't want to flow again. "Don't you mean tits?"

"No, I didn't confuse the Sheriff's anatomy or her sex," he said thoughtfully, adjusting himself to face Lyle better while keeping a clear view of the distant trailer. "You see, there are balls, and then there are *BALLS*, and she sure has a set of them even if they don't dangle. I would put Annie up against any damn hard-leg lawman out there, State Police too, and I am saying this with the utmost respect.

"Now, don't go thinking I am saying she's a butch Helga or anything like that. No, she's all 'Woman' under that uniform, and I am sure her ex-husband can vouch for that, but she still has *BALLS*."

"Well, she sure is a tough one. I'll give you that," Lyle concurred, following most of what the doc had to say, but figured he had nothing helpful to the conversation in the end.

"Tough?" the doc huffed, shooting Lyle a sideways glance and shaking his head. "Most men can't stomach seeing death, let alone when it's messy; they just puke all over the place, present company in complete understanding because of the circumstances, mind you."

"Thanks," Lyle swallowed, swishing some water in his mouth, which he spat to the ground.

"All I am saying is I am sure happy she's here," Chet mused, his mind running through a catalog of a dozen other lawmen he knew and found none who reached the bar. "It would just be a mess if it was someone else."

"Share a bit of information with 'someone' who is a 'no one,' doc," Lyle said quietly, turning towards him with an inquisitive look. "What the hell's goin' on here? I mean, Deputy Porter said that this here's the second murder today—"

"Deaths, Lyle," Chet corrected, twisting off the cap to his bottle of water and taking a long pull. "They are officially called 'deaths' until I have ruled otherwise."

"Well, you call 'em what you may, Doc," Lyle mumbled, then shrugged. "But unless you call that bloodbath in there accidental, it looks like murder to me, which don't happen 'round here! When I went in there… what I saw, it's… it's just horrible."

Doc Holster was silent as he mused over what Lyle was going on about; his eyes focused on the trailer home across the way, waiting for his queue.

Lyle was correct on both counts, and despite his apparent lack of education beyond the ninth grade, there was simply no hiding the truth. This—just like earlier when he had to bag up the body of Mrs. Rose McAllister along the edge of her rose bushes, taking great care not to disturb the narrow-spaded hand shovel protruding from her armpit—was murder.

Sure, people had accidentally stabbed themselves with garden tools before. Such things tended to accompany human nature and its remarkable ability to become entirely too comfortable with even the most mundane tasks. But accidentally stabbing oneself eleven times before finally locating the proper meat sheath between the ribs just beneath the armpit was another basket of fruit altogether.

Someone made damn sure Rose was dead, and they took a brutal route to get there.

Per Lyle's deductive proclamation, murder did not happen in those parts. Of course, there was an occasional hunting accident involving alcohol combined with wearing the wrong colors to go out and do such a task, but all-out concise, deliberate, animalistic murder? They left events like those for big-city life and television.

Lyle burped soundly with an uncontrolled shuddering spasm and then grimaced.

"Sorry... thought I was gonna pop again," he whispered.

"Hey, Doc!" exclaimed a voice across the gravel road, crisscrossing the trailer park, drawing both Doc's and Lyle's attention. Deputy Paul Mossen was currently just offside the trailer's steps with his hands on his knees, sucking in the air by the furious lung-full. He was waving the Doc over, never looking up.

"Well, Lyle, guess they're ready for me," he said, clearing his throat and pushing away from the car while patting Lyle on his back, then reaching through the rear window and collecting up his bag.

"What do ya think I ought to do?" Lyle whispered; his eyes wide with panic. "They ain't gonna need me to go in there and show 'em 'round, are they?"

"No, Lyle, you've done enough," the doc said, giving him a thankful nod and an encouraging smile. "We'll take it all from here. They will come to find you if they need to ask you any more questions.

"Maybe you ought to go lay down for a bit... get your mind off what you saw in there. Try to eat light foods, like crackers or toast, that will take the edge off your sour stomach. Also, finish up that water. That's good stuff, it is."

Lyle gave him a nod and obediently took a solid drink, satisfying the doctor that he would, in fact, be a good patient while distantly acknowledging that, yes sir, it was some pretty good water as it passed his palate. Slowly, he trudged towards his trailer where a cardboard sign displaying OFFICE hung beside the door. He wasn't the swiftest man to ever walk the Earth, but it seemed wise to take the good doctor's advice. As for Chet, he headed towards the crime scene with his bag and bottled water in hand.

-3-

"Hey Doc," Sheriff Johnson sounded, looking up from her squatting position next to the bloody body of a man, being only known since he

5

had been in his underwear and his penis half hung from the seamed edge. His face, however, was missing. "Glad you could make it."

"Annie… Deputy" he nodded to the Sheriff and then to Deputy Lou Frank, who was standing pale as a sheet next to a small television as he stepped into the cramped trailer and set his bag on the narrow counter, followed up behind slowly by Deputy Mossen, who was wiping slimy matter from his mouth.

The doc paused for a moment and scanned his surroundings of the cluttered living spaces, but his eyes weren't focusing on the piles of newspapers, empty beer cans, the pile of dog shit in the corner, or the small sink overflowing with dirty dishes and amassed by flies, no. He was taking in all the blood and tissue which covered almost every surface in some macabre, quasi-paint. He shuddered and then dug around inside his bag.

"You are looking a bit peaked over there, Lou… maybe you ought to go get some air?"

"Uh, yeah, good idea," he swallowed hard against his gorge and looked down at the sheriff. "Sheriff, if it's all right with you?"

"Yeah, go ahead, Lou," she nodded, taking a swallow from her travel mug and waving a mass of collected flies away from the faceless head of the body. "Get something to drink. You too, Paul."

"Oh, got just the thing," Doc Holster snapped his fingers, unzipped the chiller compartment to his bag, pulled out two bottles of Happy Springs, extended one before him to Deputy Frank, and then turned to hand one to Deputy Mossen behind him. "Stay in the shade until I get a chance to look at both of you."

They nodded without words and exited.

"Sheriff, you want a bottle too?"

"No, I am fine with my coffee, Chet," he smiled thinly and raised her mug a tad. "Wish it was bourbon right now, to be honest."

"Well, I am sure you will need to come over to the office later," the Doc huffed out a chuckle as he pulled on surgical gloves and squatted down next to her. "When you do, I have a nice twenty-year-old in my bottom drawer with your name on it."

"That sounds like a plan," she added, shifting so as to give him some room. "How many of those bottles do you have? You had three of them this morning over at Mrs. McAllister's?"

"Just one left in my bag," he shrugged and produced a sly smile accompanied by a clever wink. "I got six cases of it in the trunk."

"Jesus, Doc, I know it's been warm, but what's wrong with what's coming out of the tap?"

"Nothing," he shrugged, donning a pair of narrow-lens glasses. "Just when it's a free promo, why not indulge? They're handing them out by the four packs over at the Piggly Wiggly, and when they found out I was a doctor, they loaded me up as the pharmaceutical companies do me with their samples. Said maybe my patients would like them, but by the looks of it, this fella here has had all the bottled water he's ever gonna have."

"Yeah, I noticed that." She nodded, glancing about herself and making a mental note of seven empty Happy Springs bottles, which joined the collection of beer bottles and cans. "Mrs. McAllister had herself some by her when she was killed, a few in her fridge too."

"Well, they've been giving them out freely, and everyone likes something new, especially when it's free. You ought to try one… best damn water I ever tasted; refreshing too."

"I'll take your word for it," she breathed and moved back to let the doctor do his work.

Slowly the doc touched and examined the man's bloody and torn T-shirt. At one time, it had been whiteish and then tilted the head from right to left using a jutting shrapnel piece of his jawbone. Occasionally he would offer a soft grunt or the all-present 'Mm-hmm' sound in the back of his throat, but without that, he was silent in his preliminary examination.

"How are you holding up?" he asked without looking up or pausing.

"Me?" the Sheriff blinked. "I am fine. Why?"

"Well, these things can get to you," he shrugged as he went through his routine motions. "These parts, as you know, see little of this… just wondering since you looked quite off earlier."

"It's just these damn cramps," she responded, twisting at the hip, hoping to stretch her fist-like uterus into more tolerable flaccidity.

"That bad?"

"Got clots the size of gophers but with sharper teeth," she added and snorted a brief giggle at the thought. The good doc acknowledged her with his sounds of amusement and nodded.

"Well, maybe I got something in my bag for you," he added and leaned back, looking over the man on the floor. "But I think it's more about the stress of today… got a mad fire of a headache going on myself. Maybe I am a little dehydrated, hence all the water I have been drinking."

"So, Doc, what do you think?" she smiled and nodded towards the body.

"Well, he sure is dead," he offered his coroner's comedic pass, then stood, joined by Sheriff Johnson, who posed with her hand on the butt of her gun and mug in the other.

"Hammer?" she hypothesized with her head cocked.

"Maybe… that, or a heavy wrench," he shrugged. "See how the bones crushed inwards in these narrow sections?"

She looked where he was pointing but only could find chunky red porridge in the mix, albeit she nodded anyway.

"A big crescent wrench could do that or a golf putter, but then there's not enough ceiling height in here to beat in someone's head like that. No, this was up close and personal… angry."

"Jesus," she whispered, then pinched the small space between her eyes. "Got any more aspirin in that bag for me?"

"That headache still bothering you from earlier, too?" he asked, turning towards his bag. "I wish you'd take the Tylenol-three, Annie. It will knock that right out."

"Nah, gotta stay focused," she shook her head, her eyes locked onto a fly making lazy circles around a half-deflated eyeball hanging loose from the side of the destroyed head below her.

She wondered if the little pest had come in through the window or if it had been that proverbial fly on the wall when it all went down. Either way, it cared little about the condition of poor Mr. Hollis Chaplin's face as it bobbed and dipped through the chunky, torn soup of blood, bone fragments, and brains. Left alone and given a little time, the insect would be as happy as any creature could hope to be.

"Anyway, codeine locks me all up."

"Well, I tell my patients who need it to eat plenty of fruit while on it… it helps."

He handed her a small white packet containing the aspirin and extended her a frosty bottle of water.

"Yeah, I know you and your coffee," he smiled. "But you need to drink that down with plenty of water. Also, on hot days like this, coffee is going to do nothing but dehydrate you. It's a diuretic, you know?"

"Always the doc," she smiled, taking the packet and the bottle of water.

"Hey, Doc?" Deputy Mossen said quietly, his head barely appearing in the doorway. "Ambulance is here for the body and—"

"All right, goddamnit!" Chet spun and exploded in the voice's direction, sending both the Sheriff and the Deputy into a sudden convulsed expression of shock. With wide eyes, she held him with confusion and concern for having known the man for twenty-five years, and never had she seen him lose his cool.

Gently, she placed a hand on his shoulder.

"Doc?" Sheriff Johnson spoke quietly, narrowed her eyes, and studied him. "You all right?"

"Uh, yes, yes, sorry," Chet stammered and wiped his mouth, his eyes darting and bobbing, confused. Quickly, he took a long pull on his water bottle and wiped at his forehead with a handkerchief. "Don't know what's come over me, sorry. Hot in here."

With shaking hands, he retrieved a handkerchief from his back pocket and mopped up his leaking forehead, which drew another concerned look from Annie.

"Sorry, Paul, for my outburst… it's been a long day," he begged, attempting to provide a comforting smile for his actions, which resulted in a quivering grimace from a disobedient set of lips. He pinched tightly between his eyes and shook his head. "I think I may need some aspirin myself."

"Why don't we go get some air," she soothed, extending a hand to her side. The good doctor followed without protest.

Red splotches remained on his face, bordered by pale, clammy skin left behind by his outburst. Sweat coated him and showed no sign of slowing, thick and syrupy as it rolled down his temples.

She didn't like the look of him. Once outside, she intended to quietly mention her concerns to the EMTs and have them take a look at him.

The day had been hard for everyone and will get harder still.

It was just past noon.

-4-

Sheriff Johnson was rolling along Double K Road under the speed limit she helped govern. Her eyes were on the road, but her mind was not there; it was focused on the two homicides her sleepy little spot of the world now had.

These were not the first murders she had dealt with. Eleven years earlier, a drifter stuck up a small convenience store on the township border called Handsom's Holdings and shot the clerk twice in the face over twenty-nine dollars in the register. Since the crime occurred on the county line, Sheriff Billy Franklin—the lawman on the other side, whose daily excitement rarely exceeded watching paint peel from the station house walls—claimed jurisdiction and removed her and her deputies from the scene.

She also had her down-home homicide where no one could step in, drop their cock on the table, and ask her who was bigger.

Six years earlier, a man named Lester Peterson, who ran the John Deere repair shop out by the interstate, came home to find his wife in bed with none other than local Reverend Harold Mays. Lester had called off early from one of his usual twelve-hour days with a migraine and a sour stomach, only to discover his wife Sally upstairs carrying on something fierce.

Ever since the Handsom's Holdings robbery years before, Lester—like most shop owners in the area—carried a handgun of some sort. In his case, a black-matte snub-nosed .38. With it, he entered the bedroom and shot the good reverend four times, one of them squarely in the berries.

When Annie arrived on the scene with two deputies' cruisers in tow, Lester was sitting on his front porch smoking cigarettes with a half-empty bottle of rye whiskey next to him. After his arrest, she asked him why there were still two bullets in his gun, and he replied simply with a shrug,

"Felt like doing her too, but then I would have had to have done myself as well," Lester said calmly, with a single tear rolling his cheek as he smoked heavily on his pack of *Marlboros* at the station. "It's easy to put down a dog... not so easy to put down someone you love, even if she's an adulterous whore."

After that, Lester got himself a free vacation downstate, and Sally packed up and moved off to some unknown destination, and since then, Sheriff Johnson's little spot in the world had been relatively quiet.

"Sheriff?" squawked through the ham radio just under the dash. Calmly, she retrieved the handset, bringing it to her mouth, and depressed the key. "Deputy Moran here, come back, over."

"Yeah, go ahead, over," she spoke into her handset distantly as she came to a stop at the T junction between Double K and Thornton Road.

Her head was pulsing.

"Sheriff," the deputy's voice came through quietly, with a long pause. "You got your cell on you?"

"Yeah, I do, Al," she sent back, idling. "What's up?"

A moment later, her cell phone rang. It was Deputy Moran.

"Sheriff," his empty voice came through the earpiece quietly. "There's been another."

-5-

First-Deputy Al Moran was leaning against the fender of his cruiser, pulling hard on a cigarette when she rolled up, lights on and siren off. He had positioned the vehicle so it blocked the entrance to the forest preserve's recreation area.

Families came here for barbecues and reunions. High-school kids came at night to drink and fuck. The place was mostly for tourists—of whom they saw precious few given their distance from any major city—but it remained the preferred destination for anyone seeking a quiet patch of nature to camp, fish, or simply get away for a while. It brought welcome revenue into town through the grocery store, diner, bait shop, and, of course, a respectable number of traffic citations.

Sighing heavily, she collected up her hat from the seat next to her, donning it, and took up her travel mug and the bottle of water she had gotten from the doctor. It was just past noon, and the day was just getting started.

"Hey, Al," she breathed when she came to a halt before him, extending the bottle of water and taking a swallow from her mug, which was running close to dry. "You look like you could use this."

"Thanks, Sheriff," he replied with a nod, taking it and popping the top off with little thought. Half the bottle disappeared before he spoke again. "I sure did."

"What do we have?"

"Over in the picnic area," he mumbled, his eyes off across the road and focused on nothing. "Between the campsites… There's a lot of them."

"How many?" she whispered, stepping in front of his distant stare and snapping her fingers, bringing Deputy Moran back to reality with blinking eyes. "Al, how many are there?"

"Let me show you," he whispered, pulling himself from the fender, and began moving up the paved drive with the Sheriff at his shoulder.

-6-

"Jesus fucking Christ!" she gasped as they stepped into the picnic clearing to the mayhem beyond.

"I know," came a whisper just behind her.

"You only called this into me?" she asked quietly, forbidding any of her deputies to speak on 'sensitive' subjects over the air (a lesson learned since the Holdings incident all those years before).

"Yeah, just you," he nodded, coughing into a balled fist as the stifling breeze brought him the smell of death. "Thought about calling the doc, but well, I think he's been pretty busy this morning. When do you think this happened, Sheriff?"

"I have no idea," she whispered, sluggishly stepping into the clearing cautiously as if they filled the grass with sleeping vipers.

What surrounded her was bedlam.

Two families of campers, separated by an empty pitching slot carved into the trees, had converged on the picnic area in the center of the clearing and, by all first-hand observations, apparently torn one another to pieces. Unconsciously, Annie covered her mouth with an open palm as her eyes trained on the mass of bloody people, forever frozen in time at the moment of their deaths.

One woman lay sprawled open-legged across a picnic table, her face a ruined mess as she was repeatedly stabbed by what appeared to be a tent spike still dangling from her murderer's dead hand. The dead man slumped over her, his mouth hanging open and a camper's shovel protruding from his back. Behind him lay his own executioner, a heavily muscled man coated in blood sprayed from the gash along the side of his neck. Someone had used a hatchet—or perhaps a machete—on him, and his head had flopped nearly parallel to his shoulder like a *Pez* dispenser.

Whomever killed him nearly took his head off.

"More are over there, Sheriff," sounded the deputy, but she barely noticed him speak. She followed his pointing finger. Slowly her eyes traveled along the arm and past the pointing tip where, in the haze of her mind, she found more carnage. She swallowed soundly and moved in the direction without a word.

All the while, she wanted to scream.

There, in the grass just beyond one of the built-in barbeque grills, carnage littered the picnic area. A woman lay on her side with a tent pole driven clean through her chest from front to back.

Annie eyed the grill top as she crept past. Several bratwursts sat charred and smoldering long beyond the point of being edible. To her left, a body smoldered much the same and, from a distance, resembled one as well.

The woman appeared to be clutching something to her chest, perhaps the critical piece of evidence that had started it all. As Annie rounded her feet for a better look, a cough caught in her throat. She choked it back and abruptly pivoted away.

Whoever impaled her did it with such force that not only did it pass cleanly through the woman but as well as the infant child she was holding.

"Jesus Christ!" she whispered sharply, hands on her hips and face toward the sky, which beat the sundown on her, slowly shaking her head as she fought back the tears.

"Sheriff?" the deputy spoke softly from behind, closely, and then fell silent for a respectable moment as he noticed her shoulders bouncing as she sobbed quietly. He had already let his waterworks flow after he called her and had plenty of time to remove any trace evidence.

"Yes, Al?" she responded, using her wrists to wipe away the tears, her back towards him.

"What are we going to do?"

"What are we going to do?" she echoed, her eyes slowly scanning the rest of the scene, cataloging another six bodies in one state of death or another before settling on the smoldering carcass near the fire pit.

Someone had hacked off an arm at the elbow and a hand at the wrist. For a brief moment she wondered if the damage had been done postmortem, a small mercy hidden somewhere within the chaos. That thought vanished when her eyes settled on the stumps. They had charred as thoroughly as the rest of the body. No, the poor soul had suffered a bit before the flames arrived.

Her gaze swept the area in search of the missing limbs. Nearby, not more than eight feet away, lay a severed hand.

Clearing the tunnel vision from her mind with a quick snap of her neck, Annie scanned the picnic area around her with a composite image locked in, blinking each time her eyes spotted a match like a camera's shutter.

Happy Springs water bottles are littered everywhere.

What the — is as much as her mind could muddle a question, but any answer was as far away from the reason to ponder. She blinked twice, turning slowly towards her deputy while giving her numb cheeks one last wiping attention. She then cleared her throat.

"I want you to call the State Police, Al." She took a deep breath and exhaled. "We are shutting down the town."

-7-

Voices, almost distant, rained on her from every direction for over two hours. She had replied to each of them under the weight of the questions, sometimes with only a head gesture of 'Yes' or 'No.' However, if asked later what she had told them, she wouldn't be able to recall, let alone remember, who had asked her in the first place. The day was forfeit, much akin to hopes of having a sunny day at the beach when a thunderstorm rolled through, but not so alike was the fact that in this case, when it was all over, there was nothing but bodies to count.

"Sheriff, we got two more just up the north path...."

"Sheriff found one in the woods... looks like he was the one with the machete... he tripped and fell on it, dead...."

"Sheriff, over by the outhouse... in, I mean, well... all over the outhouse...."

"Sheriff Johnson, can you have your men block off the road down by the junctions at both ends?"

"Sheriff... there are children... Lots of them."

Slowly, she rolled past Albert's Crossing, pulled to the side of the road, and finished the last of the coffee from her travel mug while she thought. Her cell phone rested in her lap. It had rung constantly through most of the afternoon since her arrival at the picnic-camping grounds, and the lone bar remaining on the battery threatened to blink away at any moment.

She had called her ex-husband twice, each time hoping her voice might cross the airwaves and find its way into his arms. She just wanted a good cry; something he had always allowed her, even though all the problems that eventually drove them apart.

Yet, she only spoke about her day on the second call.

"Are you okay, Annie?" he had asked with that certain clarity, which meant he was genuinely worried about her, a tone he rarely used and one which she was still in love with him for.

She closed her eyes against the compassion there, her mind flowing over the horrid visions her day had provided, each one taking on a surrealistic three-dimensional caricature with subtle motions, reaching for her. She took a deep breath, holding it while listening to her thudding pulse in her ears.

"Yes, just a terrible day," she responded with a soft, monotone voice, knowing how her tone could always betray her to his perceptive ears. She wanted to cry, to let it out by telling him the 'all,' but she had to play by the guidelines she set for her deputies and keep it confidential for now. "It just seems like the world woke up crazy."

There was a long pause, and she swallowed; she knew what his mind was doing. He could detect the deceit in her voice, but he couldn't levy a supposition towards it. He was going to probe or let it be.

She prayed he would move on.

"Yeah, that's how it is sometimes," he replied with a slight inflection, which meant he was close to digging, but perhaps her tone gave way to a warning that doing so might not be the best course of action. Cautiously, he continued: "Do you want to come by the house?"

Yes, I fucking do! Her mind screamed out towards the receiver's end, stomping invisible feet and scurrying towards the offer, but her response started with a long, exhaled sigh.

"No, not now… maybe later," she shook her head, opening her eyes to a passing ambulance with its lights on but siren mute. The vehicle's sides were marked with Bloomington-Normal colors, which were paired cities not too far away to the northwest, heading in the direction from which she came.

They ran out of vehicles for the dead, she thought to herself as it passed, having noted that the local two ambulances were busy, and there were plenty of ones from Fulton County already on the scenes. *So many bodies.*

"Will you be in all night?"

"*Night?* Yes," he responded, surprised, knowing she usually clocked out at 8:00 PM. "Whenever you want to, I am free."

She sat staring off into the distance and thought of calling him back for the third time, this time telling him she was on her way and needed him when her eyes caught a glint of light reflecting off the windshield of an approaching vehicle. Her eyes shifted to her driver-side mirror and then down the road.

A delivery truck was rolling her way.

It came and passed, following well within the speed limit as her radar gun informed her, but she hit the lights and siren just the same as the painted words **Happy Springs** glowed at her, stenciled in large print on the side of it.

-8-

The chase was short. Really short, she only had to hit the driver with two quick blurts of her crowd siren. She had no reason to stop him; he was entirely within the law, but something made her do it; a feeling, perhaps? Pulling up, she kept her distance just as she would when pulling over any violator, siren off, lights flashing as she pulled up the CB handset.

"Station, this is the Sheriff. Come back, over," she blurted, then released the key. There was a brief pause and then a voice.

"What's up, Sheriff? Kinda busy here," returned a female voice full of irritation, causing Annie to blink.

"Excuse me?" she retorted into the handset, confused and irritated. "What kind of radio etiquette is that?"

"I ain't got no time for that etiquette shit right now, Sheriff!" the voice shot back aggressively, causing her to jump.

"Agnes? Who in the hell do you think you are talking to?"

"Annie, I have papers up to my chin, the phone is ringing off the goddamn hook, and the water guy is late! How in the hell am I supposed to do anything with these interruptions?"

"Agnes, you will not talk to me like—"

"I said to put those goddamn waste cans on the side of the station!" rocketed the dispatcher's voice through the CB's speaker, sending a surprising jolt through Annie's body. With a cocked head of utter bewilderment, she was about to depress the key once more when Agnes' voice came back, relatively calm. "I am sorry, Sheriff, but this has been one of them days. We have been waiting for calls back, and that damn water delivery truck is late!"

Annie blinked, her eyes down along the side of the delivery vehicle she had just pulled over. She focused on the vision of the driver's burly arm hanging out the window with his license and registration in hand and waiting.

"What water delivery?" Annie spoke calmly and quietly as she extended a leg out her door, her eyes moving from between the extended burly arm from the truck window in front of her and her Mossberg pump shotgun in its riding caddy just to the right of the transmission hump in the floor.

"The goddamn Happy Springs water service I ordered!" screamed back to her over the set. "How am I supposed to keep you high on coffee all day without no goddamn water? Just goes to show you that people don't pay no goddamn attention to what people tell you!"

"You've been using *that* water for the coffee?" Annie whispered, depressing the key, which felt like it took all her strength. She slowly eyed her travel mug as visions of all the mutilated dead from the day raced in on her, followed by images of the water bottles scattered about.

"See, I go out of my way to do something nice," the voice returned to her in an astonished, disbelieving tone. "Instead of giving you the swill from the tap, I did something nice, and you shit on it!

"I said put that shit on the side of the station! That's it, moron; I have something for you!"

Five sharp reports tore through the CB's speaker close to the other end's microphone, each ending with a high feedback whine.

"Agnes?" Annie gasped into the handset and paused, standing erect outside her cruiser and looking towards the west, where the station sat several miles off. After a long clenching of breath, Annie reheard those shots as distant echoing rumbled over the tree line, finally reaching her.

"Ma'am?" Came a man's voice before her, and she spun away from the car door and snatched at her sidearm, tugging twice on the automatic there before wrenching it free. Instinct had taken over, and she was down on one knee just around the side of her open door, pointing outward with her finger cupped over the trigger guard, ready.

"Don't you fucking move!" she screamed as sweat shot into her left eye, blazing the delicate tissue and forcing the other to wince and water. She rapidly blinked twice and then shrugged a shoulder towards

it to wipe and then zeroed in on the center mass of the once approaching—now hands up and frozen—delivery truck driver. *"Stay where you are!"*

"Whoa! Hey! What's all this?" he begged, his license and registration falling from his hands, his eyes dancing and jumping like a fishing bobber in a pond during a rainstorm. "I have my license and—!"

"What's in the truck?" she screamed, her finger drifting from the trigger guard to the business curve beyond it with a steady hand. Her head throbbed fiercely between her ears. Two flares raced up from her belly, the second so violent she nearly made a fist that would have blown the back out of the thick delivery man standing before her. Somehow, she maintained control.

For now.

"Huh?" Mr. Burly responded, glancing up at the picture on the back of his truck where a couple and a happy child were raising water bottles in a unison toast to all who would bother to look.

"I said, what's in the fucking truck?" she barked, readjusting her stance and aiming from the center mass target to the face.

"Just water," he replied calmly, despite the dime-sized maw of the barrel pointing at him.

'Simmons?' a voice crackled over the driver's CB in the distance. *'Where are you with your deliveries? Over?'*

"Ma'am? Was I speeding or something?"

"Don't you fucking *'ma'am'* me!" she screamed, stepping closer. "Where's the manifest?"

"It's in the truck," he snorted and picked at a sore on his cheek, examined whatever he removed, and flicked it away without so much of a thought. "Wanna see it?"

"Don't get fucking smart with me!" she blared, stepping up and leveling the pistol with his face, palm oozing sweat. *"Get the fucking manifest!"*

"Chill out, little lady," he smiled, turning his hands up shoulder height. "I don't mean you no harm. Let me get this for you."

"Hurry!" she coughed out, panting, her mind filling with images of painting the side of the truck with this man's head, and she had to force her finger off the trigger and return it to the guard. Sweat was peeking and rolling from her forehead, coating her cheeks and stinging her eyes.

"Okay, just got to get it out of the truck," he said, looking back over his shoulder.

"Just get it and get it slowly!" she commanded, receiving a nod of acknowledgment.

Calmly the man reached up and took the hand bar and stepped up into the door, reaching in and fussing for a moment, then turned as he hopped down, and that's when Annie started firing.

She saw his gun.

The first round vomited from the barrel with a deafening roar, seemingly so unexpectedly that she almost lost control of her firearm as it rocketed back. It bore a hole clean through his chest right at the throat line, not her intended spot, but the second and third shots found their marks, disintegrating his face and head just above the lip line, dropping him like a laundry bag full of wet clothes.

She stood panting and then dropped to one knee, the barrel of the gun inches from the mash of what remained of his head. Breathing heavily, her eyes darted over him as unexpected death spasms shook him. Annie flinched and fired twice more into the carcass, silencing him for good.

Standing, she kicked at his hand to move his pistol out of harm's way, and her mind followed the offending manifest papers as the breeze took them up the road.

"Whu—?" she sounded and caught her breath, her eyes blinking rapidly as the pink and yellow manifest papers danced up the road.

He had a gun! Her mind begged towards reasoning while her ears picked up the delicate meaty plops of brain matter that succumbed to gravity from crawling down the side of the cab coming to earth. *HE HAD A GUN!*

Head thumping in pace with the pulsing glow behind her eyes matching her heartbeat, she panted heavily through a clammy mouth in desperate need for water.

In the distance, the CB in her cruiser squawked again. It was Agnes. Somewhere nearby, her cell phone started ringing as well, and it was whomever the fuck it was.

In the present, her heart and head were thudding madly.

It was ripping time.

"Sheriff? Where the hell are you?" it was Agnes, irritated as before. *"We weren't done talkin' about the damn water!"*

Annie did not know why she did it, but it just felt right.

She slowly squatted in front of the bloody mess on the ground and ran her hand through the gore until it was thoroughly coated. With a blank, child-like expression of wonder, she held it before her face and examined it, unaware of the occasional giggle escaping her throat.

She began smearing it across her cheeks and neck in long, deliberate strokes, pausing once to bring it to her nose. Her expression remained one of confused fascination. Then she licked it and laughed.

"SHERIFF?"

She holstered her firearm and stood, licking at her hand once more. She giggled as she hoisted the delivery truck's side panel door up its runners, hefted out a case of water, and carried it to her cruiser.

Without hurry, she opened the trunk, placed the water inside, removed the Mossberg shotgun from its caddy, and returned to the driver's seat, closing the door behind her.

"Sheriff, are you ignoring me?" Agnes' exasperated voice came in over the set.

"No, Agnes," she responded calmly into the handset with her eyes closed, her pulse flashing red in the darkness there. "I am not ignoring you, over."

"Well, I had to take care of that moron you had cleaning up around here!" Agnes barked back through the set, irritated. "Sorry, but the station is a bigger mess now. Now, what are we going to do about that damn water?"

"No worries," Annie responded calmly, eyes opening and seeing the world on fire. "I got your water. I will be there really soon. I also have something I think you will really like."

She dropped the handset, glanced at the shotgun dipped over the passenger seat, then smiled, turning the ignition and slowly rolling away from the side of the road, heading toward the station.

—

For the remainder of that day, that sleepy little picturesque township—that no one outside of it even knew its name—became a bloodbath, and for many days following, everyone outside of it quickly learned what to call it.

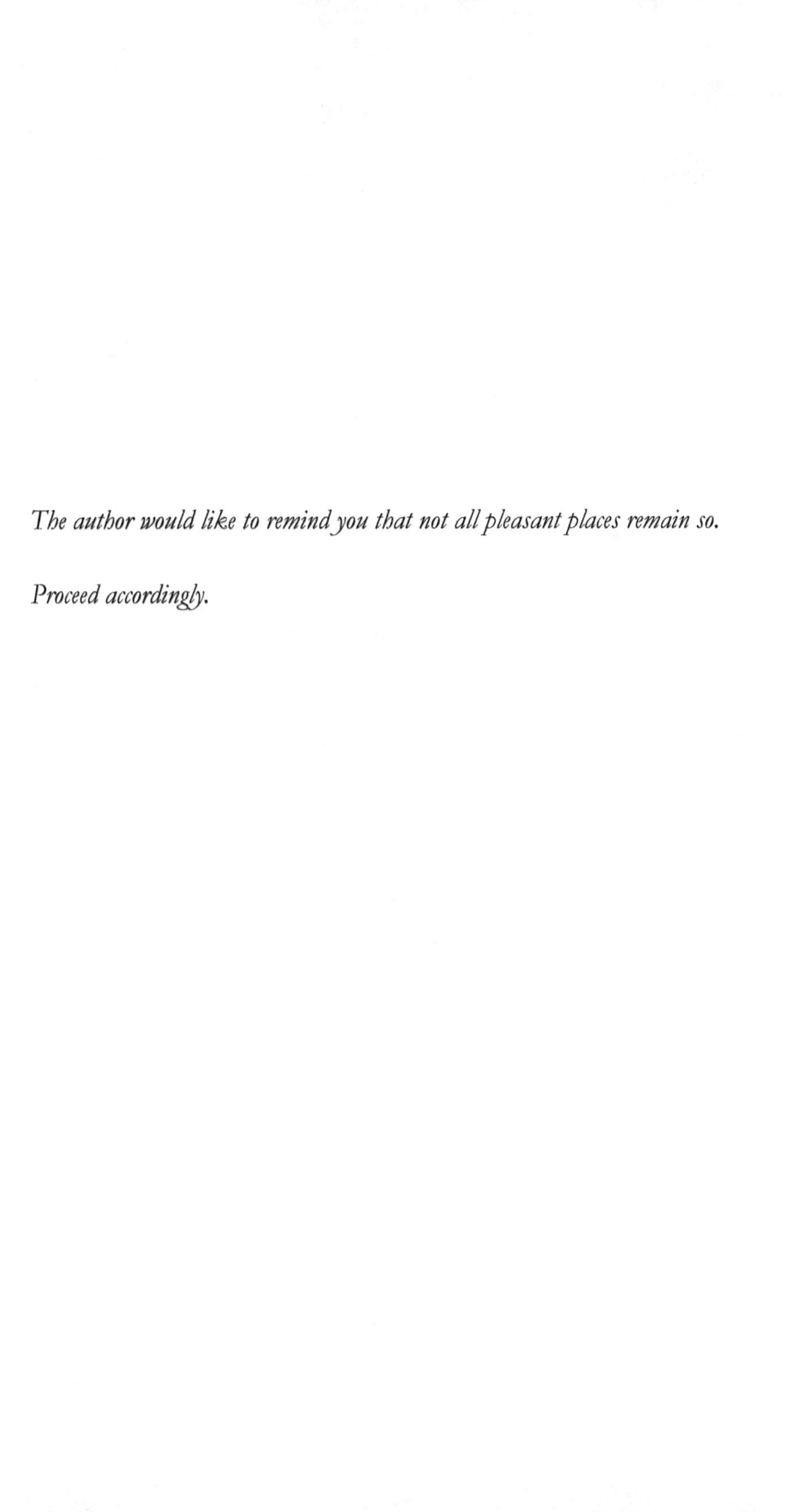

The author would like to remind you that not all pleasant places remain so.

Proceed accordingly.

Flakes, the Snowman

Flakes, The Snowman

*

I am going to write this once, only once, and then I will decide if I have any sanity left. It's been twelve years since it all happened, and in the latter four of those years, I sat in utter denial while the shrinks insisted that I should write it all out.

They all agree that it is for my greater good—the doctors that is—and to this moment, I am not sure what good a 'greater' is to come or can said thing exist.

"It will bring you 'closure,'" they perpend, regurgitating their dictation as patronizingly written once by a man who knew not of the word. I scoff at their arrogance encapsulated in a fancy frame on their office walls.

"You will feel better when you have let it all go!" my family concurs with the former and impedes their wills upon me, but I say it will kill me this time like it almost did—should have done—all those many years ago.

I don't know...

Sometimes I think that the past should stay exactly where it died, rotting like so many discarded leaves in the fall and clumped under a porch stoop, low. Then again, it is the mind that drums it back to haunt you, to torture you with it, and the brain is a sick masochist for pain when it should be a potbellied hedonist.

Since I have begun, I might as well continue until my hands shake so badly that my fingers can no longer find the keys and my nose begins to bleed again. That, or perhaps until the story within splinters my mind for good and I simply fade away.

Either way, the horror is almost done.

That night happened just like this...

-1-

That night was crisp and clear; the air was cold, with a light breeze from the west carrying the icy taste of snow with every breath. Fresh snowfall was not expected for another day and a half, which suited me just fine. It would be the weekend then, and I wouldn't have to worry about digging myself out to go to work in the mornings to come.

I loved nights like those—airy, but with a sharp enough bite like opening the freezer door on a warm day and catching just the essence of frost—and when you looked up, you could count more than a hundred stars in the sky (despite living in the inner city where the air and light pollution would usually drown them out).

Clean somehow. A natural pureness despite the human reminders of arc-sodium lights illuminating the parking spaces a few hundred yards behind me, and there, on the hill—*OUR* hill—my son and I was enjoying our time out on the sled.

A chuckle found and escaped my throat without me knowing it was rising when Toby careened to the right when he should have gone left, bounding over a drift-mound near the bottom of the hill. Knowing him, he had aimed for it intentionally to send himself airborne, which he did so spectacularly. Upon contact, he went one way while the red and silver sled shot the other, sending his yellow, snowsuit-clad body cartwheeling like a puffed-up doll over the surface.

"Are you okay?" I called down to him through cupped hands, attempting to hide my humor which had quickly changed to laughter.

"Did you see that?" he shot right back up to me, followed by a hero's dance in calf-deep snow.

Quickly, he trudged through the snow, collected the guideline from the sled, and began moving his way back up to me. I laughed soundly, enjoying his successful crashing stunt, and waved my hands over my head to let him know I had. I loved him so much, and I still do.

"That was awesome!"

"Want some of your cocoa?" I called down to him when he reached the halfway mark, straining against the raw material there from a nasty sore throat I was nearly past having. Earlier I had told him that sledding might have to be off our nightly list of things to do because of it, but I folded once I looked into his disappointed brown eyes, which begged for reasoning. He didn't whine like most children his age might do. No, he simply held me with those wantful eyes and explained that in a few days, when the new snow came, it wouldn't be *'slip-slidie'* enough.

A six-year-old with deductive qualities was a worthy opponent any day.

He was right, fresh snow and a steel-blade sled did not work well together, but it was not his reasoning that won his argument that night, just my inability to disappoint him. As I write this, I wish I had ruined his hopes of a night out sledding and kept him home.

Oh God, do I wish I did.

"Yep!" he beamed up to me and dropped the sled line bunched in a thick yellow mitten that matched his snowsuit perfectly.

I retrieved the insulated *Thermos* from the inside of my jacket and began serving up a cup of the double-sweet brew. Without delay, his mittens were off and hanging from the coat sleeves by a strap his mother had sewn into them so they wouldn't get lost. She had a knack for little things like that; adding 'just enough' to anything to make it function better. At times, I almost took her up on her jesting to allow her to do the same to my clothes so I wouldn't misplace my car keys, cell phone, or briefcase.

"Here ya go, Mr. Knievel," I smiled at a joke only I would understand and handed him the aluminum drinking cup. He took it with both hands and drank hungrily past panting cheeks. "That will warm you."

"That was so cool, Dad!" he nodded, dismissing me, and pointing toward the bottom of the hill. "Man, I flew so high!"

"That you did," I smiled, taking back the cup, and securing the *Thermos* in my inside pocket. With a little effort, he began tugging his mittens back on, only requiring assistance to ensure the elastic edges were snug around the ends of the sleeves. With a quick lift of the edge of his scarf, his face disappeared like a fighter pilot snapping on his oxygen mask. "You getting cold yet, little man?"

"Nope!" he quipped over his shoulder as he gathered up the line and waddled over so to position the sled for another run. "I'm gonna hit it head-on this time, watch!"

I briefly glanced at my watch and saw that it was going on 8:30 and nodded. We had only been there for twenty minutes, too soon to apply my authoritative veto on the night despite the redness of his cheeks or the tightening of my chilled fingers. The temperature was more than bearable with the double-layered flannel coat I was wearing and the trusty full-body thermals I had close to my skin. No, we had plenty of time, and Toby had more than enough willpower to go a thousand more times if he could.

A few more times, I told myself as he plopped down on the sled, taking up the steering line in both mittens. With a quick, confident glance shot back towards me, he signaled that he was ready for my running boost to send him on his way.

"Push me really hard this time, Dad!" he commanded through his scarf, and I did so as ordered; digging in deeply with my toes and darting forth, shoving my son into the snowy oblivion down the hill.

Like a yellow bullet, he zipped downward, holding the steering lines tightly, leaning slightly to the left as he guided the nose of the sled directly for the drift, screaming laughter the whole way. He did exactly as he planned and found the drift dead center. It seemed almost magical how he caught air and soared; for a moment, he and the sled seemed captured motionlessly in time.

Happy travels, Mr. Claus, I thought to myself, watching the twin contrails of powdery snow follow him.

That is the one image I remember today: Toby on the sled in contrasting colors from suit to vehicle, his high-pitched cry of excitement escaping him and the whole while knowing his eyes were wide with excitement as he flew.

For every breathing moment, I wish that image was the only one I carried of that night, to be powerful enough to wipe away all that later followed, but it is the only one that still allows me my sanity.

-2-

It was drawing on 9:20 when I told him it was about that time, and just like before at the house, he didn't whine; he held me with those brown eyes and spoke directly to my mind and my soul.

"But I still want to go a few more times," he said quietly without as much as a movement.

"I know, champ, but it is getting colder now," I countered without a hint of a lie because it *was* getting colder; that or I was succumbing to it, standing in one spot for most of the time that night. "And it's very late. We can come back on Saturday."

"It's not that cold," he added confidently, although his bottom lip had quivered uncontrollably since the last trip down. "Just a couple more times? *Please?*"

I stood there with my hands in my pockets while my feet stomped around the snow to chase away the numbness in my toes. My eyes scanned from his to the bottom of the hill. I attempted to calculate the extended time the trips down and back up would take, save he didn't get stuck in a drift like he had two trips down before. I shrugged, thinking 'No,' but I so wanted to please him.

"I am not sure," I said but caved regardless. "Okay, once more."

It was not the complete answer he was looking for, but at least it was halfway there. I had the chance to see the corners of his mouth curl up in a satisfied smile just before everything from the bridge of his nose down disappeared under his scarf. Spinning, he turned and pulled the sled back to the absolute edge of the hill, and I assumed my position behind him, planting my palms squarely on his tiny shoulders.

I took a deep breath as I anchored in my toes and—

That's when I first heard it.

Swish! Swish!

I paused, looking about us, unsure from which direction the sound had come and whether or not I had heard anything at all. The cold, just like the heat, can play tricks on sound waves, and on a night like this, the sounds could have happened blocks away and still sounded up close and personal.

"This time—" he pointed outward with a puffy-mitten-clad hand. "—I'm gonna go between those two bushes, around that park bench, and fly over that spot I crashed!"

"Oh, okay, one second," I acknowledged almost dismissively as I sought the source of the noise. Distantly, I could hear Toby babbling away about how he would lean into the curve this time so he wouldn't topple over and maybe even use his hand as a rudder in the snow so his turn could be sharper.

"Da-aad!" Toby whined this time, scooting forward twice, letting me know he was ready to go. "You have to push!"

The sounds rose again, sounding like heavy passes of a straw broom on a ceramic floor, and as I looked about myself attempting to pinpoint the source, Toby was insisting he was ready to launch. We were alone that night, all the responsible parents of other children having their little ones fed and bedded by now, but yet here were the noises, nonetheless.

Toby whined my parental name several more times, drawing me to him and away from the sounds. Perhaps a cross-country skier out practicing had to be someone hidden in the distant shadows of mounded snow and densely packed trees; who knows? I canceled any and all possibilities with a regrettable shrug.

"All right, all right," I made mocking faces behind his back and dug in. *"Here... we... go!"*

Off he shot with my laughter trailing behind him as I straightened, watching the little yellow blur glide away from me into the darkness. I realized that the air had gotten slightly warmer, not a lot, but just enough that snowflakes were coming down. I remember how I stood there bemused as a child watching ball tricks done by a magician as my mind locked onto the impossible oddity.

The breezes were still coming in from the West, yet the flakes were blowing in from the East, stronger than the prevailing winds.

-3-

Halfway up the hill on his last ride for the night, Toby had paused and was looking at something to his left, leaning forward in the direction of his attention. At first, I thought he was stalling, putting off the inevitability of us packing up and going home for as long as he could, but then I saw him lean forward even more, intently looking at whatever his keen eyes had picked up, like the attention of a pointer.

To my right was Toboggan Run, or so it had been named up until I was about twelve years old when I used to come to this very hill with my father. There had been a straight toboggan track made of wood, and a few local high schools practiced on it when there were still competitions around.

Nowadays, Toboggan Run was called that only by us older generations who still remembered it as such. The hill was very steep and ran a lot longer than our hill, where only the older teen daredevils and a few brave adults ever sled. The park district used the area often as staging and storage enclaves for various machinery, and during the winter months, one or two pieces could be buried over there under a mound of white. Most avoided the run for this reason, others simply because reaching the bottom often meant dodging obstacles half-hidden in the snow, only to take ten minutes to get back to the top.

Despite the dangers I associated with Toboggan Run, something was over in that direction, and it held my son's curiosity.

"What's wrong?" I called down to him, feeling my throat scream against the stress. Toby looked up my way and then returned his attention towards Toboggan Run, pointing. "Come on up, little man!"

Toby quickly broke into a waddling run, blasting away packed snow with his boots with the sled trailing behind him. His round red cheeks were puffing as he neared, and his wide eyes glowed with a culmination of worry and excitement.

"Toby?" my hands shot before me to slow his approach, for his forehead was still at groin level.

"*A snowman!*" he screamed at me and shot a straight arm toward it. "A big snowman is down there! *Look!* He has a scarf, carrot nose, a hat, and everything!"

Toby was already moving to that side of the crest, and by the time I caught up with him, he was jumping frantically in place. As I slowed, his fast-talking became jumbled, sounding much like when radios still had dials and you could spin through the stations to create some made-up, mish-mashed language.

I narrowed my eyes to see what he was so excited about through the falling snow, and he was right. There, at the bottom of Toboggan Run, was a snowman—tall, three-sectional, and seemingly very out of place.

'In the meadow, we will build a snowman,' I remember mocking that yuletide melody, a song to this day I can no longer bear to listen to. Someone had decided to build a giant fat snowman there for whatever reason was unknown to me; a place where no one would ever see it, well, that is, except for the sharp eyes of a six-year-old that saw anything and everything most people could not, including Santa.

"That's odd," I said aloud to no one in particular as I narrowed my sight to a fine slit and could barely make out the trail from when whomever rolled up the snow-boulder-like bottom of the thing.

"I want to smash it!" Toby was beaming at me and every dim and distant light out that night twinkled in his eyes.

"Not tonight, sport," I said and began to move away. "We have to get going."

"*Pluh-ease!*" Toby whined loudly as he took my arm, halting me. He had never been so insistent about anything until that night. "Last slide, I promise! I want to fly down and bash it!"

"No, son, that hill is way too danger—"

Swish-Swoosh-Swish!

My eyes shot down the hill towards the snowman from where the sound came; I shook my head and started to turn back to Toby when my eyes went right back to it. At the time, my mind accepted that my eyes might be playing games because it was cold and dark, and that snow was falling, but I swore it had moved forward.

"I am big now, and I won't try any stunts!" He was begging me with his mitten-clad hands forming a yellow pleading gesture up at me.

"No, sorry, too dangerous," I said flatly, focusing on the bottom of the hill. My vision was getting fuzzy and confused with distance as the thickening snowflakes fell. "Your mom would have my butt if she knew I let you go down there."

"You told me you did at my age!" He shot up to me, and then his expression suddenly drew blank, and those big browns of his leveled on me. "So, I am not big like you were at my age?"

He knew he had me dead to rights, and I wish I had learned to keep my big mouth shut to this day.

Slowly, he let go of my jacket and let his arms drop to his sides, and quietly, without a whimper, he went to retrieve his sled. He never looked directly at me once he collected up the guideline, and with careful steps, he walked past me towards the parking lot with the sled in tow. At the time, it didn't matter whether this was theatrics or genuine acceptance, but the pang that shuddered inside my chest was real. I was letting him down, my little trooper, and worse, I was telling him that I had no faith in him.

"Tobester!" I called out to him when he had gotten no more than a snowball's throw from me, turning. From there, I could see his big eyes scanning me, shaming me. "Once, and I mean *only* once!"

His face expanded with utter joy and brightness, and he moved so fast back to me that I still don't recall his legs ever moving. One second, he was standing at a distance, upset, and hurt, and the next, his forehead was rebounding off my abdomen with his little arms squeezing me like a vise.

✴✴

I'm going to get some coffee right now, have a cigarette to calm the nerves, and if the neighbors don't call the police because of my screaming, I will be back to finish this in a moment.

-4-

"Remember, you get one shot at this," I told him, squatting down in front of the sled with a finger pointed at him to enunciate my words, hoping to drive the message well past home.

He was sitting motionless on the sled before me with the guideline held firmly in his mittens, his face nearly gone due to the scarf, but I knew he was paying attention to everything I said; his eyes told me so.

"You miss, and that's it, got it?"

Toby nodded slowly with a muffled sound confirming, *'Got it!'*

"I'm serious now. My dad should never have let me go down that hill when I was your age, just as I shouldn't be doing now, but you are big, just like I was, maybe even bigger."

I took a moment and glanced over my shoulder down the lip of the hill. It was still down there, waiting in the snow where someone had built it, more than likely with some garish smile made of twigs or stones. I could barely make it out directly, but it was there, waiting for the oblivion my son and his sled were about to send him.

Turning back, I held Toby's eyes for a long reassurance.

"Okay, little man, I'm going to give you a soft push to get you going. That hill is steep enough, so you are going to be moving fast, quickly. I want you to hold onto your steering line tightly. No tricks, no stunts, and no ditching if you get spooked. Jumping off your sled at the speed you'll be going, you'll tumble halfway across that field.

"Got it?"

Toby released the line for a moment and gave me a confirming thumbs up.

"Once you pass those trees, you'll be fine," I continued, my mind effortlessly recounting the warnings my dad had given me all those years ago. "If you get scared, just hold onto the lines tightly and close your eyes, ok?"

"K!" was my answer, so I nodded and moved behind him.

I was looking down the hill in the line of his path, and we had gotten the nose of the sled pointed right at it. I wanted to pull him off and tell him that I had changed my mind but knew I was committed.

The snow was coming down very thick then, its angle sharp and direct, although I didn't feel any wind.

I counted out loud to three and then nudged my son into the abyss.

I watched how the sled picked up alarming speed in a hurry as Toby zipped into the fury of the falling snow, the hill accepting the blades of the sled without any resistance. A fan of icy white trailed behind him, his form shrinking as his speed increased, and in that moment heat flooded my bowels as my heart shuddered like thunder.

The snowman—that damn thing down below with its silly scarf, hat, and garish smile—*moved.*

With a wild ballad of swishing sounds, it tore toward Toby. I remember screaming his name—raw, instinctive—as my feet lurched into motion, sending me stumbling downhill with flailing arms and desperate, pumping legs. In pure horror, I watched the thing close in on an intercept course, its branch-arms stretching, reaching, clawing for my son.

"Toby, no!" I screamed as my bumbling feet fought through the thick snow, catching me up and I stumbled, flipping head over heels down the hill until slamming flat on my face. My lips mashed and ripped against my teeth, drawing blood but I didn't care. I had to save him, and as I lunged forward and downward, Toby began to scream.

The night had gone silent around me, and all I could hear was my rapid panting in unison with my beating heart. I raced forward, tumbling, faltering, flipping, cursing, standing, and then lunging the remaining distance to the bottom of the hill. All my reasoning blinded me through fear and the thick snowflakes that seemed to fall from every direction.

"Toby?" I whispered and then began screaming his name. I got no answer.

My hands were waving in front of me blindly, and I could barely chance a glimpse before another sharpened flake collided against my pupils, snapping them shut.

He is close; I know it…

I was at the base of the hill, and the snowman had been not too far from that…

It wasn't moving toward my son…That only happened in cartoons!

He must've hit the snowman as planned and hurt his face on impact! Yeah! That's why he was screaming! He was—

I froze at the sight of the sled, and my heart stopped for what it seemed. It lay spread over the snow in several mangled and broken pieces, many disappearing quickly under the falling flakes. I shuffled towards it while my eyes scanned for Toby as my fear escalated to pinnacle proportions, fearing that he was scattered across the snow like this too. I know now that I was sobbing—loud, broken—while I clawed through the drifting snow, dropping to my hands and knees as I tore at it, searching for any sign of him.

My fingers were numb and shaking when they finally closed around one of his mittens.

It was bloody.

I couldn't scream any longer, for I had no breath to bear, and all the rationality had left the world as my mind began to fall away. In a panicked effort, I raced toward the field only to run into something significant, compacted, and cold. I was rebounded to the ground instantly, my face stinging with water and ice as if a fast-moving snowball had just plastered me, and as my senses cleared, I opened my eyes to 'It.'

My eyes locked onto the icicles—its teeth—glinting wetly as they clicked together in a jagged, hungry smile. Its two glass eyes jittered and danced with a life they shouldn't have as it drifted backward through the snow, never breaking its gaze. One eye flashed with the harsh shine of an old bike reflector, the other a warped lens from a pair of sunglasses, both of them catching the light in ways that made my stomach twist. It wore everything Toby had described—the hat, the scarf, the branch-arms—but Toby had never mentioned the streaks of red paint smeared across its body, red so dark it looked like blood.

It was Toby's blood.

With a continual swishing sound, it slipped into the haze of falling flakes, leaving me where I lay, too stunned to notice my bladder had emptied. As the last shadow of its form dissolved, my mind finally caught up and understood what dangled from one of its rough-branched hands; it had my son.

I exploded from the ground with a surge of terror and rage fierce enough to bring the heavens down, tearing after it in blind pursuit. I'd made it only a few steps when something in the field to my left snagged my vision, and I skidded to a stop, feeling my brain catch fire and burn away everything I knew.

A little snowman stood there, no more than twenty feet from me. I could make out the bottom and middle snowballs, rounded in haste, and I remember—God help me—giggling at the idea of someone making a snow child.

I trudged towards it, giggling, then laughing, then screaming.

The snowman had been topped with the severed head of my son.

The only thing I remember from the remainder of that night was that I was screaming when they strapped me onto an ambulance's gurney.

✱✱✱

I don't think there is anything left to write, and besides this closing statement, there is nothing more I want to write about. I have done what the doctor suggested: to lay it all out just as I saw it, yet I still don't feel any better.

No, the police never did find my son's body, although they searched for days using volunteers and dogs.

Dogs to find my Toby; creatures that drink from toilets, lick their balls, and chew on their own shit: dogs.

I will forward this to the doctors in the morning, and they will all concur that I am insane and should be committed, but I don't care anymore.

It started snowing outside a while ago, light at first with gentle flakes coming out of the West and gaining strength. A few minutes ago, they shifted and are now coming from the East.

I will take a walk now. I have someone to look for, and he probably knows I am coming for him.

I have kept this small jar of kerosene near the door and a flare gun I picked up at a sporting goods store just for this moment.

I hope it works.

Goodnight.

My Angel Across
the Way

My Angel Across the Way

✻

The air was crisp that night as I watched her from across Mulberry Street, my angel across the way. The occasional breeze would rise, pushing in the sheer curtains at her window, then sucking them back out again as if the city was breathing. It couldn't have been a better night than this; clear, clean, and alive.

Just look at her move…

The subtle pendulous motions of her perfect hips, the edges of her abdomen rolling and tightening with natural muscle tone without signs of a child ever birthed. I wanted my hands there to feel that motion… to feel her life as she sways to the music of a three-piece mariachi band playing through her radio. They were singing something about new-love-found, and old-love-lost like so many fallen autumns leaves down a rolling river run.

A quick snap of the wrist, then curling over gently as the hand spread… those long fingers whispering empyrean grace without so much of a sound, bestowing the air with the very presence of her delicate touch. Almond eyes, dark like polished ebony—free of the cloudiness that old age brings—blink, then narrow, and slowly grow wide again with glints of reflected light, catching it just so and sending shimmers of it across the way to me.

I smiled as she sang along with the Mariachi; her voice was a mouse compared to the radio, but I could read what her lips were saying. Those lips… magnificently full and youthful with an edge of ivory teeth peeking past them, daring me to kiss them with each animated parting while her soft tongue arches her words.

God, she is so beautiful, and I love her so…

The streets were alive with bustling people below me two floors down like a pulse in motion along the veins of the city in a rhythm of a spring jogger, paced and with purpose but without any real urgency to get wherever they were going. Of course, there were the saunters, normal couples who were arm-in-arm, hand-in-hand, strolling along in their careless worlds of romantic bliss.

I watched a strolling couple from the rear windows as I smoked slowly on my cigarette, my mind and soul needing a break from the angel across the way. I stood eyeing them as the amber of my cigarette pulsed with every drag; hidden in the cover of a cupped hand as my eyes followed the motions of the kissing couple below. They were holding each other in genuine passion, an experience of which I had never known.

They didn't care about the world around them or that I was there watching them. It was their night together, and I was merely a spectator. It wouldn't have mattered if they had looked up or not. I was a ghostly shadow blended in with an assortment of other shadows in varying levels of grays and blacks. They were only into each other, but I wondered if they had seen me, would they have cared? More than likely not because I had no purpose for them; my intention was for her, my angel across the way, and this couple had nothing to fear from me.

I envied them all, even the beggar up the block who occasionally chortled into the night, having heard something comical in what the night breezes whispered to him. At least they were free in their personal bubbles. Free to move about to flow and bob and dip amongst the arc-sodium lights like careless night bugs in flight. I was not free; I had something to do, but for now, I would watch her olive skin move in the dim lights of her apartment from across Mulberry Street as that three-piece mariachi band played through her radio.

I moved back across the empty apartment towards the window, keeping just inside and away from the night glow outside, blending into the shadows around me but close enough to smell her perfume that rode the breezes. Flowers with cinnamon and a hint of anise were lightly applied to her wrists, her neckline, and the back of her knees. Every motion of her grace pulsed more of it to me, mixing with the scent of her hair… her skin… her soul.

I rechecked my watch but could not tell the time. This was an involuntary motion on my part that carried no weight upon the evening. There was only her, and she was timeless: my perfect angel across the way.

For a moment, I swore she could see me, and I stiffened, wondering if I had betrayed the trust of the surrounding shadows. Maybe she wanted someone to be there, watching her move, admiring her beauty, and absorbing her skin tones.

She never moved away from facing me as her hands glided over her thighs to her hips, upwards along her abdomen, and found a presence under her perfect breasts.

She was dancing for me, her body swaying to the mariachi music and torturing me with pure physical yearning. I wanted to be there for her, but I was, in a way… I was there to witness her last performance before the night got too late, as the ravens took flight, and the city went to sleep.

My pulse quickened as the music paused, ending the lost-love song and rolling into another. Her dancing had stopped, and she allowed her hands to fall to her sides. Those sparkling ebony eyes held firm to the shadowed rectangle frame of the open window where I stood beyond. I could see her shoulders rise and fall with breath as the occasional breeze ruffled her flowing hair, and she was looking into me, sensing my presence close, and yet she didn't flee.

Why didn't she run?

Did she know I was there, and why?

Had this been the moment she had prepared for?

Did she bathe first and then lotion, taking her time while I moved into place?

Did she carefully apply the sweet perfume in all the choice places so I would notice?

I couldn't assume anything because, in the distance, there was only the nothingness separating my angel across the way and me. Then—carefree and intentionally—she moved with that signature slow grace, her fingers trailing up and curling into a ball, leaving only the index finger, which she stopped above her heart. She was pointing there for me, asking me, choosing for me, and I knew it; her slow, reassuring nod confirmed such.

She tapped there twice…

Her mouth parted slightly to breathe…

I saw a tear run down the curvature of her cheek…

Her eyes were wide with release…

She mouthed to me, *'Please.'*

I fired once at the spot she pointed; the muffled cough left the barrel with no alarming sounds, and I heard nothing from across the way as she collapsed.

I quickly exited the building without a glance back and became one with the flowing pulse of the city as the mariachi music played on above me, hauntingly.

God, she was so beautiful, and I loved her so.

DEMAGO

DEMAGO

-1-

"Give me what you think she's worth," the burly man with heavy arm tattoos shrugged with such passiveness, one could tell straight off that to him this was not the sale of the century.

Grant paused as his mouth moved to one corner, accompanied by a questioning *Hmmm* sound, and then lifted the heavy guitar from the counter again. Grant hated bartering of all kinds; purchases should have a price tag and nothing more. If you want it, you dished out the cash; if not, you hit the pavement for maybe—just maybe—it wasn't meant to be. The thinking sound rose in his throat again as he set it back down on the counter, his hands laying heavy on the counter glass to study it longer.

"Mind the glass, friend," the burly man said with that plain irritating passiveness again, his mind elsewhere as he rooted about one nostril with an outstretched finger, removing it, and then studied the tip for a moment. Slowly, with the same finger, he pointed to a long-faded note under the glass and gave Grant the summary. "Just like everything else here: if you break it, you buy it."

"Yeah, all right," Grant rose from the counter, wiping his hands together as if he had set them in something dirty. "Sorry."

"Not a problem, if you know what I mean by that not being a problem," the man said, cutting Grant a sharp wink.

"Yeah, I get you," Grant played along, and honestly, he didn't know a damned thing this man meant.

"Good, so what do you think she's worth?" the man asked, and Grant wasn't all too surprised to see the same finger of the opposite hand climb its way up the darkened wind row of the second nostril. "It's getting late."

"Hmm," the sound had come yet a third time, a signal telling him he had better get his act together quickly or lose the show entirely. "Are you sure this is a Fender?"

The man removed the finger—thankfully coming out without any green morsels—locked eyes with this young cocker, took up the guitar slowly, paused, turned it over, and showed a tarnished metal plate on the bottom side. In clear, crisply engraved strokes, the letters formed the words in perfect, comprehensible order:

FENDER STRATOCASTER:
DEMAGO

Giving a quick wink with a nod, the proprietor lowered the guitar to the counter, making sure the hanging price tag didn't get caught up under the weight. Grant double-checked the tag from the corner of his eye, reading over again what he had read before, being only a blank, off-white card to begin with.

"Yeah, all right," Grant said, licking his lips and nodding quickly with a pulse of uneasiness running through him. There was something utterly wrong with this guitar altogether, but how do you argue what your eyes told you? "But you see... I-uh-I have read a lot of books about—"

"Do you like her or not?" the man cut in quickly, leaning forward, eyebrows rising.

"Yes, it's gorgeous, but—"

"She," the man said calmly.

"What?"

"This instrument is a *She*, friend," the proprietor said with a snap, his right hand gently coming down flat on the finely polished cherry wood, softly stroking it with a calm motion that one would soothe a whimpering child just as the nightmares left for the evening. "Just like a good ship that will bring you home safe from the sea's storm, I would say… or a wife you would race home to, eager to smell her hair and to touch her skin. Yes, sir, this here guitar is a *She*; magnificent, full bodied, elegant, and when you meet one like her, you snatch her up and never let her go."

"Yeah, okay, sorry," Grant nodded, correcting his memory and his speech for future note. "She's beautiful, perhaps the most beautiful guitar I've ever seen, but as I was saying, I've read many books on Fender, and I've never heard of a model called anything remotely close to a Dem—"

"She's unique," he said, his hands going to the glass counter, his weight shifting to the wrists, and that is where he stood, staring. Grant blinked, eyes glancing to his right, where a small sign under the glass warned against such actions, and he dismissed it without saying a word about it. "She's the only one of her kind."

"Yeah, I, um, never heard of a Demago," Grant smiled, his head shaking with disbelief.

"How well do you know your guitars?" the man asked quietly.

"Really well, I mean, they are my passion, although I haven't owned many good ones."

The burly proprietor nodded and straightened, stretching out his back with audible popping noises.

"Ever hear of the Marauder?" he asked, folding his arms and receiving a slow shaking head from Grant as his answer. "Don't worry yourself, son; not many people have because it never made it to production. Thing was too damned expensive to make because back in the late sixties, it was way ahead of its time, kinda like the Rolls Royce of guitars. Rumor has it only eight were ever constructed."

"*Wow,*" Grant sounded; sincerely.

"Well, the Fender Corporation loved a lot of what it had and thought of things that it didn't, and they took the Marauder and melded it into the Stratocaster, mixing them up like a half-breed baby. You know, like a white man and a black woman, or a black man and a white woman, you know? Making little panda bunnies, if you know what I mean?"

"Are you serious?" Grant begged, ignoring the man's attempt at humor and only focusing on the guitar. His mind raced over the extent such a purchase would mean to him, his pocketbook, and the possibility of owning the *Fender* is like discovering a Rembrandt hidden under the paint and gesso layers of a Picasso, wealth beneath wealth.

"Look here, boy," the man leaned forward, putting two fingers under his eyes, pointing at the bloodshot there. "You see these eyes here? Do they look like they're bullshittin' ya'?"

"No," Grant said, cowering.

"Then I guess you have your answer."

The man leaned back and dug into one pocket of his shirt until he produced a half-spent cigarette and placed it between his lips. The response was instinctive. Among smokers, one person lighting up was all it took before everyone else suddenly remembered they wanted one too. A cigarette found its way between his own lips and he reached for his flint.

"Sorry, son, ain't no smoking in here by the customers," the man spoke up. "They ain't ever careful enough. Rules, ya' know?"

"Oh, yeah, sorry," Grant stammered, putting the cigarette quickly behind one ear and suddenly wanting to leave this place, but then again, there was the Fender.

"All right then," the man said, dragging hard, exhaling, then tossing the cigarette to the floor where he stomped it into a curled mass of fiberglass filter and yellow stained paper. "I'm going to be closing up soon, so you had better make your decision quick. I never stay open past five, even to make a buck. Rules, ya know. So, how about it, then? How much?"

"Three fifty," Grant heard himself sprout out, and immediately he considered ducking a blow that would surely be deserved for making such an insulting offer for a piece of beauty like the *Fender*.

"Now we're getting somewhere," the man smiled. "We're bartering like they did in the old days!

"'How much for your horse?' Well, that depends on how many times I get to pork your wife and how many chickens you have to offer!"

The man broke into a wild fit of boisterous laughter; his mouth gaped wide and unnaturally off-centered as if his whole jaw was unhinged. Grant's eyes shifted, not knowing if he should join in or remain quiet. He had to swallow, but he chose to hold off just in case doing so was not allowed in the shop.

"Go ahead, boy; light yourself a smoke, and let's continue to haggle over her!" Grant paused, reflecting upon something the guy said about customers smoking, shrugged, and then did as he was told, lighting up quickly.

"Alrighty, then! Three fifty sounds like a good start, a perfect start, but I'm afraid we are pretty far off. Now I'll give you a number, and then we'll see.

"Three thousand, plus tax."

"*Whoa, three thousand?* No, no, no," Grant shook his head, having never seen three thousand dollars in one place at one time in his life.

"Well then…" the man smiled, arms folding. "Give me a counter price."

"All right," Grant nodded, understanding in part the game. Carefully he pondered, thinking of a good comeback figure, then went for broke. "Let's say then... five hundred bucks, without tax."

'There you go! Barter me, son!" the boisterous man was smiling widely, bearing his tobacco-stained teeth, the counteroffer came. "Twenty-two hundred!"

"Seven hundred," Grant smiled as he began to enjoy the bartering game.

"Seventeen, without tax, case separate," the man chirped and grinned, snapping a sharp wink

"Nine hundred, with tax, a case coming home with her," Grant smiled in return, snapping a reply wink.

"There you go," the guy laughed, clapping his large hands with fat fingers together. "Twelve hundred, tax, no case, no amp, and no cords."

"Screw that, shit!" Grant laughed back, exhaling smoke. "A thousand for everything, including an amp with cables, and you hold the door for me on the way out!"

"*Oh shit!* This boy knows how to barter like a charlatan on the Mississippi selling air over China!" the man roared, head towards the ceiling as the laughter exploded from his lungs. "I will get you here and now! There's no way you can counter this, and if you even tried, you'd feel like a bastardly fool!

"I'll give you the package: the Fender, case, amp, the whole effing rig, *and* the tax, for a solid price and even shake your hand! Four hundred and forty-four, son, and boy have I won the game!"

Grant froze, blinking twice.

Did he just undersell himself? He raced his mind, trying hard to understand that what the man had just said must have been what he had heard in error. A moment later, he was unfolding bills out onto the countertop without a word.

The man began to laugh deeply, having won the bartering game once again, and began moving about, gathering up the guts of the package plan.

What the hell just happened? Grant begged his inner reasoning, daring not to open his mouth until he was alone in his loft, laughing his ass off to the shadows in the corners.

It took five minutes for everything to be gathered and another one for Grant to stand at the door, ready to exit with his parcels held close to his person. The man slipped a packet of picks into Grant's jacket pocket just for good measure and then gave him a gentleman's wink.

"You're gonna love her, boy, and she'll love ya' just as dear!" the man laughed, his hands flipping through the three hundred and fifty dollars made up of twenties, fives, and ones. "She won't miss a riff like them cheap ones, and you'll never riff without her *ever* again! Enjoy her! Love her and play her until the end of it all!"

Laughter trailing, Grant stepped out onto the city street, finding Chicago to have grown dark quickly in his time in the little pawn shop. He felt a pleasure deep within, one which the drivers of prototypes by GM must feel the first moments in the captain's chair.

Halfway up the block was the bus stop that would drop him off at home an hour later; he glanced at his purchases in his hands and reconsidered the notion.

He hailed a cab two minutes later.

-2-

Twenty minutes from purchase, Grant sat on one of his many bean bag chairs in his studio loft near the wall of his sectional living room. The case was open before him like a large awaiting oyster with the pearl of all pearls inside.

His eyes danced over the red and black swirled lacquered beast, its strings bright gold as if spun from a magical knitting wheel in some off-beat fairy story. The thick leather strap wound around the bell of the guitar and hung off the lip of the case, bridging the amp cable, which ran straight to the amplifier off to the side. There was a constant echoing pang deep in his chest as his heartbeat drummed rapidly, and his eyes pulsed in unison with the beat. The guitar flirted with him to reach down and touch it, to caress it and hold it as he would a lover, a whore.

Grant shuddered and swallowed quickly, feeling the pooled saliva in his mouth dare to pour out of the corners of his mouth as drool, all the while not noticing the solid erection in his jeans.

"I love you," he whispered to it as he wiped his hands on his shirt, then moved quickly to a small desk he had lodged in the corner of the room.

Quickly he snatched up his notebook and started flipping through songs he had written which had neither been good nor bad, just things he had played with and nothing more. His hands shook madly as he flipped through the pages until a feedback moan rose from the amplifier. His eyes shot in that direction, and he swallowed, eyes shifting back to the open page before him to one entitled *Lamprey's Addiction.*

With slow nods, his eyes read the title repeatedly as his mind's ears listened to the melody of the notes below. This was *his* song, one he had hoped would turn into a hit, but the music died somewhere along the way.

"Well…" he spoke to no one, clearing his throat. "Let's see how this little ditty sounds on the new addition."

Grant sighed, moved back to the guitar, and slowly hoisted the Fender by its neck. A thin vibration ran the length of the strings, crossed the bridge, and raced back through his hand. He yelped and shifted the instrument from one hand to the other before looking down at the pressed inscription in the velvet lining of the case.

DEMAGO was all it said.

Without realizing it, he mouthed the word as his eyes followed the letters.

Blankly, he pulled the ivory pick from his shirt pocket, set his fingers, glanced once at the lines of music, and brought up his hand to play.

In one swipe, the picking hand came down like flowing gelatin and gilded over the strings, rippling out a perfectly balanced chord that seemed almost too perfect. His eyes watched as each string took it without hesitation, and to his dumb wonder, it was how the pick took to the cords in an almost cartoonish way. The pick sliced apart section by section as it flowed over the strings, falling away like peeled potatoes on a cutting board.

A faraway thought pulsed in the preservation side of his brain, yet his body did nothing to slow his hand. As the chords strummed from the final two strings, there was no more pick to slice, leaving only the plump hardened tips of his fingers to do the work. The blood came in two thick splashes, lashing down the neck of the guitar in a fan spray. White hot pain raced up his arm and into his head like an acid-laced high ball, jerking him backward.

"Shit!" he screamed, snapping his hand so as to ward off the pain to no avail. Blood became thick lines on the floor and surrounding furniture with each motion; his cheeks flowed with gushing tears.

In a split second of reckoning, he caught himself halfway through the urge to rip the strap from around his neck and hurl the guitar across the room; to break its back and shatter its frame.

Instead, the guitar came off quickly and was dropped onto one of the beanbag chairs. A second later, he was dashing for the bathroom, holding his injured fingers tightly in a balled fist.

-8-

The flowing cold water was merciless needles of torture as the liquid met the meat. Grant bit against the screams which begged to escape his throat, grinding his teeth together as the cries were reduced to hissing whimpers.

He squeezed the two fingers tightly at their joints while his feet danced in place, forcing the raw bleeders to remain beneath the stream. He wanted to vomit, scream, faint, fart, and shit. His bowels had turned soft and hot, threatening mutiny at any moment.

Through watery eyes which flowed constantly down his cheeks, Grant dared to examine the damage. The instant he saw bone, he winced away.

"Oh God!" he whimpered, bending, feeling acid lash up his throat and into his mouth.

His forefinger took the brunt of the strings, slicing down where the bone tip showed brilliantly like a bloody pearl. The middle fingertip was also gone, millimeters from joining its partner digit to the bone.

Reaching out with closed eyes, Grant snatched a wash-towel from the bar over the toilet and thrust his hand inside.

Get to a hospital, man! His brain screamed at him as he sat on the toilet with shaky legs.

Panting heavily, he calmed himself while his brain desperately searched for logic in everything happening and assembled a game plan. He would pick up his keys from the entry table with his teeth, go downstairs, and hail a cab to the hospital. The plan was quick, decisive, and about as painless as having exposed bone could possibly be, but it was still a plan.

Breathing deeply, he began counting backward from three, preparing himself to stand and follow through.

Three, two, whu—.

TWANG!

Grant paused at one and caught his breath as the riff echoed from the amplifier in the next room. For a moment, there was nothing else: no pain, no breathing, no emotion; only the reverberating pulse of the riff echoing through his ears.

Must've finished settling, his mind diagnosed the situation, for he had dropped the thing in haste. He released his breath, which had grown hot and stale, then slowly rose into a precarious standing position and moved toward the door.

TWANG, STRUM, TWANG!

The amplifier sounded, stopping him in his tracks. Slowly Grant peered around the bathroom entrance to the living room, and there, as set, the guitar was waiting for him.

You gotta get to a hospital! His mind begged as his pulse quickened, his eyes fixing on the guitar.

Slowly he shuffled forward, moving towards the front door while his eyes never left the guitar. His dragging toes caught carpeting, tripping him, and down he went, frantically trying to protect his wounded hand. A sudden yelp escaped his throat as he landed on his side with his hand pulled into a protective hold close to his chest, and there before him, Demago pulsed.

"You want me to play you?" Grant's voice came far and away from a place he didn't recognize, and slowly he sat up, dropping his hands to his lap. The guitar pulses twice with a shadowed hue, and its strings begin to vibrate, forming a constant hum.

Slowly, Grant stood, mindlessly using his injured hand as leverage to right himself, and as the towel fell away, the tips began to flow red again. He remained motionless as his eyes focused on the guitar.

His mind began to soar to a place where he saw himself on a grand concert stage. He was strumming and riffing while the audience screamed and cheered, and the panties! Oh, how the panties flew from the crowd, skidding past his feet and landing on his face. He was on top of the world, playing his songs while they screamed his name, and every time he wrenched the echo bar, he knew women in the crowd were losing their minds.

He was *their* guitar god; he was *their* voice and made *their* music; he was *their* playing saint!

Calmly, Grant lifted the guitar by its strap and then fed his head and neck through it, feeling its weight rest snuggly through the strap pad. A thin smile parted his lips as his left hand slowly glided up the neck, caressing the smooth lacquer skin with every pore and crevice of his fingers.

He nodded to nothing as he bent down towards the amp, cranking the volume up to max, and moved across the loft, stopping before the tall paned glass windows.

In the reflection of the glass, he could see himself but not quite himself; there he stood in a rocker's outfit of leather pants and a ripped baggy shirt with the arms cut off. His hair was sweaty and hanging despite the sparkling mousse which held it. The Grant there was smiling widely with a sparkle on his teeth.

So he matched what he saw, and the corners of his mouth rose then spread despite the screams which wanted to break free from behind them.

He took another pick from his shirt pocket and held it momentarily before his eyes, studying its pear-like opalescent shape, which became red with blood, and then tossed it to the floor. He had wanted to go to the hospital, but the guitar wanted to play, and that's what he was going to do, damning everything else.

Grant adjusted his fingers along the neck, a quick tweak of the whammy bar, then closed his eyes slowly while the bloody tips came up to strike the first chord. There was a brand-new song in his head that came out of nowhere, a fast-paced ballad that could best even Hendrix by its fierceness and vivacity. The chords echoed in his mind sounding so raw and sweet; it would be his best piece ever and his last.

There were no lyrics, just the inspiration of notes chaining together like strung festival lights; each one daring his fingers to find their rhythm and glow.

He took a deep breath and exhaled, parting his eyes to find himself in the reflection again just as his hand came down, strumming the beginning chords that ripped the air with blazing sounds and flying meat.

Faster and faster, he played, his eyes filling with tears as the pain raced sharper up his arm into his chest, feeling the warm splatters of blood as they lapped against his neck and chin. He couldn't take his eyes off the reflection, watching his phantom rock on, tearing up the stage, howling over the music he poured from his *Fender*, his Demago.

'She won't miss a riff like them cheap ones!' the pawnshop vendor's voice echoed in his mind, taunting and mocking him. *'And you'll never riff without her ever again! Enjoy her! Love her! And play her until the end of it all!'*

"I love you!" he cried as the riffs climbed and bloody flesh fell. He did love her, and he was enjoying her, and as he screamed continuously and strummed with bloody stump-knuckles, he knew he would never let her go.

Despite the wailing screams tearing out of his throat, the other dwellers in his building could only hear the guitar.

*

A man walking a small dog past the lofts paused on the street below his window. The dog tugged against him but was disciplined quickly by a tug in return, for he wanted to listen for a moment and then sent a pleasant glance upwards. He had not heard guitar playing like that for quite some time, bringing back memories of when he used to tear at the cat guts just like the person was doing two floors up.

Someone up there was rocking!

"Sounds pretty good, doesn't it?" he sounded to his pooch, who was more concerned with sniffing a stained spot on the building's wall than with anything his walker was saying to him. "Man sounds like he's trying to beat the Devil up there."

The little dog whimpered and moaned, treading half circles in place, the poor thing not knowing whether to tuck its tail or wag it in desperation.

"C'mon, Tyco, let's go."

The man and his dog moved on, leaving the music behind, and for the next forty minutes, the guitar riffs poured forth, ripping the airwaves until, finally, nothing.

* *

The little bell over the door chimed as a would-be shopper stepped into the pawnshop on the edge of the Loop, ushering in the cool, crisp air of the late morning.

The proprietor chanced a glance upward as his index finger worked diligently inside his right nostril in search of hidden treasure. With a humph, he wiped his hand on his jeans and stood upright behind the waist-high display case.

"Looking to buy a guitar?" the man said with a growing smile.

"Yeah, I'm looking for something special…" the young man grunted, scanning the shop walls at the various axes on display. "Something different."

The man behind the counter grunted, his eyes sizing up the nervous looking young man across from him. With a nod, he reached back, gripping the neck of a fine-looking *Fender*.

"I have just the one for you, *if* you are a bargaining man."

something different
FORGIVENESS
something different

Forgiveness

Dark Interlude I

You want forgiveness for the damage you have done?
I have it right here in the guise of a straight razor,
and although its edge is sharp and piercing,
its soul of cold steel, ever lacking remorse for what it does,
will aid in your redemption.

I will show it to you in just a moment,
Formally introducing you to it and welcoming you to oblivion.
You may deduce that it is a rude thing
—cruel and harsh without so much as a merciful air—
 but you are mistaken...

It will gladly accept your apology.

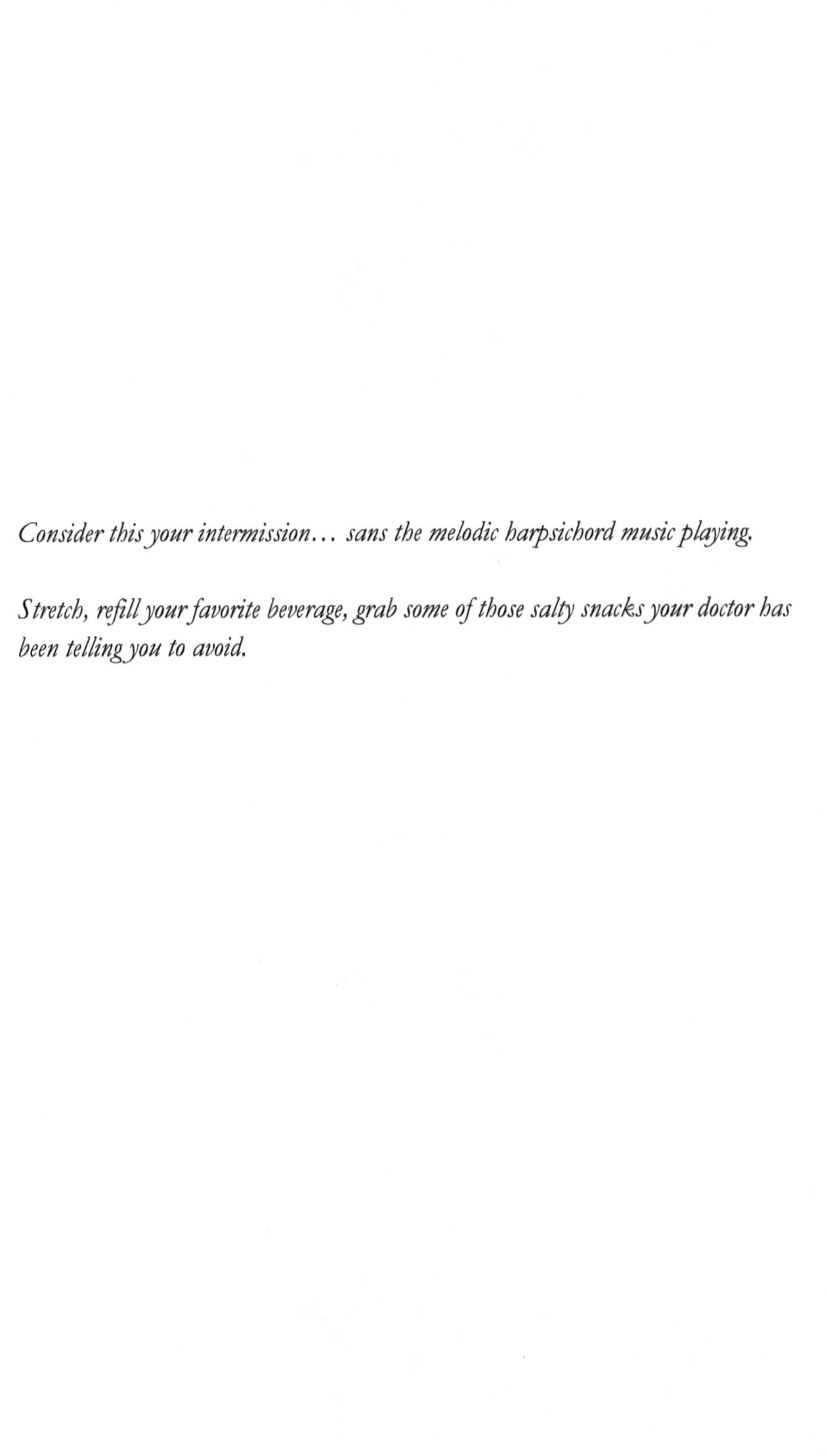

Consider this your intermission… sans the melodic harpsichord music playing.

Stretch, refill your favorite beverage, grab some of those salty snacks your doctor has been telling you to avoid.

THE ROOM DOWN THE HALL

The Room Down the Hall

An Amusing Breath Betwixt

The door to the east
faced the wall to the west;
It opened up sideways,
then down, then abreast.

Just inside it, and into,
not to here, but to there,
Sits a room warm and tidy
with a despicable air.

You can laugh if you want to,
You can taunt with your jeers,
But it's that room I do tell you
that everyone fears.

Not the decor or the windows,
or the lamps or the rugs,
Or the shadowy high corners
full of webs and dead bugs.

What people dreaded most,
from the warm little space,

Was not the warmth or the cheer,
but the feel of the place.
Having been carved out of shadows
and teardrops of gloom,
The little room pulsated
oblivion and doom.

Guests would not enter
and the maids would not clean;
A repairman once entered
only to bellow and scream:

"There is evil most present!'
said the man as he fled.
"You must burn the place down!"
Waving hands overhead.

I've tried candles and crosses
and the waters from church,
Even erected an effigy
which had been carved out of birch!

Yet the room is still there
at the end of the hall,
Waiting quietly and patient
perhaps for nothing at all.

One night in the darkness
the door opened a peek
and there in the shadows,
two eyeballs did peep.

Bedtime Stories

I stood stark in the hallway,
feeling sweat on my back,
as those eyes held me unmoving;
bright orbs against black.

It stared and it breathed
while it examined its prey,
Which was me in the hallway
like an open buffet!

I could hear my own pulse,
as it whacked in my head,
Knowing at any one moment
that I would be dead.

The moment had come--
Life's final cruel joke--
So I closed my own eyes
when the little thing spoke:

"I want a glass of water,"
the little thing said.
"Of course," I replied
patting my son on his head.

With glass in his hand,
and his paw in my mitt,
I led him back to his bed
without even a fit.

"I'm going to bed now,"
he smiled as he dozed,
I nodded then left him
promising to leave his door closed.

Yes, he is my own monster,
cantankerous and true,
And you would act as I act
if you had my son too.

I Have What
You Need

I Have What You Need

-1-

Mackenzie left Dr. Forrester's office completely drained after vomiting a week's worth of built-up aggravations and nearly incomprehensible teen angst. He gave her a pack of tissues and a fatherly pat on her shoulder as she departed. Despite the weight on her shoulders, he reassured her that there was a boy out there in the world who would see her as herself and that her mother's insistent bitching was just a way of expressing parental love. Finally, her braces didn't make her look like she had been chewing on tin cans.

Another client served while adding another two hundred dollars in the bank from a parent who would never need to pay it if they had listened to their children in the first place. Smiling, he took off his glasses and dropped them on his desk, concluding another helpful and lucrative day, and stretched back in his office chair, thinking.

He had so many clients like Mackenzie—or Kenzie as she preferred to be called—young, emotional, and very hormonal; their maturing bodies moving faster than their young minds could keep pace with, and all of them overtly idealistic about how life should be but often very wrong about how things were. Life was far more complex than the free-loving, 'make love, not war' Utopian vision that seemed reserved for teenagers like her and the potheads. No, war was never a good thing or a solution, but at times it had proven a necessary evil no matter how one looked at it. People did not have to like you simply because you thought they should, and although a beautiful song insisted otherwise, *Oz* truly was not over the rainbow no matter how much one wished it to be.

"I wish a prince would come to save me!" were Kenzie's exact words, which came through sobbing tears, and although he was empathetic and listened to her every word. *Grow the fuck up* was echoing in his mind at the time. They all wanted a *'Prince'* or to *'Disappear'* or the all-famous *'Wish I was never born,'* but those words never sparked any genuine interest as he jotted down his notes as she rambled on.

He was looking for *the* words which would send the flares up into the skies, the absolute catalyst of concern: *'I wish I were dead.'*

"Do you truly wish that?" he had spoken flatly over the lip of his steno-pad, his eyebrows standing high and arched above the rims of his glasses. "To die?"

She had been looking out his office window with her dripping eyes focused on nothing significant outside, then turned to him with the most serious face and nodded.

"Yes."

"Have you thought about hurting yourself again?" he returned flatly, flipping several pages into his notes without looking at the topic heading. Here he had cataloged where Kenzie had expressed many sessions before about the numerous cuttings and beatings, all of which were self-inflicted.

"I am tired," she exhaled a heavy breath. "Is my session over with yet?"

"Not quite," he replied, his eyes darting to the wall clock behind her. "You have twelve more minutes, but you haven't answered my question."

Kenzie's eyes had locked onto his unblinking, allowing the moments to pass in deep thought. Slowly she wiped her face dry with the backs of her hands and stood, turning away from him and pulling down the back of her baggy gray sweatpants. On both buttocks were horrible marks where cigarettes had been extinguished on and into young flesh. After a moment, she pulled them back up and returned to her seat.

"Why did you do that to yourself?" he whispered, feeling that if he attempted a higher volume, his voice would crack and shudder.

"Why, does it matter?" she snipped, eyes narrowing at him. "No guy wants to see my ass anyways so that no one will see them!"

"Kenzie, you are only fourteen," he shook his head without judgement, straightening in his chair and closing his notepad. "Why do you insist on thinking that you have to have a sexual relationship with someone? That's not love, Kenzie. That is an empty solution to a much deeper problem that—if you would just let me in—maybe we can find a solution for what haunts you."

"Whatever," she shrugged, looking away.

"And Kenzie…?" he sighed, feeling the aggravation building in his chest. "Please look at me when I am talking to you."

Her head snapped blazingly in his direction, eyes full of wet anger and inner rage.

"Thank you. Kenzie, hurting yourself is *never* going to solve anything. I know you are reaching out for help, but—"

"Well, no one knows they are there but me!" she shot forward, screaming, the tears blasting from her eyes as her hands clutched the armrests. "I am not some freak self-mutilator that wants everyone to pawn over me like some of the little bitches at my school who show off their scars like fucking trophies! No one except *you* even knows that they are there!"

"I know; you just showed me, Kenzie."

"Wanna see the ones on my tits?" she suggested grabbing at the bottom of her shirt, but thankfully this time, it was only a daring bluff.

Slowly he folded his hands on his lap and stared at her.

Kenzie was angry, there was no doubt, but this was the first time she had truly shown it. She had talked about whipping herself in the past with an extension cord, making sure she held it by the center loop so that the plug and the receptor tore into her back flesh. She stated how she forced herself to sleep on her back that night so that the welts screamed through her body, reminding her of her hatred, her pain and that she was a worthless bitch. She had talked about how she once drank two bottles of *Maalox*, and after two days of bloated backlog, she beat her swollen abdomen with a sock full of pennies from her piggy bank until both the outside and inside of her belly was bruised.

He had asked why she had done that, and her response was simple: so that she could hurt in every possible way by simply breathing.

Yes, she had talked about many things she had done to herself in the past, quite creative ones for even a person in his position would expect to hear, and now, having seen, he truly believed she had every intention of doing far worse.

"No, Kenzie, I think I have seen enough," he said, standing, and moved to his desk while she broke down in tears. Slowly, he lifted a small pad, scribbled on it for a moment, removed it, and then moved towards her with it extended before him. She wiped at her flowing eyes and sucked in twice, withdrawing loads of free flowing-mucus back into her head.

"Whu-what is this?" she whimpered, taking it and glancing at the writing through blurry eyes.

"You've been coming to me for several months now, Kenzie," he said calmly and sat on the coffee table between the two chairs. "You have been looking for something to help you, and I think that is what you are looking for."

"It's—it's a prescription to the *beach*?" she puzzled with a rising inflected voice.

"Yes, that's exactly what it is."

"I-I don't understand," she shook her head, sniffing back tears as the confusion overwhelmed her pains. "How would—"

"There's a nice spot which no one ever goes to—" he spoke over her calmly and moved to the wall where a large framed colored map of the area hung on the wall and then pointed. "—and there, I promise you, you will find what you are looking for."

Slowly Kenzie stood and moved in close and narrowed her eyes at the position he was pointing. There, just about a mile from the boardwalk was a slight indent where the waters pushed in, and under the glass, the tiny words spelled out: 'Reflection Point.'

"What am I supposed to do there?" she shook her head, confused.

"Don't you ever go to the beach?" he interrupted, his voice gentle.

"Well, no, not anymore; not since I was little. I mean, I go to the boardwalk sometimes to boy-watch, but—"

"Then you can find this place then, yes?"

"I think so," she shrugged. "But what does that have to—"

"Kenzie, you need to listen," he smiled, hushing her, and took one of her hands and led her towards the door, pausing at a desk where he retrieved a personal travel pack of tissues and handed them to her. "You overthink simple things, and that's why you suffer sometimes.

"There, at Reflection Point, are wondrous things and have helped many like yourself begin their journeys from that very spot."

"To healing?" she asked, her tone begging.

"Exactly, Kenzie," he smiled widely and gave a reassuring nod to accompany it. "Towards healing.

"I want you to take these tissues and clear up your eyes, and then later today, I want you to go to Reflection Point and take in all the place has to offer you. The best time is just after five o'clock when the water is perfect. Get your toes wet, and for a little added fun, wiggle them around a bit; the waters are warm this time of year so enjoy yourself. I assure you that in no time at all, you will find exactly what you need."

"I will?" she squeaked, her eyes brimming with hope.

"You will," he smiled and patted her shoulder, seeing her out. "I promise."

———

He checked the time on the clock from across the room and acknowledged it with a nod seeing that an hour had passed since

Kenzie had left and it was moving quickly to his five-o'clock quitting time. Calmly he stood, lifting his valise to the desktop and opened it, then gathered up particular items from his desk drawer. He was humming something tender and sweet as he locked his office door, bidding goodnight to his receptionist as he headed out into the late afternoon air.

-2-

Mackenzie filled Dr. Forrester's prescription to the letter:

'Go to the beach…dip your toes in the water… relax… think happy thoughts… be you!' is what the small prescription order said, and until she dipped her toes for the first time in the waters there, she thought that maybe it was the good doctor who needed help instead of the other way around.

She had gone home and changed from her baggy clothes into a pair of loose jean shorts and a simple top. Mackenzie stood for a moment in front of her full-length mirror to ask herself what she was doing and to ensure that none of her abuse marks showed. Confirming that neither thought was a real issue, she rode her bike the mile to the boardwalk and the additional mile along the shoreline to the spot she saw on the map. There, barely visible by the passing eye, was a small trail leading away from the road towards the waters beyond.

It was here that she actually found some solace in her tortured mind and giggled like a typical young teen for no apparent reason. She squatted low in the waters with her hands over her mouth, hiding just in case anyone of any importance may be about to witness such a rare act of hers. There was none; this was a hidden special spot prescribed to her by the one and only person who seemed to care even in the slightest way about her life and problems.

Giggling again, this time unrestrained and loud, Mackenzie splashed around in the water, enjoying it.

"I knew you would like it here, Kenzie," a voice spoke calmly from the shore behind her, and she jumped, startled. There stood Dr.

Forrester with a pleasant smile on his face and adorning eyes as he posed relaxed with his hands in his pocket.

"Dr. Forrester!" she cried happily and charged him with an open hug.

Laughing, he allowed the hug to come and returned it, bending the side of his face to the top of her head, welcoming. She had a vise-like squeeze around his midsection, he noted; the grasp of a lost child searching for a missing father figure in a world filled with dark things. Yet for once, there was no despair in her. She was smiling and showing that somewhere deep within, a light still remained. She thanked him repeatedly for his gift, this place of total enjoyment, and for giving her such a fantastic voyage to the 'healing place.'

"Oh no, my dear," he smiled, looking down into her eyes at an arm's length. "This is only the starting point, Kenzie, not the end of it. This is where you find that place of sheer enlightenment."

"Oh?" she sounded, her lips twisting into a confused, knotted expression. "I thought this was it, you know, what I needed?"

"Oh, it is," he smiled as his hands slowly slid along the tops of her shoulders towards her neck. "And I promise, it won't take long to get there."

Slowly, Mackenzie's eyes grew wide and her mouth fell open like a cave as his gloved hands tightened around her throat. Her tiny fingers locked around his wrists as she struggled and twisted against his grip, feeling tendons squeeze and pop while the blood collecting in her head grew hot.

A choppy gurgle managed to break through as his hands made a slight adjustment, tearing open the tender lining of her throat. The spray raced forward in a bloody spattering across his gloves. He slowly closed his eyes and began to hum a sweet melody in his throat, his smile broadening as the pattering sounds of uncontrolled urine escaped her body and found the sand below.

Dr. Forrester grunted once, forcing his thumbs in deep with a satisfying crunching mix, much akin to gritting gravel rocks against one another, and then a sharp reverberating snap as her esophagus gave way.

In a moment, she went limp.

All quiet now, the world rolled into another minute as the waters lapped at the hidden shoreline, uncaring.

*

Dr. Forrester stopped to buy an ice cream cone at a concession stand along the boardwalk just as the sun arced closer to the horizon line in its preparation to conclude yet another day. Calmly, he enjoyed his treat on a bench just inside the boardwalk with his briefcase sitting next to him and a gentle smile on his face.

It was really good ice cream.

His eyes happened upon a teenage girl trailing behind her apparent mother with an angry expression. She was near tears, he could tell, and oozing angst with every stomping step. The mother turned once on her with a pointed finger, and although he could not make out exactly what she was saying, the garbled tones and expressions assuredly meant someone 'has had it,' and someone else 'was about to get it.'

He slowly stood, tossed the partial cone into the receptacle, and moved towards the retreating woman and her daughter.

"Excuse me, ma'am," he spoke professionally and friendly as he extended her a business card. "My name is Doctor Forrester, and I have what you need."

THE ATTIC

The Attic

Water dripping hollow somewhere deep in the shadows...
Sharp plinks in the echoing spaces around him...
Soft thuds of heavy blood-borne from him, landing and pooling close at hand...

-1-

The portable lantern flickered again, sputtering without warning as it had twice before in the last several minutes. Beyond the bell-shaped casing, the LED cores were alerting him that soon that would be that; there would be no more juice to ride on, and the darkness must come. Carter wanted to look at his belly to reassure the mind what the deep pulsating pain already told him: that he was torn open from the navel to the ribcage, perhaps even worse.

It got your guts! Carter's mind begged as he shifted his weight onto his left shoulder, jostling the hanging bits of his insides, and he almost fainted as pain blasted across his midsection, rebounding off his lungs like a cannonball bouncing around inside the bilge of a ship. Unforgiving tears poured from his eyes, and he winced back against them, daring not to cry out, or they will come.

Panting rapidly through pursed lips, he forced his body into one more daring move to glimpse his ruined midsection. Fresh smells rose, stinking of collected blood trapped in stale air pockets of his body cavity, forcing him to cough and gag away. Mustering against his repulsion, he had to check for that the one scent he feared he would detect, a smell that would mean certain agonizing death if he didn't get out soon.

Slowly his head bobbed towards his belly in rapid darts and sniffs, dipping with waning strength and rebounded by spikes of pain, and there, rank and sour, he could smell it: the odor of fecal matter.

He no longer had to guess anything; it had gotten his guts alright...no fucking doubt about it.

Carter choked and moaned into his elbow as his mind raced through the probability of him surviving an open gut wound with lacerated bowels oozing clumps of feces into his body cavity. If he could get away from this house, he might survive—providing the docs intravenously fed him the right combination of strong antibiotics to stifle the toxins pooling inside him—he could make it. If not? Lingering in a hidden attic where no one knew he was up there with a gut wound with open bowels?

He shook his head rapidly to dislodge the thoughts because those two were not a good combination for anyone.

"Shit!" he grunted, then hissed as he boosted himself back on his elbow, countered by a white-hot jolt that sent his head slamming into the wall behind him. Loose things that had once been tethered to other things inside his body slapped and shifted against one another, slopping around like a hearty stew.

He doubled over with a choking cough, something thick and wrong spilling out of him and hitting his lap with a wet, sickening weight. The taste of acid surged up his throat, and for a heartbeat the world tilted as he realized something inside him had shifted—had slipped—had no business being where it was. A cold, coiling pressure pressed against his hip, and instinctively his hand twitched toward it, desperate to push it back, to deny what he already knew. But before he could touch it, a long, low creak rose from beneath him, freezing him in place.

With a shaky hand, he gripped the blood-soaked handle to the shotgun and raised the barrel from the floor a mere inch; its maw poised and ready at the attic door hatch, waiting for the eyes. They were fast and ferocious; chameleons in the shadows save their innate curse of having glowing eyes to assist him by blasting them where the glimmer showed. He took one down that same way already, but then he had his wits and guts together then; laying the bead right between the glowing eyes and hammered down, turning it into meaty confetti.

There were eight and one in the pipe, Carter recounted the shotgun shells rapidly to himself. Compared to how many of the things he had seen, subtracting how many he had disintegrated earlier with his tool, then balanced it all out with how many shells he had in the tubular chamber. *Five had come…you got three of 'em, including the one whose claws were in your guts. Shot that fucker twice! That leaves you with five shells and only two of them left…*

His half-masted eyes blinked rapidly, then he gave it a snapping shake and then a nod. Yes, five shots, no doubt about it.

'Ya sure you had eight shots, old buddy, or was it nine?' the cynical side of his mind quipped. *'Like, absolutely sure? I mean, it is usually a safe bet to assume you came fully loaded and ready to rock, but when was the last time you touched that thing anyway?'*

Eight shots… I had eight shots! Carter's mind demanded Reasoning and Circumstance for their mutual concurrence as he slowly pulled himself into a sitting position, his legs out before him in a spread 'V.' Trapped air pockets gurgled and burped from his exposed innards, sending acid up his throat, which filled his mouth, nearly passing his lips, an event that would have caused madness as acrid vomit met open wounds.

In a shuddered lurching motion, he leaned, allowing the chunky gut-stew to pass off to his side, forming a pool of sightless matter in a larger collected pond of his own spent life.

'Now that was close!' Mr. Cynical spoke up, chuckling. *'Ya almost made some pretty interesting gut-gumbo there.'*

"Shut up!" he growled soundly, pulling the shotgun over an extended leg and slowly begging the stale attic for a full breath. "I had uh-eight, I mean nuh-nine shots, and there is only whu-one of them left down there!"

'Now you are completely losing it,' Cynical huffed, waving him off dismissively. *There are two, remember; two of them left down there? You counted them yourself, and since you are so sure about how many shots you had, you should be sure about that too.*

"Shut—!" Carter began to fire back at Cynical when the floor trap thudded against the latch, and the shotgun exploded to life without him even knowing what had happened. Floorboards became brown powder and flying splinters moving in a fanning motion as the shot roared forth, blasting away the metal latch and pelting the far wall like a pegboard.

Panting heavily as all things quieted, Carter slowly trailed down to see that the recoil had pushed the butt of the gun inside his gutted center.

Carter fainted away.

-2-

'I would wake up if I were you,' his mind whisperer spoke, mentally nudging him.

Slowly Carter's eyes parted to a pained blur of sweat-matted hair and two yellow spheres peering in on him from a space in the floor trap. Without thought, his hand moved the shotgun out and away from his intestines, planting the butt firmly on the floor, and he cycled the pump. The heavy metallic sound of the spent round ejecting and a fresh hot one entering the chamber was enough for his watcher, and the eyes disappeared with a thud from the trap.

"Fu-fu-fuckers," he mumbled as snot ran from his nose as his mouth begged for water.

He was still alive. He knew that well, those things had not come to get him as he had feared through the night, and surprisingly the lantern still had enough power. Unlike your standard bulb, which would slowly dim to a mere orange blip in the darkness as it used every remaining volt the batteries had to offer, LEDs were on, and then they were off, leaving no room to play.

"Fu-fucking fuckers!"

'Oh, that they are, Carter ole buddy,' Cynical walked across to the trap door and moved the splintered wood about with the toe of his boot. *'Fuckers to the very core, each and every one of 'em, but are you sure there are only two left?'*

Carter attempted to draw saliva and spit at Cynical but only managed a bit of drool which sputtered through chapping lips. The point was delivered, and that was all that truly mattered, and with a wavering hand, he rested the shotgun back across his leg to be on the ready for them. He curled his finger around the trigger and waited; however, this time, he had the forethought to slide the gun back past his hip so that the butt pressed against the baseboard at his back.

Below him, he could hear their critter-chatter: fast, foreign, alien... where certain grunts were obliquely ominous and obviously directed towards him.

'I think they are talking about you, Carter, my man,' Cynical took a seat against the wall next to him and patted away sweat from his clammy forehead. *'As a matter of fact, I know they are.'*

Silence fell, a cold, deafening silence that happens right before the storm, and you either survive it, or it kills you.

'See, I don't mean to be a killjoy, but I do believe I can tell you what's about to happen next.'

Carter's head rolled towards the direction of himself as if it ran on a mechanized track while a thin smile stretched his pale rubbery skin. He attempted to swallow, to rid the patches of cold tackiness from his throat, but the motion resolved half-mast and fell away.

"*Ha!* Nuh-no ya' don't," he grinned while his head bobbed up and down, side to side, as unconsciousness played with his senses.

'You know they're going to come up here, don't you?' his self-image proposed, the final words climbing with an upwards inflection. *'I mean, you don't think they went through the trouble chasing you around the damn house just to give up now, do you?'*

Carter jerked with what could have been considered a shrug, his eyes narrowing and studying.

'Why do you keep looking at me like that?' Cynical questioned with a scrunched brow, confused. *'I am not the one they are after, remember?'*

"Ya kuh-kinda look like muh-ee," Cater fumbled with numb lips and huffed once with a chuckle that bore in pain. He winced away from it but half shook it off, nearly falling. A soft laugh rose, and he continued, a faint smile returning. "Just like muh-me. Suh-same uh-eyes and everything."

'Boy, they cut you really deep,' Cynical replied and sighed, folding his arms while shaking his head. *'Now you are starting to see things.'*

"I-I-I wuh-will be fuh-fine," Carter smiled to Self, and Self smiled to him. "Buh-barely hurts…"

'I like your spunk, my man, I really do, but I am not sure you have it in you.'

"Fuh-fuck you," Carter spat, his eyes lazily rolling loosely. "Juh-just fuck you!"

'Yeah, fuck me,' Cynical shrugged and nodded away towards the hatch, extending a pointing finger. *'But if I were you, I would look out 'cause here they come.'*

Carter's head rolled back towards the trapdoor where Cynical was pointing, and he was dead on. They were coming, pulling themselves up one by one from the hallway below in a blur.

Adrenalin met his hot empty stomach exploding into a blazing fire; his eyes widened as reality set in that his count was not simply off but grossly inaccurate. One by one, small rippling bodies spread out and poised themselves in front of the trap door for their onslaught while critter-chatter raced amongst them as one pair of eyes became two, then four, then eight.

"Shit!" he hissed and wrapped his hand around the gun tightly, and with every inch of strength he had left, he centered the shaking barrel towards the center of the mass, hoping the spread would take some, if not all, of them. *"Die!"*

Click!

Carter's mouth dropped as if on a greased hinge as his eyes grew wide while eight assemblies of teeth curved into open-maw smiles. His mouth moved to say something, anything, but in a stampede, they raced forth with claws clacking, throats growling, and eyes blazing.

'Told you that you counted wrong,' Cynical added just as they bore down on him as everything went red, then white, and then black.

—

That night as 'things' ate, opossums played in the shadows outside, scurrying about for this and that; their motions were accompanied by the singing night bugs and glittering fireflies that could care less about anything that was going on above them.

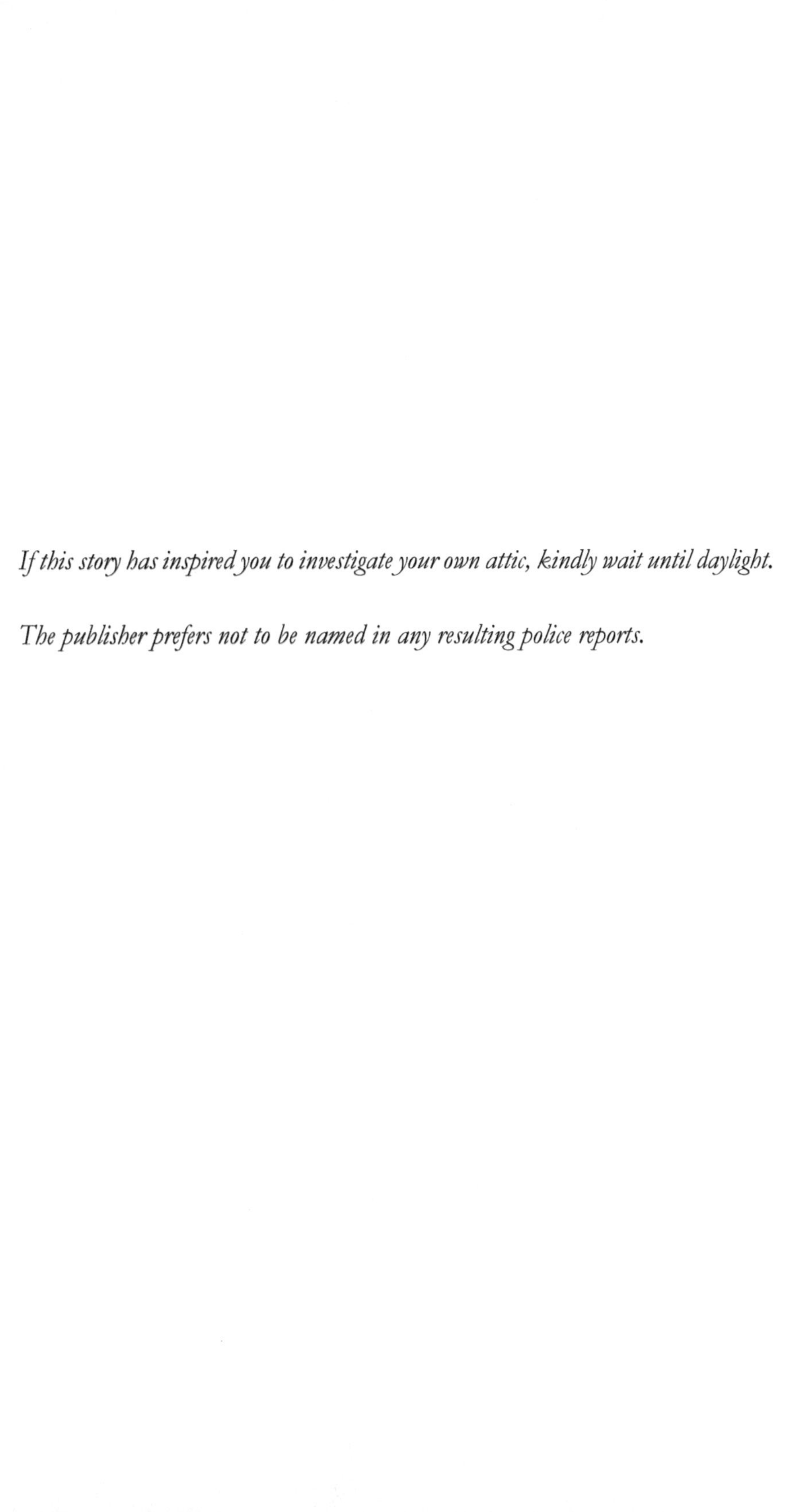

If this story has inspired you to investigate your own attic, kindly wait until daylight.

The publisher prefers not to be named in any resulting police reports.

THE FOLLEY OF MURDER

The Folly of Murder

-1-

Murder waited in the shadows, although he didn't need to. He was everywhere and nowhere at once, just like Justice or Compassion, or many a named god for that matter. No, he didn't need to hide, lurk, or be inconspicuous in any fashion; he just liked the darkness because it made him happy.

Schoolchildren laughed and shrilled as they passed the building's darkened alcove canopy where Murder was waiting, and no one in the little gaggle noticed him, which suited him just fine. There were five of them, each dressed in matching school colors of black, gray, and white; two wore pants, the remainder skirts. He watched them lazily as they passed without much a care in the world, for none required his services… yet.

Two of them suddenly felt a shiver crawl the lengths of their spines when their eyes scanned over his hiding place, brows ebbing with uncontrollable beads of sweat despite the day's mild temperatures as their lower guts gurgled sour.

Death will come for each of you his own way, Murder thought with a foretelling sigh, then checked his watch, which read 2:41, and then snorted. *Too early… but getting close.*

He shrugged and returned his eyes across the street and into Kimi's Salon & Beauty parking lot. Nine cars in the small lot were shared between the beauty salon and Earl's Red Hots, running a weeklong special of two hotdogs with everything plus fries and a drink for $3.99. Most of the vehicles there belonged to the salon staff and patrons since most people walked to the neighborhood food stand to fill their gullets on tasty—yet heart-clogging—*'Everything on them'* franks.

Murder could care less that that was a great deal or of the shop's convenient location. He wasn't hungry in the least, and as a matter of fact, he was never hungry.

He was simply waiting.

Thoughtlessly, Murder shifted himself in his collapsible nylon chair and switched his right leg to his left, folding them. He usually wouldn't come to the parties to admire his work. He was surely never invited by the victims and their families, but in his line of work, someone always welcomed him, even if they didn't quite know his name. Today, however, he had put it on his calendar as a must-see event, and the result will assure him that his task had been completed and perhaps draw out new business as well.

"Well, if that asshole cuts my hours one more time, I'm going to kill 'em!" a passerby was barking into her cell phone as she stomped along the walk wearing a uniform for a pharmacy store chain.

Murder smiled and shook his head as she passed, noting that she had all the proper vigor to carry out such a deed, but inside she was simply a coward who ran from ants when they crawled too close to her.

You will die wearing that getup, Murder thought to himself with a huff and distantly mused how Fate was such a sinister comedian when it came to her job. Although in the past, this woman had drawn Murder close to executing a work order on her by other people, she was still just a mouthy crybaby with a poor attention span which would get her killed soon by an eastbound bus. For some people, even operating feet while on a cell phone can be a hazardous and terminal event.

At 2:49 PM as the time displayed, calmly, he folded his hands in his lap.

-2-

Unlike his counterparts in the day-to-day business of life, Murder usually was one of the more patient ones, having at times waited decades before his initial spark set off the dynamite which would complete the overall goal.

Once, around 1952 or thereabouts, he gave a young boy the spark after the child witnessed his mother being raped and murdered before his eyes. The culprit—a nineteen-year-old named Justin Bigelow—was arrested, convicted, and sentenced to life in prison for the crime.

The boy grew up. He went to school, got married, had children, paid bills, celebrated birthdays, buried loved ones, and lived an entire life while Mr. Bigelow sat behind bars. Then, fifty-one years later, the prison gates opened and Justin Bigelow walked free.

By then, the boy was a fifty-nine-year-old man.

He waited calmly outside the prison eating a ham-and-cheese sandwich on rye. When Mr. Bigelow emerged, he gunned him down where he stood.

Some praised *Justice*. Others claimed *Time* had been his accomplice. Most pointed a finger at *Fate*.

But Murder had simply finished the job, even if it had taken him a little while.

"Bigelow wasn't killed!" Murder had vented to his antagonistic associates. *"Kill isn't one of us; a 'killer' is one of them, and they answer only to me!"*

The others laughed and chortled; even *Fate* added in how such events of his notoriety taking a nosedive resulted from her will, and since then, Murder hasn't spoken a word to the whole lot.

Fuck em!

Yes, he was usually patient, but for some reason, that day, he was edgy with a slight twang of anxiety curling the edges, and why he didn't know. It wasn't like what was about to happen was going to be all that exciting compared to any other day in his life, and since he could not remove himself from *The Order* simply by not speaking with them, he knew all the others would take their just credits for all the work he has done.

Maybe, just maybe, this one involved something more profound in his being; perhaps he even felt passionate about what was going to happen.

It would be best if you did not care one way or the other, Fate had told him countless years before when he had felt this way.

At the time, Murder was sitting restlessly, waiting for *Time* to do his part as well as a dozen others who were to be involved. He wasn't quite pensive with his thoughts but instead overly anxious because what was about to be, he *wanted* it to happen.

This should not be for someone like him in the business; none of them should care one way or the other; it was simply business as usual, and it kept Life going. Yet then, like now, the overall events were going to happen regardless of what someone did to prevent it, and much akin to a child the night before their birthday, the excitement was overwhelming.

Fidgeting away his last moments of calmness, Murder boosted to a standing position, collected up his folding chair and collapsed it, tucked it roughly under his arm, and quickly crossed the busy street to get a better viewing spot.

~3~

He took up a spot just to the right of the salon's door, to the left of the parking lot's entrance, with the chair's back legs planted firmly on the sidewalk two feet from the curb. Here he could watch the whole show go down, and since he never had to use the restroom, there would be no reason to miss a thing.

His watch read 3:09, and Murder giggled despite himself. He already knew the score before anyone fathomed the possibilities, and he leaned back with a smile as his mind pictured the events:

His client got off at 3:00 PM on the dot, never taking on another client despite their needs and demands. The clippers would be brushed and then dipped twice in the cleaning disinfectant, then brushed briskly once again to ensure no hair remained. All his wares would go into the drawers at his barber station and then be locked away, followed by a few careless sweeps with the broom to collect up his last client's bits and pieces.

His client would then joke with this stylist and that one; he would respond to being called a 'punk' by calling someone a 'ho'; there would be laughter and more laughter; the 'take it easy'-*ees* would follow, and finally, the collection of his shoulder bag. Everything was just like clockwork, which Murder could not dispense his gratitude for *Time* and his promptness, and then on 3-2-1, Mr. Terrance Banks would leave Kimi's Beauty & Salon with his 'down-low' boy-toy where *Fate* had laid out the stage for the masterpiece to be carried out.

If Murder were an egoist, he would have patted himself on his back.

At 3:14, the door to Kimi's opened, and out came *his* customers, giggling at each other about something said between them. Once sunlight met skin, Mr. Banks straightened up his posture and added a masculine swagger to his step just in case anyone who might be *anyone* might be looking at the time. Behind those doors of the salon, he was free to be who he wanted to be and did so quite well, but out here, in public, Terrance Banks was so deep in the closet that he was behind all the old shoes one forgot was there anymore.

Funny, Murder mused, watching. *They are actors right up until the end.*

Mr. Banks 'friend' shouldered him with a nudge after a short grunt about cutting his playing out, and Murder could have sworn he heard the friend call Terrance a bitch. Amused, Murder intertwined his fingers as he sat upright in his chair, his eyes briefly glancing at the built-in cup holder in the arm and thinking that maybe, for once, something cold to drink would have been nice. There were other times to think of such things. For now, the finale was reaching its apogee, causing him to squirm.

"Naw, man, I can't go," Terrance said as he adjusted his bag as the two turned into the parking lot. "I have to get home to—"

"You sick motherfucker!" screamed a voice as the driver-side door of an older model *Ford Escort* slammed shut by a short pregnant woman with blazing eyes of rage and tears.

Terrance and his friend jumped, startled, expecting to find a horde of attackers bearing down on them, only to find the young woman who was stomping her way toward them with a noticeable belly under her shirt.

"I didn't believe this shit until now!"

Calm yourself! Murder screamed inside his head as his fingers came undone and wrapped around the ends of the armrests. Murder's eyes darted over the stage rapidly from Terrance to the woman to the friend, feeling the excitement build each time.

"Baby—?" Terrance attempted only to have his words cut short by one of the pregnant woman's open hands, rocketing his head back. The 'friend's' reaction was expected, him being of the more promiscuous and feminine out of the duo, challenged forth, placing himself in the center of the engagement with his own open hands swinging. She took several slaps to the face but didn't slow, and when her own hands became fists, she planted one straight into his nose, forcing out the blood in gushes as he crumbled, sobbing to the ground.

Here it comes! Murder was dancing in his seat, excited as a small crowd began forming on the sidewalk, for they also wanted to catch the show. They will never know his excitement, all of them thrill seekers who were not around for the story-developing plot, but they will all see the climax! Oh, indeed, they will.

"Sheila, stop!" Terrance commanded and moved in low so as to scoop under her arms and subdue her before any more fists could fly, but she was ready—very ready—for the whole day. In one motion, Sheila snatched from her shoulder bag a black revolver and jabbed it into his throat, sending him reeling back in both pain and terror.

"So, this is him, huh?" she screamed, panting, the barrel going from Terrance to his toy and sending all the would-be onlookers to head for cover. "If it was some ho-bitch I could deal with it, but a *fucking dude?*"

"Shu-Sheila," he gasped and stammered, glancing at his friend, who was screeching like a little girl while curled into a perfect ball on the blacktop. "It's not what you think!"

"You sick fucker," she said, growling, leveling the barrel directly between Terrance's eyes which responded by growing wide at the sight of the large caliber maw staring back at him. "You go out and put your dick in this, this, *this thing* and then come put it in me? *Into your wife? The mother of your child? You put your dick covered in his shit inside me?*"

"*Shei—*"Terrance started, only to be silenced by a blurring motion of Sheila's arm as she reaffixed the pistol and squeezed the trigger three times towards the hysterical ball on the ground. Two found their mark, one blasting through the 'friend's' neck and the other tearing through the jaw, removing it in a chunky red spray; the sounds were deafening loud, and reverberating to the soul.

Hell yeah! Murder screamed as he shot into a standing position with his arms above his head, cheering, and then glanced about himself with a disconcerted look because he was the only one applauding.

He shrugged, uncaring, for no one saw him there, regardless.

Terrance was pressed back against the trunk of a car, panting heavily with wide, bugging eyes while his legs became warm with urine. In an instant, Mr. Banks scanned the destroyed head of his lover connected to a body that twitched through death spasms, the flaming eyes of his wife, and the hollow of the cannon she leveled back onto him. During that time, Terrance did not see his life flash before him as one would expect for that particular 'miracle worker' had the day off; all he saw was the future of what would happen to him.

Flowing tears ran the length of Sheila's cheeks as she held her husband with dead eyes of shame. Slowly, she wiped them away with her free hand, cleared her throat, and then spat.

"*Shu-Shu-Sheila, puh-please, duh-don't—*" he attempted, and calmly she lowered the gun to her side.

"Shut up, Terrance," she said flatly, then turned her face towards the sun and briefly closed her eyes to it, bathing in its splendor. Calmly she returned her eyes toward him and then looked at the gun. "You know, I planned on coming here and killing you both? You and your little bitch, but I'm tired now. I just don't feel like killing you."

Slowly, Murder moved in close, rounding the woman from behind, and paused momentarily to watch the final throes of death in the mess on the ground. Curiously, Murder looked over his shoulder to see Death sitting on the trunk of a car, jotting down something in his notebook, and then received a thumbs-up gesture from him. There was something very wrong with it all, and Murder didn't like it one bit.

'I just don't feel like killing you,' replayed in his mind, but he wouldn't worry yet since Death had yet to move in to claim his prizes. If Death had moved in, then that would be it—the show would be over—but for now, the darkened figure scribbled away. All things change, which meant Fate was still polishing the edges of her plan.

"That's guh-good, baby," Terrance stammered with a hand forward, motioning his wrist in a downward fashion. "Just put that gun down, and we can talk; it'll be ok, baby."

"Don't 'baby' me, fucker," she said flatly and pointed the gun again toward him, sending him cartwheeling back to the car's trunk. "You are a liar and a cheat; even worse, you were cheating on me with him. I would ask, 'how could you?' But all I would hear is more of your lies."

"Bab—"

"Don't!" Sheila commanded, cutting him off, followed by a loud metallic click of the gun hammer being drawn back. In the distance, sirens were calling, advancing. Slowly Sheila turned her head toward the oncoming wails and then sighed, turning back towards him. "Doesn't matter though; it's almost over with. I hope you know we are through?"

Terrance said nothing; his only response came in the form of his nodding head, much resembling the bouncing needle of a sewing machine. Murder stepped in close between them and leaned forward so he could look right down the cavern of the barrel and then over-dramatically shivered.

She came packing the big stuff, Terrance, my man! Murder quipped and then waited. *She is really going to fuck you up!*

"You know, Terrance," she said quietly and monotonously. "If you really wanted to stick your dick in someone's ass, all you had to do was ask. I might have let you; it's the *'IN'* thing now amongst couples, but no, you had to stick it in one that came with a dick attached."

Terrance was sobbing now; the masculinity show-of-shows had long packed up and moved to another theater. Calmly, Sheila dropped the bag from her shoulder as she held the gun up, arm bent in front of her. Murder's smile grew from corner to corner, and if he could pee, he would have been dancing as if he had to. He was clapping his hands and squeaking at the back of his throat, his eyes dancing between them when suddenly he stopped.

Sheila's head cocked unexpectantly as her attention picked up something nearby. It was close, she could feel it, and it was cheering. She glanced toward Murder's direction and then fixed directly on him, and he even saw her bottom lids flex slightly as an uncontrolled reaction forced her eyes to focus, dilating and then narrowing.

Did she just look at me? Murder's mind panicked, and he became deathly still. Her head tilted slightly, much akin to a curious puppy seeking something that was or wasn't. There was an expression of peace on her face. *She couldn't have! No one can see me!*

Sheila produced a thin Mona Lisa smile and then returned her attention to Terrance as the sirens wailed closer.

"I want you to remember one thing, Terrance; you caused all this. Not me, not anyone else, but you. You may think you even have gotten away with everything, and in a way, you have, but here's one thing: I will be gone, but you will be left with nothing but the scars."

Wait! What are you doing? Murder screamed, leaping in front of her, his hands flailing for her to stop. *This is not the way it's supposed to happen! What are you doing, woman?*

Slowly she maneuvered the tip of the barrel outward and then turned it back in on herself, placing the end under the soft spot behind her chin.

"You will have nothing but that," she said as she took a deep breath. "By the way, it's a boy."

The gun coughed, the meaty tissue of Sheila's head muffling the sound before the contents exited the gaping hole in her skull, and she collapsed to the blacktop below.

Terrance finally began to scream.

*

"That was such a well-devised arrangement," Death smiled and showed that in his notebook, he had underlined the word *'BONUS!'* three times. "I got an extra one… wasn't expecting that at all. Was this all your doing, Lady?"

Fate glanced at the open book and shrugged as she turned, her jet-black eyes with a million dancing stars within them shifting back to what she was staring at: Murder.

He was standing on the edge of the grass in a park with his hands in his pockets while his cohorts mused over their parts in his orchestra. Usually, she would smile at this, having been the fulcrum that kept everything rocking despite all the *Other's* efforts, but not that day, but not now. Now she was feeling bewilderment and uncharacteristically sympathetic to him.

"No, I had no part in this," she said quietly, allowing the breezes to blow her words back to Death.

She slowly left the group and approached Murder quietly from behind, clearing her throat just enough so that he knew she was there.

"Come to gloat as usual?" he said without turning as he watched each passerby go on about their living. He saw three of his future clients whom he had planted his spark in past times, yet seeing them had given him no thrill, only emptiness.

"For what?" she said cautiously, and although Murder could not hurt her in any way, she still did not wish to feel his rage. "I did not have anything to do with that woman turning the gun on herself."

"Oh? The great Madame Fate admits she had no control?" he sneered, turning towards her. "I find that smelling quite like bullshit, Fate."

"I know, I should be more puzzled, to be honest," she said quietly and sat on the grass next to him. "But the fact remains; I had nothing to do with it."

Murder reluctantly took a seat on the grass as well and then pulled his knees up and thought. Fate sighed quietly to herself and mumbled.

"What?" Murder asked.

"Oh, nothing," she smiled, pointing to a boy attempting to do some tricks on his skateboard along the railing of a bike rack. "That boy is about to break his collarbone and fracture his jaw. He had been warned about doing what he was doing many times. You know, 'As Fate would have it'?"

And with that, the boy glided along the rail with the skateboard underfoot, and by a mere flaw in the rail's surface, enough traction was found, and the boy flipped forward, face-planting into the concrete. Murder snorted, giggled, and broke into a fit of laughter as the boys' wails filled the air, but he quickly composed himself.

"So, who do you think caused her to do what she did?" Murder interjected after watching the boy's blood pool from the jutting bone along his collar. "Is your twin in town today?"

"No, Destiny is off doing her thing in Bali," Fate said passively as she played with her nail. "You know, 'love gained for love to be lost' and all. I don't think any of us had anything to do with it. I think today we all saw something none of us have seen in a while: Free Will."

"I thought that died around the same time they killed off Common Sense," Murder said with a rising inflection. "Didn't it?"

"That's funny," Fate giggled, her head shaking. "No, it's alive and well, just rare to see. You did notice that she saw you, didn't you? Just for a second when that moment of clarity hit her. I saw it from where I was watching just as plain as day. At that time, she had all the high cards in her hand and was in control of the table."

"Yes, I noticed that too," Murder nodded. "That bothered me."

"It happens to all of us at one time or another," she sighed, brushing grass from her hands.

"Hmm, I wonder what I looked like to her." Murder trailed off with his thoughts.

"Well, I must be going, Mr. Murder," Fate said quickly and stood, lowering a hand towards him. Cautiously he took it and pulled himself up. "Does this mean we are talking again, or will you still curse my name every chance you get?"

"For now, let us say we are getting along," Murder smiled. "Which way are you going?"

"Whichever direction the wind blows me," she smiled.

"I will walk you then," he smiled in return, extending a hand, and began walking towards Main Street without a care in the world.

Denouncing the
Looking Glass

Denouncing the Looking Glass

Dark Interlude II

*

Oh, you think you know me, don't you? There staring with those judging eyes; your thoughts as wicked and cunning as a charlatan selling false hopes with a straight razor tucked into your waistband!

So cruel are you in your plotting: Complete the barter with this imbecile or slice his throat if he has no interest in your wares!!

Oh, so foul is you as you mock me with your cavalier smile; so full of self-absorbed prowess that you think you know what sort of fool

I am! I am no man's fool do you hear me?!

You are the fool without so much of an understanding of why the rain falls or from where the winds come!

I spit at your ridicule, you worthless chance-child who crawled from the belly of your whore-mother by some miracle of happenstance! I am the one who knows you, you wretched harlot of modern-day society!

I see how you scheme and twist the very Fates to do your bidding, giving forth bittersweet nothingness to your Fellows to fill their empty bellies with!

I spit as I have never spat before this day; into your heartless peering eyes, and as you recoil in the pain that I give you I have no feelings of fellowship or sympathy towards your wallowing suffering.

Leave my presence, foul reflection, for I cast shame upon thee and for wish of want I care never to see you again!

The Music of My Life

The Music of My Life

The lyrics of Wyclef Jean begin to roll over me as I lean back into my office chair, and I am damned to recite the memories of Darlene, that woman who knew what it meant to have music in her life. I like Wyclef. I find solace in his words and the music which accompanies the lyrics. However, I knew that soon I would loathe them—despise them more so than the epitome of the word 'hatred' itself—and it would have nothing to do with him. I will hate it just as I now hate so many others; for each one I allowed to play, it took that little bit more of my life.

They are all dead now, the songs, just as Darlene is dead. As this smooth R&B love song begins, I know that once it is over, it too will die in me.

Let me begin...

*

"Well, that's just the music of my life," Darlene said quietly through the cloud of bluish cigarette smoke that floated around her head in the dim light, which humored the shadows with colors at the booth in the corner of the strip club. Her last comment—spoken so retrospectively and edged with pain—caught me up with a shudder because she wasn't talking to me in any conscious way, and through the expanding smoke, I could tell by her eyes she wasn't even sitting there in the club anymore. I paused, glancing between my digital recorder, on which I had captured most of my interview notes, and the small pad where I jotted down all the keynotes with many underlines for things I had to remember.

There were a lot of these underlined notes.

"Darlene?" I spoke quietly as I watched the pale whites of her eyes alternate colors from red to blue to yellow to violet as the disco lights behind us cycled through their patterns. There were old brown lines along which riverbeds of veins had stood out and eventually succumbed to the drought of years of crying until the permanent remnants were now shown. She blinked once slowly, and when they opened, those pitch-black irises were on me.

"Hmm?" she sounded as she drew heavily on her cigarette, her eyes never leaving me.

"Are you alright?"

"Yes... why?" her eyebrows arched dismissively.

"I don't know," I shrugged, leaning back against the duct tape-patched vinyl covering of the backing pads of the booth.

Usually, I would be the one smoking throughout an interview. It was a nervous habit I seemed only to possess when I would sit and listen to countless others pour out their histories to me like so much unused dirty dishwater, but not that day. That day, my pack sat in the center of the scratched and dinged pitted table with the open end facing her while she smoked them down one right after the other. It didn't matter, really. She was at least telling me everything, and I always traveled with three packs.

"You seemed to wander off a bit there. What do you mean by '...*the music of my life*? You mean this song playing here?"

Darlene leaned forward slightly, bending an ear towards the jukebox playing on the other side of the club, focusing on listening. I had forgotten that most strippers her age who had been dancing on stages like the one behind me had been doing so since the age of eighteen (and some sixteen like Darlene across from me), and now nearing forty-two, she was nearly deaf from the blasting of all-around speakers. I could hear it clearly, although I had never heard it before. It was the soft and upbeat background music for the employees during the hours before the place officially opened.

"No, never heard it before," she said quickly with a shrug and then leaned back against her own patchwork cushion of duct tape, her eyes narrowing on me, studying. "It sounds kinda pretty, though. Must be something the new girl put on because it is a bit light for this place."

"So, what kind of music is generally played here then?"

"Oh, you know, kinds you can shake your tits and ass to," she giggled, exhaling smoke as her head cocked towards one side and looked upwards, reading off her mental top-ten list. "AC/DC, White Snake, some Metallica if the girl who has it in her set knows how to move to it, Queen, if it's the right song."

"Do you prefer the prettier songs, then?" I introduced my next question as my hand moved feverishly to short-hand jot down the list of bands.

"Well, I mean, I used to like to listen to Dolly Parton on my downtime, and some Jefferson Airplane too, but none of the Jefferson Starship crap. They lost their edge."

She shrugged and took a long swallow from the long island iced tea she was drinking on. She gave the straw one extra-long pull, then returned it to the pool of condensation which had gathered where it sat, ice cubes melting. It had been her fourth in the last hour, and she didn't slur a bit.

"I am not a big fan of a lot of the shit on the radio these days. They don't have any soul."

"Dolly Parton? Really?" I asked with a smile, only to see her head slowly nodding in the fog.

My hand moved unconsciously as a self-driven hand scripted Dolly's name, followed by a question mark. Her accent, borne from growing up just close enough to the Mason-Dixon Line with a slight Northerner perfection to her enunciations, didn't create images of the big-breasted bombshell like Parton.

"Is there any particular song of hers that you like above all others?"

"Jolene was my favorite," she sputtered after a slight mouth twist as if she had only a blink of a debate to overcome and then leaned forward with her palms flat on the table. "But I don't listen to it anymore, Mr. Nash."

"Please, call me Eric," I chuckled, blushing slightly at her constant use of proper etiquette, and since I was her junior by a good fifteen years, the mister part didn't seem right. "Mr. Nash was my daddy."

"Well, Mr. Nash helped make a handsome son, Eric," she smiled alluringly. One could tell this was not her usual smile but a stripper's smile, the kind that got the truckers and the mill workers digging into their billfolds for dollars. I watched as it grew and turned upwards, following the machined lines of decades of delivering countless numbers of the same smiles, even the crow's feet around her eyes dimpled in, pulling me into the smile.

She might have been an old-timer in the business, but she was damn good at it, forcing me to clear my throat before speaking again.

"You said it was one of your favorites. Did you get tired of it?"

"Well, let's just say that sometimes when you have that one song to fall back on, if you hear it that one last time it could end everything for you."

I nodded, thinking I understood what she said, but I was shooting blindly at all the angles. I scribbled notes as she smoked, waiting for me to begin again.

"Any particular reason you liked that one?" I asked, and I was pretty sure my voice squeaked just enough.

"Well, because it had a double meaning in my life, is all," she giggled through her expression, which grew darker, deeper, and before she said another word, she had extinguished one cigarette and then lit another. "I was like her, Jolene, many times in my life... in this career.

"So, you stole other women's men?"

"Like a thief in the night," she nodded, blowing out the first drag through her smile. "But it's not stealing when they come to you. Back in my prime, there were hundreds of 'em: sons, brothers, husbands, fiancés, boyfriends, hell, even girlfriends all wanting to run off with me and marry me; promising to give me whatever I wanted."

"Girlfriends… *really?*" I looked up with eyebrows standing so high that I no longer had a forehead to speak of, and a chuckle escaped my throat, betraying my twisted curiosity.

"You seem surprised, Eric," she blew smoke in rapid bursts as a silent giggle moved with it. "Women come to strip clubs just as much as men do, and I'm talkin' ones with no male dancers. Shoot, they buy each other lap dances twice as much as the hard-legs do, and their laps are much softer than a guy's any day.

"Yeah, they made their candy-coated offers too, just like the men did, and once or twice I damn near took them up on it, but there's nothin' sweeter than the smell of a man in your arms, though."

"Did you ever take their offers, or was it just the dancing?" I was jotting quickly as my questions flowed and after a moment realizing she was quiet, I looked up. Those dark eyes were on me again, studying, yet this time they were peering to see if I was a fool or not. I swallowed hard under the stare.

"You are kidding, right?" she asked earnestly and honestly, to which I had no answer. I truly felt stupid. "Do you see that door back there with the red-light dome over it?"

I turned, looked where she was pointing, and then began nodding before righting myself back to those eyes.

"That there is no light alerting folks that film is being processed in the back. When it's on, it's *ON*, if you know what I mean. Of course, I took 'em, providing they were paying for it."

I blinked, confused, as my eyes shot back to my notepad, begging my memory for any recollection of a mere hint of what she was saying to me. I swallowed hard once more, taking up my glass of vodka and tonic and swallowing half of it dry.

"Okay, Darlene, I think I get what you mean then."

"Do you?" she asked, pointing her finger at me. I nodded and then shrugged. "I don't think you do, *that*, or you are too shy or a gentleman to ask what's rolling around inside that noggin of yours. Look at me… do I look ashamed of what I do?"

"No, Darlene, you do not," I said flatly as she opened her robe and exposed her breasts to me. She was perhaps more forward than I had expected when I took on the assignment.

I adjusted myself and studied her eyes for a moment. They were honest eyes that had seen countless things, and if I wanted to get all the 'ins' and 'outs,' I knew I had better stop being so coy and be the journalist I claimed to be. I spoke directly:

"So how much did they pay for a romp in the little back room?"

She smiled again, but this time it was a Darlene smile, content that *real* honesty had been placed on the table.

"Depended on what they wanted and who it was," she stretched for a moment with her arms up and then to the sides, the whole time knowing that she was giving me a show and I didn't have dollar bills in hand. She wanted me to see her, that I knew, but the real why behind me getting the free show was unclear.

"Can you give me an idea then?" I asked, watching the large D's move with her body, and although age and gravity had done their job claiming them downward towards earth, they were still lovely, nonetheless.

"Well, let's say you were a high school boy and just made the legal grade for walking in those doors there. You got your daddy set beside you with his paw full of greenbacks, depending on what you were looking for. I either made your daddy a happy man for showing his son what being with a woman was like or a poor man for tryin'. In the end, though, he was still a happy man."

"So, you got a lot of that then: fathers bringing in coming-of-age sons?"

"It depended on where I was dancing, but yeah," she nodded and scratched her head through her reddish-blond hair.

"And the fathers paid for whatever the sons wanted?" I continued, finding this of interest.

"Well, yes and no," her smile turned to laughter as her head nodded smartly as the memories flooded in. "Sometimes the daddies knew best because they were regulars themselves.

"If your daddy were pushing you to have your first *real* hand-job outside of your own handy work in the bathroom, back in the day, that would've set your daddy back ten bucks. That was on top of the lap-dance fee, which was ten; some places more."

"So, we are talking simple stuff then?" I bobbed my head as my shoulders moved into a dismissive shrug of no harm, no foul. "Nothing serious."

"Simple is how everything starts off, Eric," she smiled into her time's reflective, descriptive moments. "Once again, what your daddy wanted for you.

"Back then, if it was a blowjob, that cost your daddy fifteen to twenty depending on how cute you were; thirty if that lap dance allowed your pecker to dangle free dry against my panties, five more wet and an easy fifty if you wanted to put it in for a while, a little more if you wanted to shoot, but all the young ones shot off; usually kinda quickly."

I cleared my throat as I pulled my pad of paper close, so it angled upward on the edge of the table while the bottom covered my lap, embarrassed that her verbal descriptions began to affect my blood pressure. She smiled again, knowing what she was doing to me.

Call it intuition or years in the business, it didn't matter, but either way, she was damned well doing it.

"A hundred if you wanted to put it in my ass," she spat out for no reason, and I jumped because of it.

I had no idea that I was sitting with my mouth hung open wide until I felt the tips of her fingers below my chin gently lifting it until it closed.

My mind flooded with a thousand images borne from countless strippers I had seen perform in the past, as well as that of the *Polaroid* picture she gave me of herself from early in her career when her prime was top-sirloin, rare. I sat praying that there would not be any reason in the world that I would be required to stand for quite some time.

"I see," I said with a wheeze as I swallowed nothing but stale dance club air.

"Did I offend you?" she asked quietly, taking up her drink.

"No… no, not at all," my voice came with a whisper, and I glanced down at my pad. I hadn't written a thing.

"Hmm, I believe you," Darlene sighed, pulling up a small handbag from the cushions next to her. She fussed around inside for nothing in particular, then dismissed it, pulling up her cigarette from the ashtray.

"All I am saying is that there were a lot of them. All types, all ages, all colors throughout the years, each one wanting something that their wives or girlfriends didn't do, but to them, none of them were paying for it like you would if you found a girl on a corner."

She blew bluish smoke, studying me for a moment.

"Do you like music?" she introduced out of the blue, and I paused, wondering if this was a new conversation direction or a short pause in this woman's uninhibited presence.

I nodded.

"What's your favorite song of songs?" she pushed.

"I would have to say one of my favorites is 'Magic Carpet Ride,' by Steppenwolf."

"Wow! For a young man, you know your classics!" she beamed brightly, raised her glass to mine, and then 'clinked' it. "I was expecting something more modern, but good show. Yes, that was one of my favorites at one time, but I don't listen to it anymore. Too many memories, but fitting to what we are talking about, well, at least some of the words to the song, or at least the innuendos. That's what rooms like that one in the back are for: a magical carpet ride, and by 'carpet,'

I am talking about that strip of dew-laden hair between a woman's thighs."

"Are you saying then that everyone, even a guy like me, is looking for a girl like you for that little back room then?"

"No, not all of them," she smiled, shrugging, then continued. "Most of the ones who come in places like this getting some normally never cross their minds, but while sitting around that stage, they all wish they could; you could see them fucking you with their eyes.

"Those with money, providing they didn't look like they rolled out of an alley, might, and let me say again, might get something extra, and those who didn't, they paid so in dollars for the fantasy."

"So, prostitution and stripping go hand in hand then?" my journalistic side spoke out, intrigued and wanting. My comment was crass and blunt; I knew it the moment my lips began to form the words, but she wasn't stupid, and she knew where I was coming from, but her fit of laughter still made me question if I should have stayed quiet.

"Mr. Nash, you are a reporter deep down after all!" she slapped the table twice, twisting in her seat as the genuine laughter bent her. "That type of direct question deserves another drink!

"Shanna! Two more!"

Her laughter trailed to a giggle fit which lasted until a young woman arrived with a cork-top tray with two glasses of what we were drinking on top. As Darlene had told me earlier when our first drinks arrived, the girl, Shanna, was a dancer-in-training at barely eighteen. She was pretty despite her plain-looking features, the epitome of the girl-next-door and Midwestern born; fed on healthy meals, which gave her the energy to stay lean but put weight on her in the right places. She smiled as she placed our drinks before us, collecting up the stale glasses without as much as a word.

"Love ya, Sugar!" Darlene called after the girl as she returned to her duties, and with a gentle hum in her throat, Darlene took a long pull on the white straw sticking over the rim of the glass.

"Rounding back to the song, Jolene," I continued where the conversation stemmed from and hoped to eventually get back to her self-addressed comment, which started it all; I took a sip of my drink and raised my eyebrows as I waited for my response. "You said it has a double meaning?"

"Well, Mr. Nash," she began, then paused, smiling and then giggling, reaching across and giving my hand a little squeeze. "Eric, sorry. Well, Eric, you can only be a heart-breaker until your heart gets broken, and mine surely has been broken many times, but first, I need to clarify some things before you write this stuff up."

My palms rose to her as a thin smile stretched my face, letting her know I was all ears and ready to listen.

"Okay… here's the thing. Not all strippers do what I am talking about… right here and now. Stripping is a noble position despite the shadowed beliefs; just some of us know that money can be made beyond spinning around that pole out there. Most strippers, when they tell you they are doing it to support their kid or to go back to school, they are doing it for just that reason 'cause its quick money… good money… and they don't have to answer to no one, save the club manager and the dance-boss.

"Did you know them fuckers get their money up front whether you make a dollar that night or not?"

"No, I didn't know that." My head shook as I jotted the note down and placed an asterisk next to it for future reference to a potential continuation story.

"Yep, it's true," she sneered and slapped the table to show her angst. "They call it a 'pole-rental fee' as if you are the only one rubbing your cooze against it all night. Shit, you'd be lucky that in between sets, they sent someone out to wipe down the pole from one girl to the next!'

"Any bad experiences with the 'dance bosses?'" I pushed along, enjoying the side road while the rest of my interview waited for me to circle back to it.

"Of course there were, but there's this one which I will never forget if you wanna hear it?" she asked, and although I was nodding, I knew I would hear it whether I had said yes or no. "Well then…back in eighty-nine, when I was twenty-one, I was dancing in Reno.

"There was this one dance boss there named Danny Adagio, which all the girls called 'Danny the Dago' behind his back. He was a real work of warmed-up shit. The pole rental for the night was fifty bucks back then, and you were required to dance five sets that night, but any real dancer will tell you that the money is made on the floor and not twirling your slit on that brass pole."

"It's not?" I tossed the question in there, although I had an idea.

"Shit naw!" she snorted, her face twisting with disgust at the possibility. "Think of it: the average Joe is sticking one, maybe two singles into your panties a set, and a set can last three song lengths mixed, and Danny made sure each set ran four songs just because he could.

"Anyway, the money was on the floor giving lap dances to the tourists whose wives were busy dumping dollars in the casino slots and drinking mimosas by the quart. If you sat on an old timer's lap with your panties hiked between your cheeks and just squirmed a little? Shit… they'd sign over the deeds to their homes to you."

"So, I take it this Danny was a slave driver, then?" I edged her along, picturing it, feeling it, and begging for more.

"That and then some," she shrugged, lighting another one of my cigarettes, then looked off as she reminisced. "More like a pimp, really. See, Danny didn't like the idea of girls getting fed up with not making any money and moving on, and he had a lot of them scared for their lives if they tried.

"Back in eighty-nine, this girl, Nicole, danced right after me. She was barely scraping by and threatened to leave for another club. One night after overhearing her complaining in the changing room, Danny took her out back in the alley with his hand wrapped in a wet bar towel and beat her in the belly so badly she couldn't shit straight for a month."

"You're fucking kidding?" I begged, my so-called 'journalistic professionalism' flying to the wayside as my mouth dropped and then shut back on its own just as quickly. Darlene simply nodded as she dragged on her cigarette. "*He beat her?* No… why would he do that."

"Yep, that's what he did, and he still made her finish off her sets which she was barely able to do, but that wasn't even the worse thing he'd done. What was worse, since you had to dance for him, sometimes you didn't have the pole fee upfront, you were working it off any way you could through the night, but you had better have his fee by the time you cashed out, and by then, the fee was double."

"Jesus," I whispered without realizing that I had spoken and then swallowed half of my drink away without tasting a thing. "What would happen if you didn't?"

"That depended if he liked you," she said dryly, tightening her robe about herself as shame crawled in and around her skin. "If he liked you, sometimes he gave you until the next day, kinda like a double-or-nothing, or you were his date for the night. If he didn't like you all that much or had stiffed him before, a wet bar cloth would have been heaven by the time he was done with you."

"That's just…didn't anyone…wait, what about the police or—?" I was stammering, trying to find reasoning and justice for past events now gone, only to see Darlene's shaking head and her long-aged fingers reach across, silencing my lips.

"I see that this is upsetting you a bit," she comforted me motherly, her southern drawl coming in thick. "Why don't we just move on from that and let me finish talking about the business, ok?"

I nodded, angered and relieved, pinching my lips together so she could finish her story.

"I was telling you about the song, Jolene?" she started, her voice calm and professional, and I nodded without a sound. "You see, Dolly is pleading with this Jolene character with auburn hair who could take any man she wanted to leave her man alone, and well, I was Jolene for a long while there.

"At first, there was never any sex; at best, I would let preferred customers hold my ass or shake their faces in my breasts, but that was about it. I did my dance sets; I made my money; I made friends, or at least those who called me their friends. Most importantly, every night I went home happy but lonely because any decent man wasn't gonna date a stripper and then take her home to mama, if ya know what I mean?"

I nodded, knowing, and concurred that although there had been several women I wanted for myself in the past, she was right; my mother would have had a cow if I had brought them home.

"Once there was a gentleman named Dillon Hawkins who tried to love me, but then he broke my heart just like I had broken so many others in the past."

"What happened?" I asked, and although this was now beyond the scope of my interview, my empathy towards her sudden, saddened look couldn't stop me from inquiring.

"Well, he loved me for me despite what I did for a living," she sighed and then drew so heavily on her cigarette I could have sworn I had seen her cheeks clap together in the middle. "Or so I thought. Just as I was good at taking men, he was good at taking the ladies, and please understand the word I used: ladies. I am not talking about girls like me, but the high-standard ones, so, while I was his woman who would do all the things that no proper lady would do, he was busy playing Don Juan on the side with the upper class.

"On the day he left me--when he found the right-proper woman he could take home to his momma...I found out he had been screwing all my coworkers just as he had done me."

"I am sorry, Darlene," I spoke softly, and I truly was. She had been hurt badly by the events she was telling me about, and despite all that she was and is, she also had feelings that had been crushed.

"Well, don't be," she snorted. "You live and learn, and I learned my lesson all too well that day."

"Had he originally been someone who came into the clubs to watch you dance, or was he a private room fella?"

"Actually, I had met him outside of the club scene, and he came in only twice to watch me dance, but back then, there were no special rooms for private dances, yet; just janitor's closets and restrooms if you wanted to make that extra dollar.

"Ya see, after him, I moved on and poured myself into my work, and after a while, I was so damned good working for the crowds I started seeing a more professional class of gentlemen in the clubs I danced at. These men had serious money, the kind where they could drop a grand or two in a place like that and never notice it missing, if you get what I mean?"

I nodded to this, having known some people just like that.

"Well, the thing with those who have more to those that don't is, that they want quality, and at the time, I had left Reno and went down to Tampa where the weather was warm, and the clubs were in numbers. There, I landed a gig at The Pelican, which was one of the hottest clubs in town then. I started bringing home a grand a night when I was only twenty-one, and with that kind of money, I not only lived in a nice apartment in a nice area, but I could afford nicer outfits to wear while I was dancing, which just made me more money.

"I was out there shakin' my ass to songs like White Horse by Laid Back, to more sensual routines to things like China Girl by David Bowie and pieces like that. Basically, I was using songs that defined me, my mood, and my life, and since I made the clubs so much money, they let me choose my set numbers.

"Anyways, I was having a lot of fun, and then one afternoon, all the girls had to go in for a meeting, and the dance boss told us that they were opening private dance booths where we could make some serious bread."

She dragged and exhaled, eyes distant, thinking before continuing.

"They never asked us to do things, you know, but they sure hinted at it something fierce, and since the customer was going to pay for both a dance and the time, all us girls knew where they were going with it. I figured that I being a star, I would get a guy in one of the booths to do some extra erotic stuff and make him cream his jeans in a hurry, and that'd be that."

"But that's not what happened, was it?" I broke in, tapping the pad with the tip of my pen as her eyes trailed to the tabletop before her, and she fell quiet as her head shook slowly. "Can you tell me about it?"

"Is this gonna help you understand things better, Eric?" she asked, looking up, her eyes wide and begging.

"Yes, it will," I nodded, and I was being honest.

She quietly opened her little bag and reached in, finding what she was looking for immediately without fail. In her lap, she unscrewed something and then shifted, her motions clearly showing she was trying to remain still and steady. Then she raised a little silver spoon to a nostril rounded with white powder. One sniff, and it disappeared.

"Sorry," she spoke without looking up, then did the same act with the other nostril and then put everything away. "Want some?"

"No, I am fine," I replied, palms up so to show her I was sure.

"Well, one night I went in, and the club manager, Ellis was his name, came up to me and said that there was a business party in from out of town. They were trying to land this big deal with some guys from New York, and Ellis says to me: *Darlene, they are asking for the best girl, and that's you.*'

"So, I ask him are they looking for a girl to sit with them all night 'cause I was worried, you see, because at The Pelican, I also made a lot of money dancing. I had many fans out there waiting for my sets, you know? I even had this new set tape full of Blondie and The Stray Cats, and I had rehearsed this new number for about two weeks.

"So, Ellis tells me no, no dancing for me that night, but the guys from one company wanted me to give a private dance to the big wig from New York, and he looks at me with a smile and says: *They've already dropped two-grand in here, so I know you are gonna give that rich fella the show of his lifetime.'*

"He even gave me a big-ole double wink!"

She paused, head shaking as her eyes scanned the spaces around us, never looking at any one thing in particular, and then returned to me.

"I was young and dumb, and the thought of all that money just went to my head, so I agreed. So, Ellis took my mix tape to the back and had the booth operator load it up so it would play only in the private area, and yeah, that was the first time."

I blinked, staring at her as she drew quiet.

"First time you had sex for money?" I introduced.

"Yeah," she mumbled. "And from then on, I couldn't listen to those songs even though they were my favorites."

"I see." I nodded, not seeing but jotted notes anyway.

"I don't think you do," she whispered, and from my earlier assumptions of her, what was lost was proven wrong; she still had some water in those old ducts after all, and she cried silently in the shadows.

"Is there something that I am missing?" I asked, looking around myself, confused at her reactions since she had been so forthcoming and carefree for more than an hour then that she would seem so bothered now.

"You said you like music, Eric, right?" she asked, her body slightly shaking as if she was cold.

"Yes, very much so," I began, then nodded. "I have a large collection of music at my home."

"Have a song played during the bad times of your life?"

"Yes."

"Ever listen to that song ever again?" she shot right back, stunning me, and I slowly shook my head *'no.'* "I didn't think so. I saw your expression after I said, *'well, that's just the music of my life,'* but I didn't think you knew what I was talking about. That's alright, and why should you? But one day, you will. You don't have to be an old stripper well past her prime humping on a dented pole in the shit end of all shit-end clubs like this one.

"Do you know what places like this one here are referred to?"

"No, what?"

"Places like this one here are where strippers like me come to die," she sniffed hard, withdrawing mucus through numb nostrils and wiping away at one eye. "All the music that we have ever danced to once has become like that one song you won't ever listen to again because it is spoiled now. Zeppelin, Hall and Oates, Blondie, David Bowie, Duran Duran, some Blacksheep, and even more recent like Beyonce, Sia, Estelle, you name 'em; dead to me just as I am a little more 'dead' on the inside.

"That night, while I listened to Blondie sing Heart of Glass, I had this rich bastard with a big cock humping me seven ways to Sunday, while the club manager and his cronies stood behind the two-way glass jerking off and smiling. The whole while, I cried my eyes out, and none of them did nothing because, despite my popularity, my fancy outfits, and the money I brought into the club, I was nothing but a dirty little whore from Kentucky, and I was getting *exactly* what the Lord put me on this earth to get.

"After that, the music was pretty much dead to me, and from that night on, I was not only the most sought-after performer but also the most sought-after whore."

"Why did you keep going then?" I begged, setting my pen down and leaving the recorder running to take in the details; my mind was numb as if I had just snorted the coke. "I mean, you are a smart woman, you were young… you didn't have to put up with any of that."

"That's just it, Eric," she whimpered, covering her eyes with both palms, and then spoke without looking at me. "It was all dead to me from that night, and I hated all of it, so I started coming in every night to murder the music, to murder every song I once held dear!

"I had become that Jolene every woman whispered about in fear, the one they prayed their men would never find… because they always did. And when they came, I gave them everything—my body, my voice, the songs that had once been pieces of my soul. I kept hoping there would be one song left, one I could play and finally feel whole again, but each new day only brought more shame, more hollow space inside me… and another song gone cold and dead."

She gasped air suddenly and began to cry, slamming the table with her fists soundly, and I glanced about myself for wayward eyes but found none but Shanna's, who pinched her mouth together and returned to her business. I collected a dry napkin from the tabletop and extended it to her.

"Darlene, please, everything is all right," I whispered, tapping the back of her hand with it so that she knew it was there, which she collected without looking. She began wiping at her eyes and forehead, blew soundly into the napkin, and then looked at me with begging eyes.

"Eric, please, I feel so bad," she begged, sniffing back the tears. "What I am telling you is not worth the money you are paying me for this. Can I at least give you a private dance for it?"

"No, Darlene, I am not here for that," I soothed her, feeling my skin crawl along my back to be offered such a thing so clearly out of the blue and by someone so distraught and clearly intoxicated by both booze and drugs. "We pay all our interviewees handsomely."

"Are you sure?" she begged, pawing at me as I nodded quickly, attempting to keep her robe closed and saving her any humility I think she had not had for quite some time. "You think I am a dirty whore don't you?"

"God, no!" I whispered sternly, and despite whatever I did think of her, the last thing I wanted was for her to lose any other levels of control. "Don't say things like that!"

"Why? I've heard it all: *Skag, bitch, baby, whore, slut, cunt, twat, ho-bag, skank!*

"'Come on down from that piece of brass and swing on this dick here, ya fuckin' slut! I bet that slit of yours can do back bends around a horse's cock!'

"Please let me be one of them for you so I can feel better, Eric! Let me be your whore! We can play Steppenwolf, and you can ride this old carpet until you bust!"

"Darlene, please!" I barked, pulled away from her, snatched my recorder up, made it disappear into my pocket, then pulled out a white envelope containing ten, one-hundred-dollar bills and slammed it to the table in front of her. "You are drunk, high, and this interview is over!"

"Go ahead and leave, Eric!" she stood up and screamed at me as I collected up my pad of paper, leaving the pen, and backed towards the door on the other side of the club, and I didn't have to look around to know that there were several sets of eyes on me. "You ain't no different than any of the other ones! You came to hear my music for some damn money, so you at least ought to get your pecker wet too!"

"Darlene, that is enough!" I shot back, but there was no strength in my words.

"You think that it's just the music of my life that's fucked now?" she was screaming, leaning her body into the words and sending them at me like daggers. "You just wait motherfucker! You wait until you turn on the goddamn radio and try to focus on it ever again!"

I could feel her rage beaming at and into me, an essence of raw emotion that, up until that day, I had never felt. With spittle flying and tears streaming, she pursued with her verbal onslaught, and for once in my life, I thought I would have to defend myself against a woman physically.

"Darlene, please!" I begged, moving backward in a daze with sluggish, invisible mud-trudging steps, my legs in a nightmarish dreamscape.

"I was cursed, you fucker, just as I am cursing you now!" she shrieked, pointing at me with a shaking finger. *"You will be back here when it is dead*

inside you, Eric Nash! You will find your place where the songs are poisoned, and you go to die!"

I forced my legs to backpedal quickly despite the numbness there, rebounding off tables with chairs turned upside down on their tops, sending many to the floor, dropping my note pad which I reclaimed with trembling fingers. I froze, terrified when I looked up to see Darlene bearing down at me with her glass held high above her head, preparing to smash me with it. I attempted to move, but my body betrayed me, and as it arched down with her leathery aged legs moving quickly before me, I saw Shanna step in front of her with hands up and intercepting the blow.

"Momma! Stop it!" Shanna commanded, snatching the glass from her hand and peering up into Darlene's face. They stood momentarily with their eyes locked onto one another as both breathed heavily. My mind begged the ears to repeat what it had just heard.

Did she just call that woman: 'Momma'? My mind begged, but I didn't need an answer because I knew she had.

"I knew I should've watered down your drinks!" Shanna hissed and then pointed behind her. "How dare you act that way to a guest? You need to go lie down for a while and collect yourself! We're opening in four hours!"

Darlene folded pathetically, her shoulders drooping low as all her rage left her in a rush, like the air from an over-inflated balloon escaping. She nodded slowly and moved past Shanna without looking up except to pause briefly, giving me a sideways glance, whispering:

"Sorry."

I stood slowly with my pad of paper to my chest and with wide eyes, my mind numb as it attempted to process everything while the adrenalin still coursed my veins. I swallowed twice, long and hard.

"She's your mother?" I whispered to Shana, who turned to me and shrugged.

"Yeah, that's my momma, Mr. Nash," she nodded, placed the glass on the closet tabletop, then moved to me, took me by the arm, and started walking me towards the door. "Sorry about her. She's been like that since she hurt herself a few years ago and stopped dancing."

"Wait, Darlene, your mother, she doesn't dance?" I begged as my surroundings brightened as we moved to the door. "But she told me she is performing!"

"Mr. Nash, everything is fine… don't you worry, your pretty head none," Shanna smiled and attempted to adjust my collar as we stepped out into the late morning air. It was already holding a temperature in the eighties and climbing swiftly. The stale sour mash aroma with decades of old cigarette and cigar tar coating the edges left us, only to be replaced with that of spent diesel fumes and hot dust of the surrounding gravel parking lot.

She walked with me to my car, parked near the door, then moved me to my door.

"Momma has her good days and bad, but I had warned her about drudging up the past like this. It ain't good for no one."

My mind was out of sorts as it still attempted to recollect the final moments of the interview and then put them back where they made sense, and before I knew it, I was sitting behind my wheel with Shanna pushing my door closed. She was smiling down at me with perfect teeth, unlike her mother's, whose years had eradicated the simple innocence of a genuine smile and replaced it with that of a stripper. Shanna favored her mother so, a near spitting image of the *Polaroid* that was stuck inside my notebook, but there was a hint of the stripper smile in the young face before me, nonetheless.

"What did she mean about being cursed?" I whispered, my mind barely in motion on a minimalistic auto-drive set by some innate ability to keep me functioning. "Like being in the trade?"

"Naw, she claims that years ago she was hexed by some woman she did wrong," Shanna replied, toying with her bangs just as carelessly as one would a piece of lint on their clothing, uncaring. "Said because of it she gonna die, and because I'm her daughter, I'm gonna die too. We all gonna die, Mr. Nash, curse or no curse."

"Do you believe her?" I whispered, attempting to find reason in her young eyes only to see them narrow as she smiled.

"I believe she believes, but that don't matter, none," she giggled. "Either way, you got your story."

"Yeah, a crazy fucking story," I mumbled, retrieving the open pack of cigs from the passenger seat, sticking one into my mouth, then lit it.

"Well, you write your story any way you see fit, Mr. Nash," she said softly, leaning on the edge of the window edging the door, and brushing loose auburn hairs from in front of her face. "But please, don't paint my momma out to be a whore 'cause she does have a good heart; it's just been broken over all these years."

"Honestly, Shanna, I don't know how I will write any of it," I said flatly, looking at the steering wheel before me as a focal point in the recent madness. I felt a soft touch of fingers at my chin, pulling me in her direction, and she met my face with a bright, warm smile.

"My name is Jolene, Mr. Nash," she glowed and allowed a soft giggle to escape her throat. "My momma named me after that damned song, but she can't stand to call me by it no more, so I just go by Shanna, which is my middle name."

"She named you *Jolene*," I whispered and then chuckled for no reason that I knew then or now and then found those sparkling eyes and a dazzling smile on me, nodding. "Go figure."

"I know the song too, Mr. Nash, and as if those words had life, well, you should come see me dance sometime 'cause I bet I'd steal you from your wife."

She gave me a wink and tapped my wedding band once.

"So that's the music of her life?" I whispered, head shaking slowly. I quickly licked my lips as I drew away from her comments, focusing on the raw comprehension of the symbolisms of Darlene's words colliding with gray clouds of my confusion. I peered deeply into my mind, pushed the clouds away, and swallowed hard to steady my question. "Your mother said all she had left regarding the music of her life was one last song and that if she played it, that would be the end of her. Is that song you?"

"Yes sir, Mr. Nash," she giggled and took a step back. "She tells me a hundred times a day that I am her beautiful song, her Jolene, and the music has truly died without me. I can't see that as being so, but I guess I will find out tonight 'cause I ain't stayin' in this shit hole forever."

"Huh?" I begged, confused and repulsed by that young woman's callousness, which I initially received a shrug as my answer. "I'm not following you."

"You see, the only difference between me and my momma is that I love thousands of songs, Mr. Nash, and on top of them, there are a few thousand more yet to be made so that I will be around for quite some time. She has done her thing, and now it's time to do mine."

"What do you mean you will find out tonight?" I whispered as her eyes narrowed, and she leaned forward, sticking her rear out and reaching into her back pocket, where she removed a mini-USB drive and held it between two fingers.

"This here is my mix-set, and guess what? Guess the main song mixed throughout, which will be piping through them speakers inside?"

"Jolene?" my mouth moved, but there were no sounds.

"You are smart, Mr. Nash; Momma was right!" she burst into a laughing fit, returned the drive to her rear pocket, and then tapped my door. "Now, you get on back into the city, Mr. Nash, and write your article.

"If you need a good song to listen to and a hot body to watch while it plays, you know where we are. I give the best private shows Mondays through Wednesdays after six, on Thursdays and Fridays all day long; on Saturday, I give morning performances… we open then at eleven.

"Just come on in and ask for me proper then. Just as for Jolene, and we can play any song you want!"

She stepped away and hooked her thumbs into the front pockets of her shorts and then gave me a slow wink with a sultry, stripper smile. I started the car, backed out, whipped the front around, and then moved out of the gravel drive and kept moving until I had pulled into my drive an hour later.

At my home destination, I sat in the drive for quite some time as I stared at my digital recorder, daring myself to play it, but instead chose to play my favorite radio station programmed in the number one slot of my selector buttons: the oldies station.

I smiled, relieved that one of my favorite songs was beginning to play, and I closed my eyes as the sweet music of the Eagles played forth. They sang of this place of damnation hidden under the façade of a place to rest. As the words echoed forth about the alluring Siren in the doorway of that place just off a dark desert highway scented by burning *colitas*, my wife appeared in my doorway with two beers in her hands. She held them up as a waving gesture which I responded by opening my door to go to her, reaching for the ignition key when my mind raced through the lyrics to a description of escape that never happens.

'…*you can check out any time you like, but you can never leave…*' the words played through the stereo speakers, and I shuddered thinking back on the strip club and Darlene and her daughter, Jolene, who went by another name to save her mother's broken sanity.

Well, until that night, at least.

Calmly I switched off the car and then went inside with my wife.

—

Since that day, I have never listened to Hotel California *again or any other that drudges up memories of my time that I sat interviewing Darlene (which easily can be any song that plays on the radio at any given moment). Now, I barely listen to anything at all.*

Later—as I write this now—I truly understand what she meant by the music of her life: each one was a damnation of a memorable scar aging you one step further towards oblivion until there is nothing left… leaving only the silence.

Real Monsters

Real Monsters

*

Late in the day—*just like every day really*—if you go down the fourth branching trail from the second right after the cement bike path, the one *in* the forest preserve, not the periphery, *and* providing that you remember to make a right and not a left at the large downed elm, turn around two-and-a-half times (never three quarters), you will find them in a clearing; gathering.

They normally arrive alone, but sometimes in twos, often threes, depending on their moods at the end of the long day; however, believe it or not, they are usually upbeat providing they had a successful hunt. For these particular monsters living in a large city, a successful hunt was common and there was always something noteworthy to trade.

"Calm now, everyone, please!" a squat looking older fellow as he stood on a large stump wearing a comfortable looking gray-tweed suit, announced clearly; his aged hands rising slowly above his head. "The day is drawing late, and I know everyone is rather excited with plenty of stories to tell and with bellies full."

"My stomach is not quite full at all," a saddened voice muttered from the second row in of the gathered group in the clearing, drawing the dozens of eyes to the spot.

"Oh, and why is that, Nelson?" the elder one spoke, adjusting his glasses on his nose as a hand retrieved a small note pad which he flipped through until finding what he was looking for. "Were you not given the retirement home on Timothy Road?"

"Well, yes," the small little voice replied as he stepped into view with large, saddened eyes, drooping.

"Then I do not understand why you'd be hungry because I specifically gave you that location because *you* are young, *they* are old, and the chances that you would have to give any chase is practically nonexistent."

"I know," Nelson replied, head dropping as his eyes moved from the left to the right just in case anyone was shamefully staring at him. "It's the muscle rub they use there you see... I think I am allergic to it."

Nelson protruded his tongue a bit and there it hung red and swollen, dotted with blisters.

"Oh, I didn't think about that," the elder nodded, his shoulders tingling with embarrassment as he scanned the crowd. "Does anyone have any leftovers which our young Nelson might enjoy? Anyone?"

"I have a foot!" a voice called out from the crowd, accompanied by what was either a wide, flat hand in the air, or a flipper of some sort.

"And I have a thigh of a teen!" announced yet another, drawing the attention to the opposite side of the clearing, with plenty of *'oohs'* and *'ahs'* to go with it, and someone out there even licked their lips quite loudly. "Plus, a couple rather tender forearms, barely nibbled!"

"Male or female, Boff?" the older one asked excitedly, catching a ball of saliva at the corner of his mouth before it dared to drool out.

"Err, one second... it has been a long day," there was rustling in the crowd followed by the sound of two strips of tender meat tearing, chomping then a long sigh. "Based on their taste, one of each, Bellwether!"

"Excellent! Excellent!" the old leader clapped his hands together in excitement and then looked down into the face of the excited young one. "Will that do for you, Nelson?"

"Hey, I think I am hungry too!" bore a voice of no name from the crowd, followed by snickering.

"You've eaten plenty, Nom-Nom!" the bellwether barked to his right, a gnarly finger pointing. "I can smell the blubber of an Irish couch potato and the sinew of a policeman on your breath from here!"

The clearing erupted with the cackles and boisterous laughter of nearly half a hundred mouths, the ones with more than one notwithstanding, of course.

"Go now and eat, Nelson," the bellwether spoke quietly to the young one. "Just leave whatever booty you have brought in the center for trading."

Nelson nodded with a brilliant smile, his double rowed teeth clicking together rapidly like so many fingernails rolling on stone, and off he went for scrumptious teen-meat.

"So did everyone have a successful hunt today?"

"YES!" came the voices in unison (some of which by way of sounds which could be construed as such).

"Very good, very good," he spoke, raising his palms towards the dusky sky, racing quickly into twilight. "The hour is getting late, so let us tidy everything up before the *Others* come out."

Those in the clearing moved in perfect synchronous fashion. Those with larger feet stepped carefully to avoid those with tails, while those with tails curled them inward so as not to jab the shorter-statured ones in the eyes. In short order, four long rows had formed. The first row on the left faced the second, while the remaining two faced the backs of those standing before them.

In their hands each carried a sack of one size or another, and smiles stretched across maws, beaks, and proboscises alike.

This was how it was done every day for quite some time.

"Before we begin, I would like to introduce a new member who has decided so wisely to cross over from the night clans to join The Order of Real Monsters. Her name is just as beautiful as she is, please welcome, Selena."

From the growing shadows of the clearing behind the leader stepped a small frame with eyes of pitch which sparkled with a thousand stars. Amongst those in the lot she looked quite normal save her eyes and her shadowed skin, and in many ways she looked just like prey.

"Hello, everyone!" she spoke loudly with a small curve of a waving hand, her voice dancing with nervousness as she spoke loud enough for everyone to hear her. "It is so good to be here!"

"Hello, Selena!" came the half a hundred voices, some more guttural, others higher pitched, and a few resembling nothing at all like a salutation but they were understood, nonetheless. "Welcome!"

"Alright, Clannies!" the leader spoke with a smile, his hands out to his side in preparation to applaud. "Now, show our Selena how the bartering is done!"

Clap! His hands came together and, in a steady rhythm every other second, met again, giving the others their timing. The rows began to sway left in unison. The far-left line moved first, the remaining three following a heartbeat later, and as they swayed, the facing rows exchanged items from their sacks without ever missing the rhythm.

Once an exchange was completed, the second row turned to face the one behind it and the motion continued. Two rows now moved one way while the other two drifted the opposite, the trade passing steadily from hand to hand. When three rows finally faced the lone line on the right, the items were dropped at their feet, fresh pieces retrieved from the sacks, and the entire display reversed itself.

"So, let me get this straight," Selena inquired, bending slightly with her small hands on her knees so she was head level with the bellwether. "The Order of the Real Monsters hunt during the day where there are no shadows or creaking floorboards, and with so much light that even under-the-beds and centers-of-closets, are even frightening to a small child?"

"Precisely, my dear," he responded with a smile, continuing his rhythmic clapping.

"So, you get the children even before ones from my old clan get into place?"

"Them and adults too!" he quipped, proudly. "Choice depends entirely on the lust of the palate that day."

"That's why 'Thing Which Goes Bump' is always hungry," she sounded retrospectively quiet to herself. "So, you scare them, then eat them, then take their belongings when they fear the least?"

"You are a quick one, Selena," he nodded, giving her a wink. "But just like your clan, sometimes the feast is the fear, we don't eat them all, although sometimes they do smell too good to pass up."

"Did that one just trade wedding bands with the other one?" she gasped, pointing at an exchange right before where they stood.

"Yes indeed!" he beamed. "We call that a *Two-for-One Special*' Couples often taste the best with an extra helping of terror. If you get yourself a couple who is expecting a child, well, talk about a scrumptious dumpling morsel to finish up the meal with, eh?"

"*Brilliant!*" she whispered sharply, her sparkling eyes dancing with the rhythm. "But some are exchanging electronics, like that cell phone. Aren't you worried about their technology? I mean, they have location services built in now, so wouldn't the authorities come looking for them? Exposing us all?"

"We call that 'opportunity,' Selena," he bobbed his head back and forth playfully. "*If* they come looking for us, we don't have to go looking for them. There's nothing like having the meat coming to the beast, eh?"

"Double brilliant!" she giggled, her hand covering her mouth in awe. "So, to understand this completely, Bellwether: you Monster during the day when everyone's guard is down and then pounce?"

"Yes," he smiled.

"And then you take what you wish of them to later trade?"

"We do like the pretty things, yes," he chuckled, speeding up the pace to half second claps and the group followed suit without losing a beat. "'*The more they twinkle the more we tinkle*' we like to say!"

"I think I am really going to enjoy this!" she squeaked and clapped her hands rapidly together which immediately drew a wave of exasperated moans and squeals from the rows. "Did I—?"

"She just messed up the timing!" a hulking one moaned pathetically, then shrugged.

"Carl stepped on my tail because of her!" another bayed over the din of the grumbling crowd.

"Calm down, calm down, it was over anyways!" the leader soothed with a semi-sarcastic voice; monsters are whiners in the end. "She didn't do it on purpose! She was excited by the display of all your Monsterdom!"

"*Really?*" excited whispers rose and the bellwether nodded.

"Yes, really and truly!" Selena nodded rapidly, the edge of embarrassment cutting into her deeply. "It was so rhythmic! So, in time! I couldn't have done better!"

"Oh, well that's nice of her to say," a squirmy one jiggled, perhaps nodding in acceptance, to one whose stubby little wings fluttered happily with the compliment.

"Gather your things everyone and head to your dwellings!" the leader spoke, cupping his hands around his pale wrinkled mouth. "Twilight is upon us and tomorrow is going to be a big, *BIG* day!"

"I am really sorry about that," Selena spoke quietly only to receive a waving hand from him. "I didn't know—"

"Quite alright, Selena, how would you have known, and they are all happy regardless," he smiled and hopped off the tree stump and extended a hand to her which she took and stepped down gracefully. "Today was quite a successful day, I must say.

Mumbling in small groups, those present gathered up their traded goods and moved off through the woods towards destinations unknown. Sighing, he pressed back and took a seat on the stump watching them leave, occasionally producing waves to return the ones he got.

"So, where do I sign up?" she quipped, excitedly; nearly dancing in place before him.

"Oh soon, soon, Selena," he smiled, checking the time on a small pocket watch and then scanning the sky. Twilight had come quickly, the soft blues and remnant oranges of dusk blending together briefly as it awaited the darkness of night. "Just after everyone leaves."

"Okay, great!" she danced and waved to a few departures just for the hell of it. "I wonder what part of the city I will get. Downtown? The Westside? Harper's Court? *Ooh!* There are a lot of meaty tourists in Harper's Court… *Yum!*"

"Yes those are lovely places for a day-hunt," he sighed and nodded, checking his watch once again. "Haven't been there in decades myself though."

"Oh no?" she smirked, her mouth twisting to the side, musing. "Where do you hunt? I bet you have your own secret place, being the leader and all."

"Not really," he smiled, glancing at his watch and then exhaling a heavy breath with a smile on his face. "Nighttime is upon us, so glad… come with me, I must show you something."

"Alright," she smiled and looped her arm into his extended bent one and they began moving slowly across the clearing. "Well, I can see now why you call yourselves *'Real Monsters'.*"

"You can?" he inquired, adjusting his glasses with a slowly pressed finger. "And why is that, Selena? Let me hear what you think."

"Well, a 'real' monster comes out during the day," she began; her eyes up and to the side as her brain collected information. "And what makes them 'real' is because they are not afraid to do so. They are quite clever this way because they catch people when their guard is down and not expecting anything other than your usual problems."

"So far, so good, dear," he smiled, patting her arm.

"At night, when my clan comes out, Mankind is tense; no one ever wants to look under their bed, check their closets, goes down into the basement and surely never goes to the backyard shed without at least a weapon of some sort.

"Plus, look at the woods. All of my kind that used to patrol the woods stopped doing so because no one in their right mind would venture into them alone at night. Now, the Night Clans don't even bother coming in unless are fleeing *Them*, which is rare."

"Yes, this I know," he smiled and patted her hand. "That's why I Monster here at this time."

"Huh?" she blinked confused as they came to a stop near the edge of the clearing. "But that doesn't make any sense, Bellwether. The woods are practically empty at this time of night, I just said that and you agreed."

"Very true, Selena," he smiled broadly, stepping back. "The woods are practically empty at this time."

"Then what do you hunt?" she whispered dryly as the hairs on her neck slowly climbed to attention.

"Other monsters, silly girl," he beamed, checking his watch for the last time and then returning it to his pocket. "Primarily the Night ones."

"Yu-you are joking," she half whispered, half chuckled nervously as she took a step backwards. "This must be part of a test, isn't it, Bellwether?"

"No, no joke I am afraid, Selena," he sighed, advancing a step as he calmly removed his glasses, folding them and then placing them in his shirt pocket. "Remember what I said earlier: there's nothing like the meat coming to the beast, little one."

"Whu-why would you d-do that?" she squealed, her body growing cold as the old man advanced on her, growing, bulging, rising. Panicked tears began to stream her face as she backed into a tree, those old eyes peering into her growing large and brightening.

"Because I'm a monster, silly," he chuckled

"We're all monsters!" she begged, eyes scanning for a way of escape and not finding any. "You can't do this!"

"Of course I can, child!" he growled as ligaments stretched and popped while his form stretched to new heights. "Real monster's prey relaxes in the daylight; haven't you been listening? And all afternoon in my presence you were quite uneasy because of the light. Monsters in general are quite relaxed at night, aren't they, and you, Selena, were quite relaxed as darkness fell."

"But I want to join you!" she begged, cowering as the shape before her became quite monstrous from the simple squatness of the old man once before her; its heat from its mouth panting down on her as drool lashed her skin. "I will be the best Real Monster there is, I swear it!"

"Certainly, you would have!" he growled, panting. "But now I am hungry!"

"Please, I beg you!" she pleaded, her arms before her face, seeking anything to save her, to distract this one before her in hopes of escape, and because of her pleads the advancing form relaxed. Through pinched eyes she sought the one thing and blurted it out: "You said you wanted to show me something!"

"Oh yes, that's right, how silly of me," he spoke calmly and pleasantly.

"What is it?" she whimpered, lowering her arms cautiously, feeling that this had all been a ruse; the alpha-beast showing the newbie who wore the biggest claws.

"My teeth," he quipped with a smile, then lunged forth.

Screams rose as flesh tore, gurgling away to nothing as grunts echoed and jaws snapped with slicing teeth.

As meat thudded to the earth and bats flapped hurriedly into flight in the surrounding preserve, the Real Monster fed.

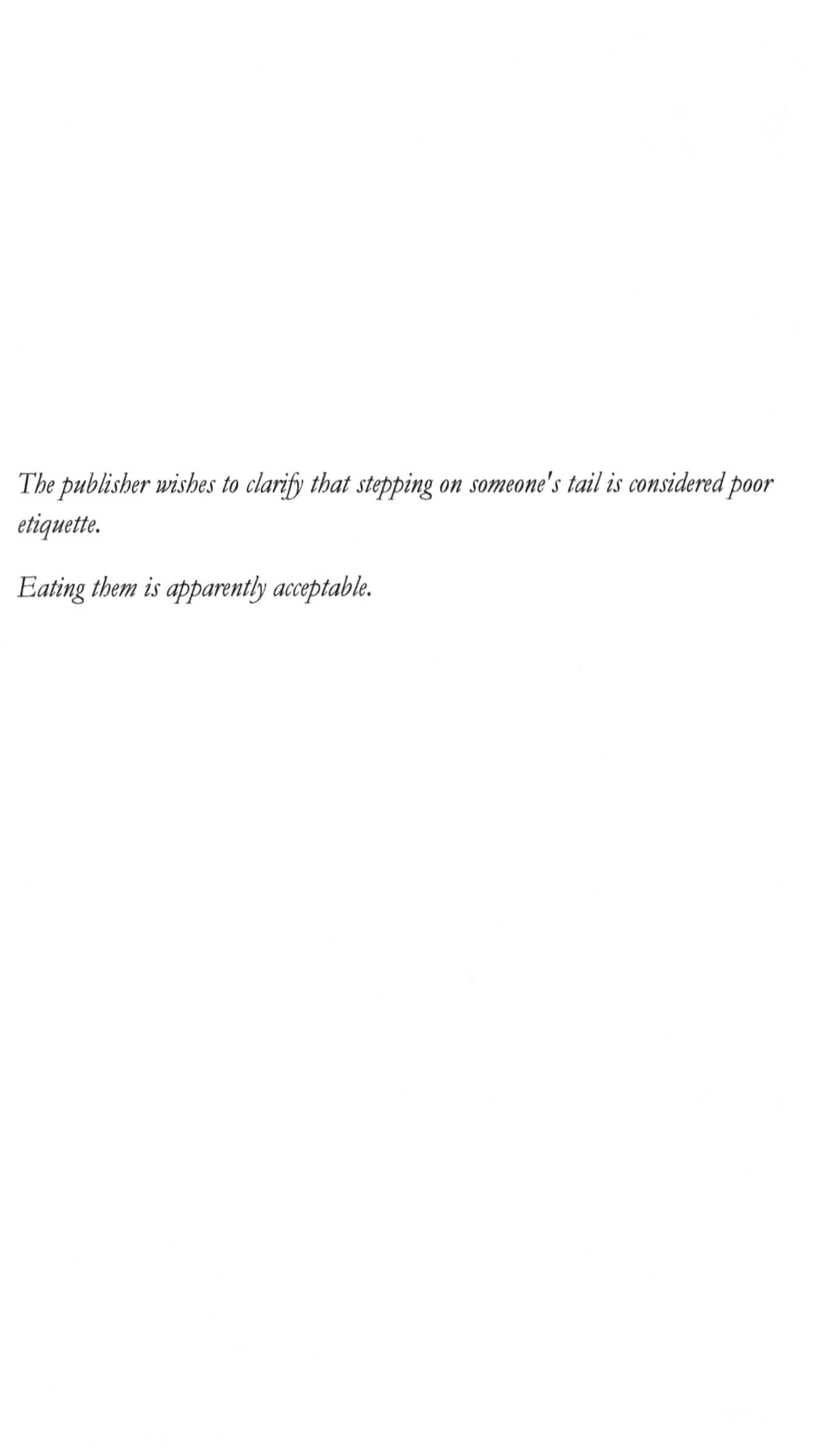

The publisher wishes to clarify that stepping on someone's tail is considered poor etiquette.

Eating them is apparently acceptable.

Whimsy
Whimsy

Whimsy-Whimsy

Another Amusing Breath

Early in the morning,
—just a little past noon—
A bright green caterpillar
sang to the moon.

He sang songs of sadness,
with a bright beaming smile,
About timeless true love
and other things vile.

Like kisses and hugs
and holding hands too!
 Praising heartache and sorrow
and other things blue.

A red fox joined in,
a black hide in the night.
Then a robin, a sparrow,
Calling out to the light.

In a matter of minutes
—about an hour or so—
A large crowd had gathered
to take in the show.

A flea echoed bass,
while a toad hit the sharps.
Fireflies played on cellos
While lizards plucked harps.

A grand party of no one,
totaling a number of three,
They sang, and they sang
as if singing to me.

So, I sat on a log,
on the banks of the lake,
and listened to nothing
That my ears would forsake.

THEO WAITED

Theo Waited

Theo waited where he always waited, nestled in a spot between three fire-thorn hedges in full radiant bloom protecting his back and sides from view. A twisted rosehip bush anchored by solid roots firmly in place stood at his front, camouflaging him completely. Despite the lavishness of all that surrounded him, he was an exclusive enclave of unfortunate possibilities who patiently endured the moment, calculating everything with precise, dark diabolism.

There were more than a dozen identical places on the edge of the property, which would have provided him similar protection while allowing him to peer out into the world, a world that would see nothing if it looked back, yet he reveled in that one chosen spot. That particular hollow warmed him with embracing arms of protection like no other. This spot was his earth-mother, and he knew she would never betray him nor allow him to come to any harm.

The ground there was softer, too, providing his body comfort for the long hours of waiting while he studied every detail around him, whether it was moving or unmoving, foe or prey. Smiles would spread, and soft sighs would rise as comforting breezes flowed through the branches, speaking to him with faint whispers of reassurance that all he was doing was irreproachable. This was a predator's mentality with the viciousness of pure animalistic drive yet controlled by a tenacious level of patience similar to mountains watching the world age by.

No, he would wait as he always waited, patiently.

Strong enough breezes would occasionally rise, enabling him the opportunity to twist and stretch tense muscles as the hedges rustled briskly around him. He was a smart one, knowing that if he didn't move with his trembling surroundings, there was that chance someone would notice a motionless object in a field of waving orange and red poms.

No one ever had, however.

People in these parts felt their world was safe, living in a suburbia-existence with manicured lawns and extra-sized garages just in case another vehicle was required. At the same time, the wives and daughters sunbathed scantily by the pools without so much as a concern of an onlooker. Expensive dogs were led about by retired couples who would walk at their lackadaisical pace along the bike paths, happy and content in their self-induced false sense of security from which he fed from.

This area was truly the *away from it all*: the city's outer neighborhoods where the rich and the arrogant set up expensive nests to roost, raising their golden chicks and driving automobiles with price tags far more significant than even the most modest home. For all the days he waited, he had not seen so much as a police cruiser rolling by, let alone anyone suddenly curious about his nestled little hiding spot. No… no one ever noticed him simply because no one felt they had to look for him in the first place.

Carefully, he drew a small Bible from his jacket pocket as he sat cross-legged in his spot and slowly thumbed along its pages with no real prescribed effort.

Theo wasn't a religious man by any sense, dear no; to him, things like that held no real purpose in a world so unevenly divided between Good and Evil, Darkness and Light, and he never subscribed to the notion that God sat on one side of the Coin of Fate whilst the Devil sat on the other.

In the end, he really could give two shits how the order went because, without question, he saw his existence to rest precisely in the middle. In truth, he viewed the Bible as nothing more than a one-sided story that spoke of great things God had done and of His supposed Son's leadership while speaking His words. It also told of all the wickedness Man had done, soiling the given life from such an omnipotent being that—for some reason—lost control over his children.

Why bring the floods for your ill-raised children? Theo proposed, thinking that one as powerful as *He* is purported to be, why does *His* punishment have to be so dire? *Can't you just make it happen?*

He shook his head, confused, finding it all hard to understand, considering he had seen so many well-behaved children under the judging eyes of proper parents. They were no more potent than their self-induced claims of omnipotence. Contrary to this, he had also seen many an imperfect child of similar right parents whose cheeks or bottoms were reddened-sore after their disobedience, adding to this paradoxical humoring that rapidly circled his mind.

In either case, there were no floods or banishments, giant locust swarms followed by amines, diseases, or outright damnations to the 'horrid' place. No, there was simply Parent-Child, Child-Parent, and somewhere in the middle, there was always some command and conquered, despite sometimes the presence of which was nearly anorexic.

Man is so weak and easily broken; couldn't you command them to act correctly? Theo thought on, scrutinizing the written logic. Is omnipotence a direct road leading to arrogance, or even maybe, perhaps, insanity?

Theo huffed and closed the book, returning it to his pocket unread. He did not need to think of such things on a day like that, for wherever God or the Devil was at that moment, they surely were not paying close attention to him or what he was about to do.

"There's my jogger," he whispered through a growing smile as his eyes focused on the shape of a woman moving towards him along the bike path. "She's right on time as usual."

His mind could not recall how many days he had watched her jog up the path; her long ponytail held firmly in a red twist which coincided with the even tempo of her pace, while small hands formed perfect little fists so as to pump forward and backward; advancing her body towards him. Each day she would excite him more than the last as her athletic outfit sang to him, expressing her flamboyant and longing desire for his attention and touch.

The fitting athletic shorts enunciated every expansion and contraction of her muscled thighs; the sports top with a 'V' of sweat-soaked fabric down the front, and the tiny tips of her socks just peeking out from her white and pink jogging shoes. His eyes would dance over the subtle bounce her breasts would project despite the athletic bra she wore, and his eyes would trail down to her crotch where that slice of feminine distinction formed perfectly in elastic fabric.

The combination of everything heightened by the sheer anticipation of her actions often made his mouth water, which would drip silently to earth in long, drooling streams.

Soon she would reach her usual resting point at the water fountain at the junction of two paths sitting directly across the street from him, and there—routinely—she would drink extensively, then exhale with an open-mouthed expression as her back arched with it, making his spine shudder. She would then stretch out her blood-swollen limbs: flexing, twisting, then bending, showing him that perfectly round bottom that would nearly explode his loins. He could picture everything beneath the stretched fabric calling out to him, teasing him, wanting him there, and deep down, he knew she did all of this for him. Yes, she will follow her routine as she had done for so many days without losing a beat, but this time all shall conclude with something more exciting than finishing her run.

As the woman went through the motions of all things expected, he drew from a pocket a small tape recorder carefully prepared with great intent for this day. Without moving his eyes from his prey, a thumb rolled forward, reassuring that the volume was to its max, and then he slowly depressed the PLAY button.

Meow! a kitten's cry rose from the player, but the woman didn't pay notice. She was busy bending to her ankles and holding there for a ten count.

Meow, meow, meee-oww! The recording played on, yet this time—predictably—the woman paused, head-turning and cocked, aware, seeking the source.

Slowly she straightened while giving her waist a slow stretching twist back and forth as she wiped the sweat from her brow. All the time, her eyes scanned the surroundings for the little kitten's meow.

Meow, meow!

"Here, kitty-kitty," she called out in a child-like voice, nibbling at the bait. She looked about her in all directions for the animal; its fear-filled calls rubbed at her heart humanely with motherly instincts.

He smiled widely, having had his presumptions proven correctly.

Meow, meow! Called out the miniature speaker's response; she did the one thing no one ever had: she looked directly at the spot where he was hiding, squinting.

Quickly, his finger depressed the PAUSE button as his heart thudded in his chest. Sudden breath caught in his lungs as her eyes narrowed instinctively and scanned, seeking the colored bushes where he hid.

Can she see me? A fear-driven response blazed in from the possibility, and he swallowed hard.

Checking about her to ensure no vehicles were approaching, she stepped out onto the pavement while advancing with a bunched brow of genuine concern. Slowly he exhaled with affirmation based on her actions that she could not make him out amongst the façade, and a smile returned to his face.

Meow, meow, meow! The kitten calls rose again with a simple motion of his thumb, and with the hook snagged firmly in her jaw, he was luring her in precisely.

Calmly, the woman leaned forward and began a slow advance in his direction, her fingers extended and rubbing together while making soft, *Tisk*-kissy sounds in hopes of luring the poor creature out of its hiding place. Slowly, he closed his eyes, absorbing her inner humanity while allowing her gentle calls of reassurance to flow over him, asserting that everything would be all right and to come to her loving presence. She drew closer—crossing the narrow road and into the grass along the hedge wall—stooping low as an adult would approach a lost, crying child.

Patiently, he set the player to the side and allowed it to roll. He envisioned the kitten he had found in an alley near his home a week before while the crying sounds rose from the recorder. He could picture it there now: sleeping in the front window, freshly bathed and wearing its brand-new collar, while dishes full of delicious food and clean water to drink waited for it in the kitchen; a king's reward for a creature that has aided him.

Calmly, he opened his eyes as she drew in, pulling his legs from under one another effortlessly, and then moved into a crouched position behind the rose hips. He could smell her hair, her perspiration, the heated musk of her loins from a steady-paced jog, and soon he would taste her as well.

"Kitty-kitty?" she sounded again, her body now low and crawling as she approached the edge of the bush, his eyes catching the perfect heart-shaped crests of her buttocks behind her. He was swollen with it all as blood rushed in cavities and extended while his jaw locked tightly for want of a rapturous scream.

Soon, he thought as he silently wept as a delicate hand appeared through the bushes-low. Tears ran from his eyes, borne from her display of pure innocence and selflessness. This one was not one whom the book said God would punish or the Devil would misguide, no; she was pureness and joy—a lone child amongst a world of monsters like him in a place where he lived unchallenged and equally unquestioned by all.

"Are you okay, kitty?"

Drawing in just past the edge of the bushes—her hair within touching distance with breaths that could be heard and a body warmly fondled—she pushed on through the bramble, searching, calling, and caring. In an instant, her eyes widened, her mouth formed a perfect 'O', and a faraway mouse squeak ran through her throat.

"Oh God!" she coughed a harsh whisper as her lungs begged to scream through an unwilling throat.

"Not quite," he replied, mumbling tear-soaked lips, his hands shooting forward and wrapping tightly, wrenching her in. She managed to squeal as a large hand clamped over her nose and mouth, and as the edges of existence slowly faded from the edges of her eyes, growing black, the glint of a switchblade sparked in her eyes.

She had begged for someone to save her from the swallowing darkness, yet the day moved on.

The breezes blew, the walking couples walked, and the hedges swayed as they always had, and neither God nor the Devil had any comments on the subject that day.

Patience is a virtue.

Waiting, however, is an entirely different matter.

THE
ROSE PETAL

The Rose Petal

The rain which is falling should have so many significant symbolisms for my mind to wander to, but it does not. Right now, my creative side should be exploring the significance of new life; the cleansing power of nature; children playing in the puddles which form and settle by morning's light, or even, perchance, finding calmness in the chaos of it all. Those would be wonderful thoughts to hold, allowing the mind to float amongst the raindrops—between them, around them, with them, becoming them—but no. These rains, like so many others in my past, call upon memories of her, Matilda, and how she danced in the cloud-falls and laughed, the only real sounds she ever made.

I remember her face being that of an olive glow amongst the gray sheets that fell, brightening them as moonbeams do unto the shadows of night. Only then, in the rain, did she ever seem as normal as you or me, a child in the body and mind of a tortured being whose only crime in life was her silence...

There was a time when I would have regarded someone like her as plain—possessing just enough facial charm to acknowledge her as pretty—but that is a fool's observation, one I was certainly guilty of; beholding the painting without ever paying proper respect to the canvas beneath. Matilda's paint—although simple by brush and stroke compared to a masterpiece—had been applied by an artisan of wondrous creation where the surface underneath was full of life: a perfectly imperfect medium that almost evaded capture by my inner eye.

The thoughts of her smile pull me back to the memories of her as rain tendrils race down the windows of my den. I stand there as distant lightning illuminates me and shows me my reflection in the patterned flashes, sometimes wincing away from what I see there. I am past hating the person in the reflection because those without a soul to speak of cannot be liked or disliked, let alone worthy of contemptuous thought. I could have done more. I could have loved her like a friend, a brother, or perhaps a savior in her hell, but instead, I chose to be a doctor of such self-induced importance, thinking my way was best without knowing her.

The psychology field at the time had a dozen different names for hundreds of similar ailments of the mind, and with those, there were countless remedies I assisted in treating her with. For my part, I will be eternally damned, this I know, and like so many a specter floating amongst this purgatorial ether, for will or not want, I cannot keep her out of my mind.

I was but an assistant then—a brazen graduate continuing my study of the human mind without so much as a low grade on my record—and in my pursuit to impress my superiors, I raced at the opportunity to apprentice at Shepherd's Grace; a mental hospital tucked in amongst the quiet hills in the country.

I was there but a month when I met Matilda: a homeless beggar half crazed out of her mind with 'the fever,' a non-existent condition which doctors assumed when they didn't have a clue of what ailed a person's mind back then.

Not much has changed in all these years; only the name they give 'the unknown' varies depending on the situation, and in retrospective comparison, doctors know just as little now as we did back then. Perhaps even worse now, doctors are armed with countless drugs to do most of their work for them, an era where medications have replaced instructed counseling much akin to how the calculator has reduced long division to an ancient—and soon to be forgotten—practice.

Matilda was a muted misfit of a young woman amidst urban society who was apprehended in a filthy alleyway after stealing a chicken from a street vendor in hopes of filling her starving belly. They found her in this squalor as she gnawed viciously on the raw meat, biting two of the arresting officers quite severely and gouging out another one's eyes. She had been at the asylum for almost three months when I first met her, yet the mark on her forehead delivered by an officer's baton still glowed as brightly as the day she was struck.

They had tortured that poor girl for her crimes, continuously spraying her down with frigid water until her lips turned blue and then beat her within an inch of her life. They thrashed her with a wet, heavy canvas that had been knotted and dragged through coarse sand to heighten the pain in attempts to draw out a confession from her.

"A confession for what?" I recall asking my mentor then, me at the proud age of twenty-one, and still as blind about the world as a newborn pup.

"For whatever they wanted her to confess," he replied as he jotted down progress reports on the patients, which rarely contained anything progressive.

"Did they get a confession then?" I asked, mumbling, as I looked over nude photographs taken of Matilda upon her arrival (a hospital's documentation policy to prove that that was how she was delivered just in case her injuries proved fatal). As I studied her dazed posture, captured so vividly in the details of the prints, I never found a spot larger than a robin's egg that did not bear a welt or a bruise.

"Does that really matter?" he replied after downing his fourth tumbler of scotch, dismissing me with it like an idle schoolboy, and from that day, I never questioned him or anyone else at the asylum about her.

No, they never got a confession from her, and as a matter of fact, they never got one single word out of her, not even a whimper. This I had learned many years later by a mere circumstance of running into one of the constables who was there the night, and as I drowned him in liquor, he allowed his mind to travel back so as to tell me everything.

"It was horrible," he managed to say through quivering lips as I poured his glass full, his eyes filled with ballooned tears daring to allow gravity to take control of them. He went on to tell me how the chief of police was one sadistic bastard, and despite any mercy God may have nested upon his soul, he was as ruthless as they came who justified his actions by right and by badge.

The retired officer went on to tell me he had been ordered to hold her wrists while another held her by the ankles, stretching her out across a wooden table. There, the chief never questioned her once as he whipped her belly and breasts until they glowed as red as a fire plug.

She never once screamed, even when the old bastard violated her internally with a police baton, and this insolent silence drew so much rage from him that he struck her unconscious with it; leaving his mark, which I saw months later.

Before you judge them right to the hell they belong, judge me as harshly as well. Although I never struck her, I did play my part in opening the dikes to her apparent insanity to their widest berth.

Ice water baths, shock treatments, chemical stimulants (both external and internal), and ice water enemas; anything the good doctor—my mentor—ordered. Even then, she never made a sound, but I knew then what I learned later on: that a person could genuinely scream with silence, and I bore witness that such silence is deafening in the end. During these 'treatments,' she never once took her eyes off mine, and in them she pleaded for me to listen to her suffering, but alas, I did not, for I did not know how to listen.

At night while I lay on my cot in my quarters, I often thought of her and her suffering through our methods of treatment which was so barbarically primitive that I wondered if she would ever speak a word, just a hint to inform me what was going on behind those eyes. As I dreamt every night, I saw her there, screaming in her silence as her body contorted under the guise of 'modern remedies.'

I cannot recall a time when I did not wake with my sheets soaked with sweat and my body cold from the visions I saw in my dreams.

It wasn't until two years later, when my mentor died from swelling of the liver, that I finally achieved my status of doctor—an achievement given in haste because no one else wanted the responsibility in such a remote place—and was placed into a position where I had the authority to deal out treatments as I saw fit. There were no more baths of icy water, no more enemas of arctic cold, and indeed the electrodes were abandoned save for extreme cases, but never again did they touch Matilda. Then, with this newly awarded power, I returned to what I had learned in my studies, started listening to her silence, and found that she had a lot to say.

"Matilda," I said softly to her one day in the garden, and although the ten-foot walls which surrounded it confirmed her confinement, the ivy which grew there gave her some comfort, I believe. "How are you today?"

She paused in her work, having collected up all the discarded rose petals in the garden that the blooms no longer wanted and arranged them upon a bench in a pretty pattern of no real significance, at least to me. She smiled and blinked her acknowledgment, pausing for a moment before selecting a single petal from the arrangement—one she chose with the utmost care—and placing it into a small palm, nuzzling it to her cheek. I was about to speak again, to inquire once more about her state of being just in case she had not heard me the first time, when she extended her palm towards me, petal up.

"This is for me?" I asked, genuinely curious because never once had she offered me a gift. Her smile widened, and her eyes blinked twice, answering me in her silent way, which I accepted without a further word. As I marveled at the simplicity of it—a near-perfect petal with a single marring flaw so effortlessly discarded from the bloom— my mind envisioned Matilda to be much the same: nearly perfect, yet so easily discarded by society for reasons of not.

I never noticed the thunder belching above me as the skies darkened, for my eyes and mind were locked upon this enigma in my palm, instinctively searching the cataloged medical texts to understand such a simple show of kindness. Shortly thereafter, the air came to a drizzle and then to a pouring rain, and for the better part of an hour I sat soaking in the downpour on the edge of the bench in the hospital's garden, watching her dance and laugh. She was laughing so gaily with a sound that made the angels weep, and I bore witness to this act as I sat holding my petal in their falling tears that day.

I could do nothing but watch in amazement while the rains washed away all I had ever purported to understand about the human mind as I sat cupping my fallen petal while she danced amongst the roses. I still have it here now, the petal she gave me, pressed between two sheets of glass within a leaden frame I carry in my inside pocket for reasons I still do not know. It is my albatross, my loathsome burden through life, never yielding me respite from the suffering I understood too late for her. All I knew was that the rains brought her voice in the form of childish glee, and to witness and study this phenomenon, I allowed her out whenever the storms came without fail.

Months of this went by, and I never understood the reasons for her change during the storms. Still, I was destined to find out until she caught the fever—a real one that time with onset pneumonia—did my true injustices show by forbidding her to dance in the rain ever again. With that action of which, I had assumed, I was protecting her from the ailments drawn from the damp and the cold; I had sealed her fate in death.

I still remember that night just as I do this very night, and I shudder to think I could have saved her. The rains had come in heavy, and she so wanted to go out in it, her eyes pleading with me as her finger pointed towards the windows. We were sitting in the common area when I refused her longings, and I thought the grief would tear her apart. I had explained to her that I feared that if she got sick again, medicine would not be able to save her, and as I spoke my reasoning facts, she cried soundlessly before me as the rains fell outside.

Quickly, she dashed to her room and returned with cupped hands holding dozens of dried, aged, burgundy-colored rose petals, extending them towards me as if they were coins of gold. This was her offering to me, her bribe, and her eyes begged for me to accept them so as to allow her to meet the rains. Once again, I refused and expressed that she should return to her room, for the hour was late, and at that moment, I should have known what her eyes said to me. They spoke softly of her intent to be there in the rains despite anything I ordered her to do, and she moved away slowly, never looking upon my face again.

As I walked her to her room, head hung low against her chest; she dropped a lone petal to the floor every third forward step so as to join the dripping tears from her cheeks; marking the trail from whence we walked in beauty and in sorrow. I provided Matilda with the prescribed medications, which allowed her to sleep, and she took them quietly without water. After I closed the door behind her—watching through the port-holed door—she stooped down in the center of the room and placed the remaining petals in a neat pile on the floor.

Slowly, she moved to the windows across the room, her eyes peering through the barred glass where a narrow-vented section above was parted to allow fresh air in. That is when my heart sank as I watched her stand on the tips of her toes, reaching up in hopes of feeling the splattering rain that had found its way in.

Quietly and with a heavy heart, I closed the porthole in the door and went to my office to sleep.

It was on that following morning, when I found that poor sweet, muted girl... dead.

Sometime after I had retreated for the night, Matilda pulled herself up to the vented courtesy window and tried to squeeze through the narrow space. She had reached out as far as she could manage, wiggling her arm, head, and shoulder through, and then sometime during her attempt, she slipped, bringing the weight of her body down on the window's metal ledge, crushing in her throat and snapping her neck, hanging her there.

I quit the asylum soon thereafter, following an authoritative inquest into her death, and spent the next twenty-five years in private practice.

Though the inquest ruled her death an accident, no verdict ever relieved me of my own. The law was satisfied, the hospital absolved, and the matter quietly placed amongst the archives of forgotten tragedies. Yet every rainfall since has reopened the proceedings, and in that private court of memory, I have never once been acquitted.

Now, as I spend my remaining years writing for psychology journals and teaching future would-be psychologists the art of understanding, I still keep the rose petal she gave me; a petal gifted by another petal of a different sort, both discarded by their blooms for whatever reasons they saw fit.

That morning after I found her, I collected up the small pile of rose petals she had placed on the floor and have kept them in a jewelry box ever since. Tonight—just as with every night on the anniversary of her passing—I will go out into it the night and lay a petal down in memory of her dancing in the rain with once muted lungs that screeched laughter towards the skies.

Without fail of expectations, each year on this night, it has rained despite foretold news of the weather, and each time it has, I have returned one of those rose petals to her. Tonight, as I stand at my windows staring out, I hold the last remaining petal, the very one she gave me all those years ago.

I know I could have done more for her, but then what could I have done being a wretched weed in her garden where the nearly perfect discarded petals fell?

To this, I have no answers, but I pray that when I place this last one down, my dear muted Matilda will talk to me; for now, I have truly learned to listen.

Though the
Heavens Fall

Though the Heavens Fall

-1-

The shadows held subtle creaks and moans as the winds stressed the wooden supports of the old building, and besides these sounds brought on by the gusting winds outside, Abernathy Parish was relatively quiet that Tuesday morning.

Father Anthony methodically stepped out into the nave during his usual morning rituals and glanced around, hoping to see at least one worshiper present, whether for prayer or solace, yet found none. With a heavy heart, he turned back towards his office, where his tea sat, now chilled to room temperature, resting next to a stack of paperwork he didn't want to work on. Giving a laggard glance towards the confessional, which also was empty, he allowed one last personal sigh to escape his throat quietly.

There will be souls to save when they need saving, he thought encouragingly to himself as he straightened Bibles along a pew, having enough OCD to be considered overtly 'neat' by his parishioners, 'tidy' by word of his wife. —*that or when the weather allows it.*

His parishioners came in all forms, from the humble to the flauntingly vain and the very subtle ones who rode the middle. Either they had a place in society to fit right into or didn't care what people thought of them one way or the other.

There of course was the one who came every Sunday, taking a seat at the very far pew in the back, away from everyone else, spending the entire service upon the kneeling bench and never once looking up. That one, he often suffered, must carry such a burden that even raising eyes toward the altar would somehow deepen the humiliation of it beyond what could be borne, let alone forgiven.

Then there was his boisterous singer. Though blessed with a voice trained since childhood and capable of stirring even the most stubborn heart, she sang with such enthusiasm that the remainder of the congregation might as well have simply moved their lips and spared themselves the effort. More than once he had considered speaking to her about it, and more than once he had decided against it, for the Lord deserved at least one person who sounded genuinely happy to be there.

Never the matter, they came when they came; however, it was almost always out of need rather than desire, with Sunday being the day the majority chose to present themselves before the Lord. Even then, Father Anthony suspected attendance was often more about appearances than devotion, lest one be thought either a harlot of the faith or a downright heathen upon the blessed day.

Small towns have a way of spreading news quickly, and the more wicked the information may be—of course, with plenty of copious *(dis)*colorations of the truth—the faster the gossip spread. At one point in time, he figured there had to be some gossip floating about him as well, lingering in the corners of Danny's Pub or being trimmed and shaped at Sandy's Styles along with the town's hair.

There had to be.

Here he was, a Catholic priest—a youngish married one at that—rolling into town and taking over Abernathy Parish immediately following the death of Father Bagley. With very few words of introduction to the flock and even less personal information for them to chew upon, he settled into the parish as if he had always belonged there. People still came then, though largely out of curiosity rather than devotion, many of them waiting patiently for the moment he might make a fool of himself. That would have made them happy enough; a minor stumble by the new priest would have kept the gossip train trudging faithfully along its tracks for months.

Thankfully, that never happened, though many surely stood ready for it all the same. In time, their curiosity waned and gave way to familiarity, and although they came to enjoy his sermons well enough, they remained much like parishioners everywhere else; most sought the Lord when the burden grew heavy enough to carry.

"What do you expect, Colin?" His wife, Catherine, smiled over a copy of *Counting Stars* as she sat on the couch beside him with her back pressed into the armrest; feet resting comfortably upon his lap, and then giggled at the moment.

It was her happy, but nervous giggle, the kind she reserved for those portions of her romance novels where the setting had moved from merely sultry to downright boiling. Although he was not a romance reader, he had secretly read this particular title by L.D.K. Johnson and found it to be the perfect romantic story with the heat, as Catherine called it, 'bearable,' albeit he would readily admit he had proven rather reactionary to certain imagery within its pages.

This was her fifth time reading it.

He leaned back onto the couch with a heavy sigh, glancing at the cover and biting his tongue. Surely if his congregation knew such a book was in his house, the rumors would spread faster than a dam break. Still, if there was to be a separation of Church and State, Catherine had delivered the message long ago about prior separation from the home.

"I am not sure what I expected," he said quietly, having once been at least idealistic of what.

"My love," she soothed with a gentle smile. "This is a small town with nine churches, each of different faiths, all of them trying to be more perfect than the next. Of course, they're going to put on the big show when others are putting on their shows like they were cars."

"*Cars?*" he had asked as he sipped at his coffee. "And how's that?"

"You know? Like the auto show!" she had burst forth, laughter unconstrained. "Everyone showing off their best and trying to be all-too perfect collector."

He smiled at this, gave her feet a loving squeeze, then rose to get her more tea. He loved her dearly and trusted her words more than any living person. Perhaps she was right; his congregation sought perfection in their lives, yet they didn't realize what they sought was unreachable whilst in the mortal coil.

As he poured her tea—P. G. Tips as always—he considered the word repeatedly, only to return to the same conclusion: perfection was merely an interpretation, a mirage fashioned from whatever ideals society happened to hold dear at the time. It forever lingered just beyond the next rise, appearing close enough to touch yet never truly obtainable. Many coveted it, but those who devoted themselves to its pursuit often failed most spectacularly, not because perfection itself was unattainable, but because they never truly understood what they were chasing.

That conversation wasn't uttered for nought those days ago, and since then, the simplicity of the message and the meaning curled around his mind slowly in a continuous loop. What he wanted for his flock was simple: love thy neighbor, be tolerant of things they did not understand, and follow God's gospels in their daily lives; to use Tolerance as a guiding force and not as dismissive mentioning in some daily anecdote of no relative basis.

He had hoped that this would be or become their guiding beliefs, their ethos, but then again, he had always wanted to be six-foot-two and a hundred and ninety pounds of pure muscle, but that sure in hell wasn't going to happen.

Taking a personal moment to ponder, he sat at the end of the pew nestled in the outermost aisle closest to his office, allowing himself a brief moment to reflect upon the paths which had brought him there.

He had been an engineer once, then a businessman. Marriage followed, and then a child, only to have cancer steal that child away and drive him toward the Protestant Church in search of answers.

It was there, in the light of that place, that he found God and realized his life's purpose was not selling high-end routing equipment to ISPs, but serving a higher power. With his wife's blessing, he entered the seminary and became a minister.

After a time, something within the Protestant way ceased speaking to him as clearly as it once had, and so he followed the road which ultimately led him to where he was now: a Catholic priest. Since then, he had held many titles; everything from deacon to vicar and, of course, 'My dearest' from the missus, whilst reserving the designation of 'Father' for those who had been in the faith since childhood.

To him, it mattered little what he was called, provided they at least came, but in times such as these, when more and more found personal guidance and solace through social media and *YouTube*, the flock had indeed grown thin.

Your halls are empty yet again, Lord, he mused as his eyes held the large crucifix hanging above and to the rear of the altar, admiring the fine craftsmanship of days of yore. *And if so, may the rain abate for just a little while?*

He sighed long and hard while his hands hung clasped between his knees, his wearied heart beating calmly as he gazed upon the large wooden crucifix in comfort.

It was old. Rumor held it to be nearly three hundred years in age, carved somewhere near Pordenone, Italy, where a craftsman first set his planer to the wood and, through inspiration or devotion, fashioned the masterpiece which now watched over Abernathy Parish.

It was also the only thing to survive the fire which razed St. Birinus Church to the ground in 1957 near Belchertown, Massachusetts. That fire had come on a stormy day much like this one, rain hammering the world outside just as it now pounded against Abernathy Parish while Father Anthony sat musing upon that Tuesday morning.

For St. Birinus, it was a Sunday.

The violent storm came in after days of steady rain which drenched Belchertown, bringing thunderheads that sent lightning into the church's steeple and ignited the straw insulation hidden within its wooden walls, engulfing the building in flames despite the downpour.

A hundred and twenty-seven people went up with the church, including thirty-seven children ranging from newborns to teenagers.

He had once read that when the smoke finally cleared, the vicar was found kneeling before the crucifix, reduced to little more than ash and bone. A burned Bible remained pressed against his chest while one blackened arm stretched outward towards the figure above, fingers of fragile ash still reaching. Through it all, the crucifix remained hanging between its stone-tiered moorings, untouched by the inferno which had consumed everything around it.

At times—in retrospect of the fire which had killed so many— Father Anthony had envisioned the eyes of the crucifix staring upwards towards the heavens as the ceiling blazed above it.

I worry for them too, Lord, his thoughts continued. *Am I to consider their absence a personal moment to reflect upon my choices or a sign that I am not reaching them?*

Should I get a Facebook account?

There was no answer for him to apprehend, let alone to follow in the slightest degree, so with a heavy sigh, he went to his office to collect a notepad and inventory the sanctuary in case anything needed ordering.

Outside, the storm continued its stormy ways and it was growing.

-2-

The sound of the front doors slamming closed echoed through the empty spaces within; heavy, deep, and with no explanation save that someone had entered, for indeed, there had been no one inside to leave. Despite a good priest's reserved demeanor, he smiled at this, whispered a quick thank you toward the ceiling, and adjusted his collar as he rose.

He was eager, though he did not wish to appear so before whoever might be waiting in the pews, and for one of the very few times since he had donned a collar, Father Anthony found himself genuinely giddy.

How long had it been since someone simply came in outside of worship hours? One year, perhaps two, and he wasn't about to count the electrician who came to repair the PA system, despite the man's habit of wearing a crucifix and crossing his head, lips, and heart each time he entered the nave.

No, the fellow was a devout Catholic, but he was also being paid to be there. A bemusing thought crossed Father Anthony then: perhaps the pews would be full if he passed out tens at the door instead of warm welcomes.

He shuddered then at the thought as he now shuddered with the upcoming salutation to whoever was present.

With one deep breath, he grasped the doorknob, turning it, then stopped short when a soft chime called from his desk; it was the confessional alert bell.

"Oh," he blinked, his smile waning.

Clearing his throat as he made one final adjustment to the collar, he opened the office door and went.

Even a confession is at least a sign.

-3-

"I have sinned, Father, so greatly sinned," out came a male's voice through the perforated screen before Father Anthony could close the privacy door.

He paused momentarily, perplexed.

Quickly he pitted the man's words against recent memories, and never had there been someone so anxious to confess, let alone making a beeline from the front door to the confessional. Clearing his throat, he adjusted himself on the cushioned bench in the vague shadows produced by ambient light allowed in through slits in the top of the booth.

"You're Catholic, my son?" he asked quietly, almost in a whisper. Despite their particular construct to preserve privacy, Father Anthony never quite trusted confessional boxes, for even the slightest story seemed to echo within, reflecting to the ears of someone not intended.

He shook his head on this and waited.

"Yes and no," the man replied, a wearied tone to the pattern, anxious even. "I was raised as one, my mother was devout, but things have kept me from it for a long time... perhaps this was not—"

"Never mind that," Father Anthony sputtered, dismissing several formalities. He felt he was about to lose this man, this soul who had come with a heavy heart, and it shouldn't matter if he were a bleeding heathen, provided he had the right direction to go in the first place. "How have you sinned, my son?"

There was a long pause, followed by a slight shuffling on the other side of the screen, followed by the sounds of tissue paper unfolding, ending with a long exhalation as the man blew his nose, thick and rich with mucus.

"Sorry, Father," the voice moaned.

"No worries, my son," Father Anthony smiled, shaking his head, albeit the man could not see his gestures. "The weather has been a bit nasty lately, to be expected. Please, continue."

Deep breaths rising, followed by a heavy sigh, reached Father Anthony through the screen.

"I have done things which He would not condone..." the voice finally came back and trailed.

"Can you elaborate, my son?" Father Anthony presented, removing a rosary from his jacket pocket and entwining the round, polished cedar beads among his fingers.

"Vile things, Father," the voice wavered with a slight inflection that came close to concluding with a squeal. Slow breaths between them in the shadows where only heartbeats sounded; the dim light to provide comfort and privacy held air growing stale with both curiosities and regrets. "Things of which cannot be forgiven, I fear."

"*He* forgives all who seek redemption," Father Anthony quickly spoke, his voice directive to shepherd this soul toward understanding and enlightenment. "To speak of such weighing sins is the first step towards virtue and to move past these darkened times in your life."

The silence was his retort as the man on the other side of the screen contemplated his words, but Father Anthony had patience and would allow him to continue when he was ready.

"And what of righteousness, Father?" the man interjected with a mouse of a whisper. "Where does that pertain to sin or the sinner? If one felt that he was being righteous in his decision and then acted, does that play out to be a sin or a righteous act?"

"Righteousness is heeded in both the mind and the spirit, my son," Father Anthony replied, unaware he was shaking his head slowly as if correcting man's views in visual presence. "Do not let these things burden either any longer."

Father Anthony sat with the shared silence of the man, wondering if his words were finding their course with him or not. Clearing his throat, he adds:

"How have you sinned so, my son?"

Silence fell, thick and hanging like so many wet blankets upon a line, weighing the moment down where only time and light could render them free. Despite the massive limestone walls, the storm's clamor could still be heard, yet it was not what drew Father Anthony's attention. It was the deep, rhythmic breathing from the other side of the screen and the steady plinks of rainwater dripping from the man's clothes to the floor below.

Guess I'll be cleaning up a mess. Father Anthony thought and then cursed himself immediately afterward. *This is where the lost come to be found, not to worry about whether the weather had drenched them, sweated them, or blew their hair all out of sorts! What in God's Earth are you think—?*

"I have killed *Him*, Father," the man said flatly, exhaling a long breath.

Father Anthony's eyes widened as the words struck like a bolt; most alarming was the word 'kill,' something of which no one had ever spoken to him in such a manner.

"Whom have you killed?" his voice came with a creak that he hoped the confessor did not sense.

"The *Son*, Father...*He* has come back, or at least *He* did, and I... I killed *Him*."

Father Anthony sat upright, his back a tense plank, eyes narrowed on the screen as he rapidly repeated the man's confession.

"Forgive my confusion," he whispered, his tone full of bewilderment. "And yes, taking a mortal life is a dire sin, but you killed whose son?"

"God's..." the man's voice wavered, becoming sullen and in a low tone without a hint of a whisper. "I killed *Him* just after he returned."

"All right, my son...." Father Anthony straightened, his posture comforting but with an edge of irritation if the man could see him clearly.

He didn't know whom he was dealing with, and although the man seemed quite sincere, Father Anthony remained unconvinced that all levels of sanity were present, if not sobriety itself. He could detect neither alcohol nor the familiar scent of marijuana upon him, yet something truly was amiss; he even dared to conjecture the possibility that someone from his old Protestant order had sent the fellow along as part of some elaborate jest. Diligently he continued, though beneath it all lingered a heavy air of caution, for he had no desire to be made a fool of all the same.

"I understand you are scared and confused, but you are saying that you killed *Him*... The return of Jesus Christ... Our savior?"

"Yes, Father... the very one."

Father Anthony had to bite back the first words which rose to his lips; his teeth clenched as his hands curled into fists. He had been fatigued as of late, exhausted really. The rainy seasons traditionally brought such things upon him, with aches and pains making it impossible to find a comfortable position in which to sleep, often leaving him tossing and turning until it threatened to drive his wife mad. The last thing he needed was dealing with someone not in full possession of their faculties or the target of some elaborate prank.

No, not a trick; not even the Protestants would stoop that low. This man was sincere—or at least as sincere as his mind would allow him to be—and he was seeking help.

Yes, this man must be distraught and confused; a person who believed he had committed the greatest of sins had likely suffered some fracture of reason and thought only of the church when seeking solace from his guilt. This was what Father Anthony was dealing with and nothing more, and with his head cocked to one side and eyes closed, he counted backward from ten—with a stumble around seven, then another at four, forgetting there was a three altogether—before taking a deep breath.

"And how do you know that this man you killed was the Lord, my son?" Father Anthony exhaled the words with wary anticipation.

"Because when I saw *Him*, he was aglow," the man replied and adjusted, the leather-covered cushion beneath him groaning as he shifted his weight. "*He* was staring down from atop the hill at Kandinsky Park over on Euclid; you know the one?"

"I do, my son," Father Anthony acknowledged as he shifted the rosary from one hand to the next, having had a vice grip on them that began to gnaw at the soft spots between the fingers. He knew Euclid Street quite well… lots of bad things have happened on Euclid.

"*He* was looking about," the man's voice began to tremble again. "*He* was in pain, a lot of it, I think, and *He* was sobbing."

"I see—" was all Father Anthony could muster as a reply, then cleared his throat in hopes some guiding words would follow, but the man burst forth emotionally, causing Father Anthony to jump, startled.

"You know *He* was to return, right Father?" the man begged, a vague silhouette filling the space of the screen in featureless details.

"Yes, *He* is, but you are speaking about things which some, even in the Church, review as metaphorical, and—"

"'*His eyes are like a flame of fire, and on his head are many diadems, and he has a name written that no one knows but himself!*'" The man quickly broke in with the scriptures, his palms audibly planting against the wood frame encompassing the screen, his lips grazing the thin perforated sheeting. "*He is clothed in a robe dipped in blood, and the name by which he is called is The Word of God.*

"*And the armies of heaven, arrayed in fine linen, white and pure, were following him on white horses.*

"*From his mouth comes a sharp sword with which to strike down the nations, and he will rule them with a rod of iron.*

"*He will tread the winepress of the fury of the wrath of God the Almighty. On his robe and on his thigh, he has a name written—!*'"

"Ye-Yes, my son," Father Anthony quickly jumped in, his monotone voice projecting authority and control of both the subject and the moment, yet his mind raced with anxious confusion at the same time.

This man confessed to having killed someone, a crime dangerous enough in its own right, but to believe so completely in what he was now claiming placed him in a category beyond dangerous, perhaps even homicidally insane. For all those parishioners he had scowled at because of their smartphones, e-Readers, and social media servitude, he wished at least one of them was there right then.

"But you are quoting *Revelations*, nineteen-twelve to be exact, and that speaks of the apocalyptical end. The Bible also tells of his return in a time of enlightenment for those who wish—"

"*He* was crying blood, Father," the man said flatly as he moved from the screen, completely disappearing in the darkness of the confessional. "*His* clothes were covered with it."

Audible weight on leather followed… a shifting of a foot in puddled water… rapid, deep breathing of staling air, then silence.

"I see," Father Anthony added and leaned back as well, shifting his eyes toward the handle and daring to reach for it while explaining why he must leave. He was frightened without a doubt, though not so much by what the man said, but by the manner in which he said it despite his apparent remorse. As he went along, nothing sounded scripted or fabricated. It was earnest, remorseful, and cogent, spoken clearly as though every word were fact.

Quietly, he licked his lips as he extended his hand toward the latch, fingers rolling slowly as they prepared to grasp and go, but then he pulled back; both frightened to flee and ashamed for wanting to.

He had seen a movie long ago where an assassin had gone to confession, and after a scripted monologue, asked the priest to lean forward so he could tell him a secret. The priest obliged, leaning close to the lattice, and in a blink, the assassin drew a pistol and blew the poor man's head off. That was what he was dealing with; a crazed man, perhaps even a Protestant on some absurd vendetta, sent to put an end to the wayward minister who had crossed the aisle and become a Catholic priest and—

Enough of that! He damned his thoughts, shaking his head; dismissing the foolishness for what it was, and then calmly placed his palms flat on his lap with closed eyes and moving lips without sound; asking the Lord for strength, guidance, and understanding for this troubled soul which came to him, and to clear his mind of silly and irrelevant thoughts.

"Father?" the voice whispered through the screen, a mouse of a voice.

"Sorry, my son," he stammered, collecting his thoughts. "Co-could this 'blood' been an injury… one who refused to heal, or-um… one you gave this man?"

"No, Father," the man said quietly, sniffing hard and sucking up runny mucus into the cavities. "I didn't injure *Him* for *Him* to bleed; *He* was doing that just fine by *Himself*, but in the form of tears."

"All right, my son, what happened next?" he asked, unsure whether he was being courteous or curious, or both.

"I approached *Him* and asked *Him* who *He* was," the man said with an invisible shrug in the shadows. "*He* told me, and then *He* asked me if the rest of the world was just as bad as imagined, and I said to *Him* that it was far worse than bad. I told *Him* of the wars, the crime, how politicians use his teachings and name in vain so to corrupt the weak; everything!

The man paused as he leaned close to the screen once again.

"*He* then vomited blood, Father…" the man's voice returned to a quivering whisper. "…everywhere."

Silence fell between them, leaving only the sounds of the storm and the plinking water on the mason floor.

"So-so what did you do then, my son?" Father Anthony broke the silence, albeit his tone barely rose above a whisper.

"I broke *His* neck, Father," the words came flatly, solid, and without hesitation, followed by a heavy suction of more mucus.

"Wuh-whu-why would you do this?" Father Anthony sharply begged in a high-pitched whisper, fully believing that this man had murdered someone in this fashion. Still, his mind was reeling in pure confusion, praying for understanding.

"So that he wouldn't suffer anymore," the man's voice returned with the rumble of a growl, deep and growing. "'*No longer in a world where the masses flock towards the suffering like flies to the light in the dark,*' or something similar I read once, but I can't remember where."

The man sighed in the darkness, followed by the sounds of a zipper rising to its top.

"I think it's time for me to go, Father; I will trouble you no longer with this. Thank you for your time."

"Wait, my son!" Father Anthony said quickly and loudly, yet he could barely hear his voice.

The audible winds picked up outside, shrieking through the church's aisles as if the front doors were open wide. The confessional walls began to shake, accompanied by the sounds of paper flapping freely somewhere out in the pews. Before him, thin pine began to stress and crack, and soon the perforated screen began to bulge inward, growing pregnant by stresses applied to it.

Something was coming through.

Light began emanating inwards, shooting golden beams that never seemed to land upon him but instead floated as brilliant rods suspended around him. He was screaming this, but through the event, he never once heard his own cries as the bedlam drowned them out. He frantically reached for the latch, yet it would not allow his hand satisfaction as it seemingly moved further from him the more he tried.

It has begun, the man's voice monotonously called out in his head, clear and understandable without the sounds of what surrounded interfering.

In a blink, the world became very, very bright.

✻

"Father?" a voice in the light called from above him, concerned. "Father, are you awake?"

"Huh?" he licked his lips as his eyes broke from a rapidly blinking blur to focus on Chip, the church maintenance man.

"Ah! Catching a few Z's on a wet and windy day like today, eh?" Chip beamed a tobacco and coffee-stained smile as he set his toolbox down and swung a utility belt around his waist as he stood in the aisle.

Chip was a haggard sort of a man whose hair had never once been accused of being kept, let alone combed through; long and graying at the roots, which showed clearly as it was pulled back tightly into a mannish ponytail. He smelled of machine oil and sweat, though not unpleasantly by any measure; it was the scent of a working man who used his hands instead of a keyboard, one which reminded Father Anthony very much of his own father. He knew Chip was a drinking man, but he drank off-duty and with restraint, never arriving with dullness in his eyes. In short, he was reliable and faithful.

"Can't say that I blame you, though; on a day like this, all you can do is watch the sewers overflow or catch up on some rest, right Father?"

"Chip? What are you—?" he paused, hand coming up with clenched rosary beads.

Slowly, he relaxed his fisted grip where perfectly round indentations had formed in the fleshy places between his fingers, now buzzing from lack of circulation. He watched as color returned to the whitened pits, then made several slow clenches to coax the feeling back into them. His attention drifted toward the confessional box on the far side of the church where one door—the confessor's door—sat ajar. He swallowed hard and drew a steady breath, only then realizing he had been holding it.

Chip was going on about something behind him that involved a body, death, and murder as Father Antony dilatorily rose and took unheeded steps toward the confessional. A glance at his wristwatch told him it was nearly half-past three, and having checked before leaving his office earlier before sitting in the pew, it was just five past the hour, then.

As he drew near the box, he was convinced everything was tidy and in order before his apparent slumber—his level of OCD would have assured this—and in no way was a door left hanging open. The latches are solid and catch with an audible click, set inside doors heavy enough to stay closed without any chance of rattling open by any means.

Someone had been in there while he slept, while he dreamt, while he heard a confession.

Upon reaching the door, he paused with an extended hand to complete the opening process someone else had begun and then contemplated closing it, a thing someone may have likewise attempted before him, and then he froze. None of it could have been real, none of it. It was all a simple afternoon dream which coasted upon the edge of a knife, with horrors upon one side and surrealism upon the other as it sliced through the everyday thoughts and frustrations of his affairs as a priest.

He withdrew his hand and exhaled lengthily, turning his head slightly over his shoulder to Chip, who was in tow while going on about something of ill events.

"What was that, Chip?" Father Anthony spoke in almost a whisper. "Someone died?"

"No, not just die; murdered," Chip said with an off chuckle, often known as the sort who could laugh at just about anything providing that the 'anything' was not happening to them. "Over there at Kandinsky Park where all those punks like to hang out at night and smoke illegal cigarettes, drink and fu— I mean have non-marital relations."

"Kandinsky Park?" he whispered sharply, turning completely, his face tingling as the blood washed from it, which he wiped at a cheek mindlessly. "This happened today?"

"Yeah, Father, earlier on, just before the storm came," Chip nodded, his eyes narrowing to concerned slits as he set his toolbox down once again. "You all right, Father?"

Father Anthony turned away towards the box, hand extended with palm up as if showing off a new sedan, then returned towards Chip, whose face had not altered from the look of concern. Slowly his hand came to his mouth, which he wiped downward twice along its edges, then took a step towards Chip.

"Kandinsky Park?" he begged again, blood returning to the ghost mask it had become.

"Yeah, Kandinsky Park," Chip shrugged. "They had every street from Euclid to Sommerset closed off. That's why I got here a bit late. I've never seen that many police cars in one place in years. I think all of Cordale's finest were there; some County sheriffs too, and I even saw a state cruiser off to the side. Hell, even Kankakee's KLBG was there with cameras and lights and that anchorman Clyde, something or another. Looked like something straight out of a movie."

"Did they say what happened or who it was?" Father Anthony begged, his head daring another look towards the box.

"Deputy I talked to said they didn't know who the fella was." Chip shrugged. "Just said someone killed him is all… broke the fella's neck. They think it might be mugging. Stripped the guy right down to his skivvies. It just goes to show you how this town and its common areas have been going to the dogs all these years.

"Like I was telling Ms. McKahey at the drug store the other day, Cordale is going to the dogs, and there should be—!"

"Di-did they say what he looked like?" Father Anthony begged, almost in a squeal.

"Nope, not really, just some young fella… someone no one had ever seen before in or around town."

"And all this happened today," Father Anthony whispered to himself, dismissing Chip entirely as he slowly turned back towards the box and approached it, hand extended.

It was only a dream, he thought, his eyes barely blinking as his hand reached for the latch. *You probably heard something about the murder on the radio this morning during breakfast with Catherine and didn't pay much attention. It just came up as a dream… just a dream.*

The latch felt cold but solid, and with his thumb, he tried the release twice, and besides the slight creaking sound of an unoiled mechanism, it appeared to be working as designed. He needed to open it, to let in the light to see, and yet again, did he want to or have to, with the former leading his contemplative spirit to shut the door and forget about it.

"Something wrong with the latch, Father?" Chip added from over his shoulder with honest curiosity.

"No, no," he shook his head, clearing his throat. "Chip, how long have you been here before you woke me?"

"Oh, I'd say twenty minutes or so," Chip added with a shrug, with a quick gander at his watch. "I would have come in as soon as I got here, but a bunch of the letters had blown off the sign out front, so I gathered them up. The wind had 'em everywhere... had me chasing them like a darn fool out there on the lawn."

"And did you see anyone enter or leave the parish?"

"Um, nope, can't say that I did," Chip shook his head and produced a smile. "Just a lot of branches and letters blowing about the lawn is all. Why?"

"No reason," he swallowed as he firmly grasped the handle. "No reason at all, Chip, thank you."

Here goes, Father Anthony thought and then slowly opened the door in full swing.

It was empty, save the one telltale sign he hoped was and was not there simultaneously: a puddle.

Vibrations from the door's movement sent subtle ripples across its surface, then coming still like smoked glass. It had collected on the stone floor of the box, which was slightly raised from the rest of the church's foundation, and although he could see it clearly, it took several blinking snapshots of the eyes for his brain to register its presence fully.

For a moment, all he could hear was the sound of his pulse in his ears.

"What was that?" he said quietly over his shoulder to Chip, who had added something to the moment but had not ascertained in the slightest.

"I said, it looks like you have a leak in the roof somewhere," he repeated as he stepped forward and past the good Father, then squatted, touching the edge of the puddle then looking up towards the confessional ceiling where the vents were and stood to examine closer. "Hmm, I don't see any water there, but you probably have a leak to get water like this. It must have dried off from the vent but look there; the cushion has some water on it too."

Without a thought, Chip pulled his red and black checkered handkerchief from his back pocket and wiped it dry.

"Yes sir; has to be a leak," he added with a nod and glanced back up. "Looks like we had splattering when the water hit the vents. When I am done putting up the storm shutters, I'll have a look."

With that, Chip stepped from the confessional, gathered up his toolbox, and set off to handle his chores. Father Anthony blinked slowly and then shut the door. He knew what he thought he knew, only to awaken from an apparent dream wherein a man had confessed to murder. Being a dream, it was all coincidence of course, and yet there remained the undeniable evidence that someone in water-soaked clothes had occupied the confessional. Shaking his head with a wry smile, he turned to return to his office and then paused.

"Chip?" he called after him, who stopped and faced him. "Storm shutters?"

"Oh, yeah, they're in the cellar," Chip smiled. "They haven't been used since long before you came here, but the church got 'em back in O-nine after a summer of bad storms. We lost some irreplaceable stained glass back then."

"Is the storm really that bad to need shutters?"

"Naw, not yet," Chip shrugged and turned up the nave towards the altar, talking as he went. "The storm's bad, but I think it's about to get a lot worse after today."

Father Anthony watched him go and then slowly turned back towards the confessional; his thoughts, heavy.

"I think you're right, Chip," Father Anthony said quietly as his eyes held the confessional, which sat closed and unoccupied. He shuddered as thunder boomed outside, brought on by a blazing light display that bore through the windows and stained glass in sheer brilliance.

Slowly Father Anthony moved towards his office, retrieving his windbreaker and locking the door. He paused at the mouth of the nave and crossed his head, his heart, and his lips, and left into the storm, heading home to find solace in his wife's arms.

—

As the day progressed, so did the storm, growing ever more heavy and violent as it moved over Cordale proper, knocking out power in some neighborhoods, toppling plenty of trees in others, and still, the full brunt of it had not yet come.

Outside Abernathy Parish, the remaining letters on the church's illuminated sign board grabbed hold of the winds. They took flight, forever erasing the posting **LOVE THY NEIGHBOR**, never to be seen again.

Some stories leave footprints. Others leave craters.

I am happy you've made it this far… there is more darkness ahead.

THE BOOGEYMAN
RETURNETH

The Bogeyman Returneth

-1-

"Are you ok?" James' wife inquired, giving him a sideways glance as she entered the room to find out why the phone was off the hook, a constant, annoying pulse blaring.

"Yes, umm, I—" James managed, setting the cordless receiver down on the back of the sofa and moving towards the hallway without giving his wife not so much as a glance.

"You okay?" she inquired, brow scrunching. Her husband was always a cool-headed man, even during tornado season, but now he looked alarmed, if not frightened.

"Alex… I need to go see Alex for a bit… he has… where are my keys?"

"In your jacket," she answered quickly, face perplexed, moving into the hallway in time to see her husband donning his jacket backward. "James! What are you doing? You are putting it on inside-out!"

"I am?" he said, puzzled, his wide eyes meeting hers while his mouth hung, prepared to speak but produced nothing but airy whispers as sweat beaded up on his forehead.

"Did something happen?" her words came almost in a whisper as her brow wrinkled, developing deep creases of concern. "James? Is everything all right? What happened to Alex?"

"Alex, oh, yes Alex…" he licked his lips, correcting his jacket when the jingle of keys clamored in the pocket gave him a slight relief. "He, umm… killed an animal… wild. It attacked him."

"*What?*" she almost screamed it.

"Yeah, it attacked him and, umm, well… I… yeah, I need to get my pistol," he nodded firmly, speaking it to no one for it was nothing more than his mind racing through a quick and dirty laundry which it desperately was trying to prepare.

"Your gun?" his wife was screaming the words now. *"What do you need your gun for?"*

"Just in case!" he snapped, pushing past her, snatching the closet door open, and immediately reached up high, using the tips of his toes to rummage around the top shelf.

Not the closet! The remnants of the terrified child in him called out, and for a step, he retreated. *It lives in there!*

He paused with eyes closed, took a deep breath, held it for just a moment, then shook it off, whisper-cursing himself as he returned to his rummaging.

"James, you are scaring me," she whimpered, having gone from irritation with the bleating phone to confusion and now outright fear, all within a few minutes. "You said he killed an animal… whu-what do you need to bring your gun for?"

"As I said, just in case!" he barked, pulling down the metal-gray lockbox and snatching open the lid as he kicked the closet door closed.

Despite the lack of daily handling of a firearm, his hands made quick work of slamming the loaded eight-shot magazine into the butt of the small Walther .380 auto, cycled a round into the chamber, flicking on the safety with his thumb, and then slid it into his jacket pocket.

Candace was now in the hallway with her back pressed to the wall, her shaking hands covering her mouth as steady streams of tears poured from her eyes. As he moved from the closet towards the front door, he dropped the box down hard on the foyer stand and regarded her with a sharp glare. Immediately, he saw the tears, and his heart sank.

"James?" her voice squeaked.

"Baby, listen," he sighed heavily, exhaling all the adrenalin-laced fear and anger in one breath. Slowly and softly, he moved towards her with palms up and gently took her by the wrists, pulling her hands from her face to his. "I didn't mean to scare you."

"But you are!" she cried, flinching away from his touch.

"I know… I know," he whispered, moving close and kissing her gently on the forehead. "Shush, baby, shush… I don't mean to scare you. Trust me, Candace."

"All right," she eked out, not wanting to be afraid any longer. "Just tell me what's going on… what did Alex say to you?"

"All right," he said, concentrating furiously on keeping his fear levels from rising again. *What exactly will you tell her and not come off as sounding insane?* His mind begged the question. Breathing deeply, he focused on the basics. "Alex called and said a wild animal attacked him. He fought it off, but he is hurt and—"

"Hurt?" she screamed, panic state reaching another crest along this furious rollercoaster ride. "What the hell happened? Hurt how?"

"Candace, quiet now and let me finish," he said firmly without yelling, which was not a simple task considering he wanted to vomit out the fear badly. He closed his eyes briefly, focusing on the pulsing of his heart, taking deep breaths to find focus in the rampaging thoughts. "It clawed him and bit him; that's all I know. I don't know how badly, but he was very rattled, so I didn't make out much about what he said. All I know is that he used a hatchet to fight it off, and it crawled into his wood cellar."

"What the hell was it?" her eyes were darting. "A coyote?"

Go ahead, spill it! The condescending area of his brain laughed at his moment. *Tell her what* exactly *attacked old Alex-boy-O! Let her learn how fucking crazy you've been since you were a kid!*

"I don't know," he shuddered to silence the taunting mind. "He just said—"

"Bu-but you said he killed it, right?" she squawked, bringing forth fresh tears.

"Yes, I know. He said that and I think it's probably dead, but he asked me to come over there and help him, which I am about to do. I am bringing my gun just in case the thing is still alive and angry, that's all."

"But why didn't he call the police? Why do you have to go over there? Baby, I don't like this at all!"

"Candace, I am not going to argue about this right now," he said, shaking, his eyes closing out the red of the confusion to where he plummeted into the darkness. "I am his friend, and he needs me, no different than when your friend Beth needed you at two in the morning in the middle of a thunderstorm. When those close to us call, we go, simple and plain… Okay?"

Eyes darting rapidly over her husband's face, Candace slowly nodded. None of it made any sense at all, and if she tried to weed through the forest of question marks, she knew she would find herself even more confused, and agreeing made all the perfect sense to her. Without a word, she propelled herself into his arms and squeezed him tightly, kissing his chest from the side of her mouth.

"Please, tell me you will be careful, okay?" she begged through tears of concern, squeezing tightly.

"Trust me, baby," he soothed, squeezing back and petting her hair. "I will be. I will get there, grab up Alex and get him off to the hospital. Once we are there, doctors will notify the police about an animal attack, and they will head over to his place, looking for it. They have to do this whenever an animal scratches someone; it's their protocol.:

"But you'll be there without the police," she whispered, the levels of her rationality making it difficult for him to counter in any way.

"I will not go out of my way to look for a wounded, let alone a dead animal," he attempted with a reassuring smile. "I promise."

"Okay, sweetie," she sniffed, moving back calmly and attempting to regain her composure. "I am holding you to that. Make sure you call me."

"I will," he smiled, wondering if it appeared sincere, and then zipped his jacket and turned towards the front door.

'Man, he came back for me like when we were kids!' Alex's voice blasted through his mind. *'But I got him! I got that son of a bitch!'*

James paused, glancing into the open lockbox where a box of .380 ammo, three-quarters full, sat.

'I was nowhere near a closet, but I got that fucker! Hacked him right in the fucking neck! You should see the blood! Oh, you had better believe I killed the fucker, and he ain't coming back no more!'

He pocketed the box of shells.

-2-

When James pulled into the long drive, Alex Porter was sitting on the edge of a wood splitter parked along the side of his house which is used to split logs into manageable-sized quarters for burning in the winter. He had had a system, Alex did: for every log he split, he would divide the quarters between two piles: personal use and one for sale. He would stack his share methodically in the cellar and the marketable half in the shed out back.

The salable wood would sit piled and dry until fall since it was early summer and the only people in the market for firewood during this time of year were the sentimental ones who lit fireplaces at night to add to the romanticism. Occasionally, someone would inquire if he had wood for sale for such events, but the usual love bug went to the stores and bought it in small bundles.

As James rounded the drive near the porch, his gut told him to park it so that the nose of the truck was pointing out towards the road, which he did, cutting the wheel sharply and allowing the tail to whip around to a stop.

Just in case, he assured himself, killing the engine but leaving the keys to dangle in the ON position as he left the cab, leaving the door open. *Just in case.*

Alex wasn't just sitting on the edge of the wood splitter; he was perched on it like some gaunt vulture, waiting for whatever might crawl out of the open cellar doors. His whole body was locked in a ready stance, eyes fixed on the darkness below without so much as a blink. John had no doubt he was terrified. The stiffness in Alex's spine said as much, and the shotgun resting across his thigh—its barrel aimed straight into the cellar's throat—made it clear exactly where that fear lived.

He looked older than his thirty-six years, worn thin, as if something had already taken a piece of him, and though summer hadn't even settled in yet, sweat poured off him in sheets. As James approached, slow and careful, his hand drifted to the Walther at his side, thumb flicking the safety off before he even realized he'd done it.

"That's where it went," Alex nodded towards the opening, his eyes never leaving the direction.

James circled a pile of logs, his eyes taking in everything around him: the deep grooves in the gravel right down to the base dirt, tattered bloody fabric, hair, and the blood… especially the blood. It was everywhere, dark and rich like thick syrup, which had fallen in heavy quantities to even pool in places amongst the gravel drive. Up the side of the house was an enormous fan spray visually detailing what Alex had told him earlier on the phone: Alex had got the thing in the neck… no fucking doubt about it.

"'It,' or 'Him,' Alex?" James begged, whispering as he moved in close.

The air seemed dramatically thicker as he got closer, and moving through it was like driving through thick mud. He stopped to the left and just in front of Alex, his eyes slowly moving from the bloodied ground to the cellar opening and his friend. Alex looked sickly pale and clammy, but his eyes—those dark brown eyes of his—blazed wide and bright.

"Both," Alex burped out. "You know what I am talking about, Jim."

"I know," he nodded slowly, looking over Alex's torn shirt, and he could see open jagged flesh on his chest and abdomen. Eyes trailing south along Alex's thigh, the jeans were gaping where a vicious mouth had latched on, sinking in teeth.

"Tried to get to my truck," Alex blinked, standing. Slowly, his eyes pulled away from his stare down match with the darkness below, and he looked up at James with a vain attempt at a smile. "Ya know, that's where I keep the Mossberg… maybe more so to get away? He just came out after me…."

Alex trailed off, going somewhere James could only assume some quieter, happier place. Perhaps, but deep down, he knew he went *Before*; back to a time when this thing plagued them both, more so Alex because he had a closet in his room whereas James did not. It would hide in there for only them to ever see, and when summer came, so did it.

"He wasn't afraid, man!" Alex's eyes bulged and darted around the area; the first time, he took his eyes off the cellar opening since the thing had fled there. "He wasn't afraid of coming out like when we were kids! He just came!"

James was nodding as his eyes wandered past the back of Alex's property, where, when they were both young, his own family's house once sat. His mind filled with the horrific after-echoes of them screaming with youthful throats, followed by the heavy metallic bang of the rear screen door flying open. He could see them both racing out towards the center line that divided the two properties, where they sat shaking, huddled, scratched, and crying in the moonless night.

No, it never would follow them out; it wouldn't dare. It would then only watch them from the barrier of the screen door with those yellow eyes as they cried for their savior, which never truly came.

"Trust me, man," Alex squeaked, eyes widening. "I damn near shit my pants when I saw his shadow coming up on me there."

Alex pointed towards a sizeable bloody patch in the drive, not too far from his own truck.

"That's where he pounced me, man, and he-he-he bit me!" Alex shifted so that James could see a similar chunk of shirt and flesh missing from his shoulder blade. "Said I tasted the same from back then, smelled the same too, but I fuh-fought! Fought him the whole time, man; like a fuh-fucking bulldog, man, but he… he was so damn strong."

"But you fought him, Alex," James said softly, attempting to soothe his friend's apparent state of shock. "That's what matters."

"Yeah… I fought him all right," Alex shot his shoulders back triumphantly. "Fought him real good."

Alex's attention shot back towards the cellar, the shotgun leveling. "Did you hear something?"

"No," James whispered, eyes over the barrel of the Walther. Suddenly, James felt entirely under gunned holding the pea shooter.

"If he's down there watching us, he remembers you too," Alex whispered, and James suddenly felt his testicular sac curl up as it drew his balls in tight. "Maybe I shouldn't have called you… maybe he had lost your scent when you moved away? Maybe I should have moved on too and burned this place down as I headed out the door."

You are freaking me out, man!" James hissed desperately while suddenly wanting to go pee. "Did you hear something or not?"

Alex didn't answer. He stood at the ready while peering in, his mouth quietly working the situation out. Swallowing against the moment, James asked the most critical question of the day.

"Alex, why are we still standing here?" James shuddered.

"What?"

"Why in the fuck are we just standing here?" James demanded the logic. "Let's get the fuck out of Dodge and get you to a hospital!"

Alex's attention narrowed as he snapped the *Mossberg* up to his cheek, his eyes becoming fine slits as he peered into the cellar through the sights. James dropped to one knee, his other hand obeying and coming up and under the pistol, leveling and steadying it like the marksman his father had taught him years before. The two of them were statues poised for the slightest movement. The only sounds were the tree branches shifting slightly in the breeze and their racing heartbeats.

Alex finally exhaled, relaxing, loosening his grip on the shotgun.

"It's nothing," he said flatly.

"Jesus, Alex, did you kill the fucker or not?" James harshly grunted through clenched teeth, feeling acid creep up the sides of his throat.

"Yes, I did!" Alex roared back. "Hacked him right in the fucking jugular; look at all this fucking blood, man! *The fucking jugular!*"

"Then let's get out of here then" James was already backing away while his aim of never leaving the cellar doors. Alex was following suit, sidestepping at first, then the two of them backpedaled shoulder to shoulder towards the waiting truck. James dared a glance over his shoulder to gauge their progress, terror-stricken that he would turn into that face with yellow eyes, or while turned, it would dash from the cellar, charging them both down.

Almost there, his mind acknowledged, and as he returned his fixation to the cellar, he was expecting teeth.

Nothing; just open doors.

"Okay, here's what we do," James said quietly, almost whispering, as their butts contacted the rear bumper of his truck. "Give me the shotgun, and you take my Walther. Go around to the passenger door and get in... you can't drive in your condition. Keys are in the ignition. Start her up, and I will cover us with the shotgun. Once I am in, we are out of here, okay?"

Alex answered with the shotgun being handed over. They hurriedly made the exchange, then Alex limped out of view to carry out the plan. James stood at the ready, his ears picking up the passenger side door opening, followed by a slight jingling of keys and completed by the engine roaring to life. Nodding, James exhaled long and hard as he moved around the rear corner of the truck, hugging the side with his hip towards the awaiting driver's door.

I hate this! James' mind screamed as his back pressed against the open door. Damp sweat pressed against him from his shirt as he breathed. *This is when he'll come! Right when I turn to get in the truck! Just like in the movies, man! Just like —*

"C'mon, man!" Alex cried verbally and emotionally. "Let's get out of here. He's dead!"

"Right," James said, sucking in deeply, then spun, throwing in his legs while tossing the shotgun to the floor of the passenger seat as he threw himself inside. Blasting pain rocketed through the side of his head right above the ear as it connected to the door seam, but there was no time for that now.

Cursing, his feet depressed the brake and floored the gas simultaneously as he snatched back the shifter, kicking up a shrapnel storm of gravel and dust behind them.

Racing down the drive, neither of them kept their eyes from the rear; Alex through the rear window while James drove blindly, fixated on the rear-view mirror. It would come now, bounding through the dust cloud with barred teeth, sharp claws, and those yellow eyes. It would pounce upon the vehicle without effort, tearing into it and then into them.

Despite what was expected, it never came, and as the vehicle met asphalt and screeched into its turn toward town, they never stopped looking back.

-3-

James left his friend and the hospital over eight hours later once he was sure Alex was stable. It was going on nine as the sun was angling towards the eliminator line of the night. As he reached his truck in the parking lot, James couldn't help himself from checking to ensure that the only thing in the bed was the bed itself.

Cursing himself, he got in and started for home.

Four hundred and thirty-eight stitches plus three pints of blood was the count they had put into Alex that day, and enough morphine to keep an addict happy for a long while. When the doctors first told him the extent of the work that was performed, he balked, head dizzy, but later, he remembered that he had read once that some shark attacks took more than a thousand to patch up a surfer. A shark attack, one might expect it; there are a lot of teeth and thrashing involved, but the ocean was several states away, and he knew it was no damn shark.

James was right, though; the hospital immediately contacted the police, who then got the fire and the state animal control departments, all of whom descended upon Alex's property as if a natural disaster had taken place. They found copious amounts of blood, plenty of animal-like scratch marks, and signs of a horrible struggle, but no animal, wounded or otherwise. James was not surprised by the news; he figured since 'He' came from 'Nowhere' damn near thirty years before, Alex sent him right back to that nowhere with his head dangling by a thread.

It took little for him to convince the doctors or the police to withhold that information from Alex until he came out of his sedation, especially after Alex began foaming about the bogeyman attacking him and chasing him into the yard. When he demanded that they locked all the closet doors and began calling out to his dead parents, the time for sedation came. However, since they had found no animal to determine the creature's health, doctors immediately began the usually painful process of rabies vaccinations on him.

Alex would be grateful after the fact that he was not conscious.

"Three to five days," James spoke quietly into his cell as he rolled along Longwood Drive towards home. His head and stomach ached, and he longed for his wife's touch and to smell her skin close to his. It had been a very long day. "We can go check on him tomorrow during visiting hours. We should pick him up some of that nicotine gum. I am not sure he would last without his fix."

"Sounds good, baby," Candace giggled, her voice coming through with clear adoration and love, bringing warmth to his soul. "I will run you one super relaxing bath when you get home."

"Perfect," he spoke into the phone, but not with any natural flair; his focus was on the rear-view mirror as the night slowly grew darker. He wasn't looking for drivers coming up on him too fast; he was looking for eyes.

'Maybe I didn't get him!' Alex's voice came into his mind, full of trauma and drug-induced panic as his brain's fight-or-flight fought against the chemicals that doctors were giving him to force his mind to shut down. *'Maybe he was just sitting down in that darkness looking up at us with those yellow eyes, just waiting for us to drop our guard!'*

"Are you listening to me?" Candace's voice broke in, shutting off his inner voice.

"What?" James blinked. "Uh, yeah-yeah-yeah; the bath."

"No, I asked you, are you hungry, and how close are you now?" she replied. James paused as his eyes darted about his surroundings to find his bearings. After a terrifying moment of being lost, he realized he had made the left turn at Longwood and Elm, went through three stop signs, and then made a right onto Evelyn Glenn with no cognizant process.

"Umm, no, not hungry, and I am a few blocks away... let me get off this phone, so I can concentrate."

Click! There was no time for formal goodbyes.

"Get a grip on yourself before you hit somebody out here!" he barked at himself and focused on the road before him, locking both hands onto the steering wheel.

-4-

James slowly pulled into his driveway just as the sun was making its final plunge into the night, coming within a car's length behind his wife's and then killing the engine.

The night bugs were out making their music somewhere off in the shrubbery and trees, carried by the night's air, which held a cool crispness like so many clean sheets on a clothesline. The world, his world—despite how chaotic all of it was today—seemed to return to a calm peace that he wanted to last forever.

He took a moment to look over all he had: the lawn, the bushes he needed to trim, the bubbling reflecting pond by the front of the porch… the front porch that leads up to his —

James choked, eyes widening and frozen on the screen to the front door. There it was, darkened and hollow, the front door open with the screen as Candace was more than likely letting in the fresh night air.

'If he's down there watching us, he remembers you too,' Alex's voice begged his brain as he stared at the screen door with the darkness of the hallway beyond it. That's how *'He'* watched them once, mocking them and knowing he couldn't chase after them, but they couldn't run away forever either, could they? *'He wasn't afraid of coming out… not like when we were kids!'*

No eyes were peering out at him, but there was that feeling nonetheless; heavy and foreboding, like a storm on the horizon. Slowly, without taking his eyes off the front door, James pressed the buttons to speed dial his home, followed by the all-present SPEAKER PHONE optional button. Through the mobile's speaker, the phone rang, followed momentarily later by his home phone ringing in the distance after the signal made all its cross-connections from the public switch telephone network. Back and forth, the ringing played their game of sound tennis, each return drawing the hairs on the back of his neck higher and stiffer.

"Hello?" It was Candace's voice.

"Honey, it's me," James exhaled.

"Yeah, I know," answered a tone of confusion. "Why are you calling me from your cell phone?"

"Because I am in the drive. I just pulled in."

"You did?" perplexity strengthened, then relaxing laughter. "Oh! I thought you had come in already… I heard the screen door close."

"What?"

"Yeah, must not have closed it all the way… now I feel stupid calling out your name to an empty house—"

"Candace!" he screamed into the phone, kicking open the truck door and hauling up Alex's shotgun from the passenger side floor. *"Get out of the house!"*

He jumped from the truck and bounded a small hedge that ran the drive length, breaking into a sprinter's dash as the shotgun swung up in front of him, his finger curling the trigger.

As James raced across the lawn in a bounding gait towards the porch, from inside the house, his wife began to scream.

THE BROOCH

The Brooch

✻

My end is quite near; I know this...

The clock is slowing under lax springs, which cannot be wound anymore; the gears are old and missing teeth, and soon the hands will crawl to their final resting spots, sealing my fate therein. Upon this moment I write, and nearby my glass of wine sits nearly empty; I study the dusty clump of material that holds the key to everything which is me.

Bound in its tattered wrappings made from old dust cloths never washed, I dwell upon what was stolen so many years ago by these very hands, which now shake liver spotted as I attempt to scribble this confession. I do not do this act of record for some last attempt to deplore all that I have done and find some glorified grace in the eyes of whom I must confront soon enough.

My soul, as with my life, became forfeit a very long time ago, and through the years of searching, I now realize that all that time, I was seeking out revenge for being born.

I whimper in attempts to hold back ancient tears that now dare to fall, each poised in a collective, clear bulge along eyelids tired and red as the haunting sounds of the violinist's bow coaxing the soft notes of Canon from the strings. I hear them now as I heard them then that night; soft and pure music filled with tones both rising and falling effortlessly as if her mere motions were that of a conductor and the instrument played along accordingly, magically.

I subdue these tears yet again, not for what she played in the dim light of the building's cellar low, although her music entrapped my soul with such gentle fingers of grace that I became a better man because of it. Instead, I mourn for her, the violinist whom I never knew her name.

If I could have had such an honor bestowed upon me, I believe my life from that point in time would have rectified so many ill fates delivered. Perhaps, if I had known it earlier, I would have never snatched the brooch from her neck in the busy morning market. I would have forbidden my coveting hands from seeking hastened rewards. In turn, I would have damned them, for they had never performed an honest day's work to earn anything other than from vulgar thievery and my most internalized contempt.

Perhaps...

Perchance...

I still remember her startled eyes, which grew large as I snatched the brooch savagely away from her, and how that moment of fear turned into that of sorrow. Not for herself as I held my shoddy revolver on her, no, but instead she sorrowed for me. She never screamed nor ever cried out, and never did she cower under the weight of the moment. She simply looked at me from head to toe as I stood poised in the best of my worst and then nodded, producing an understanding smile as she whispered to me: 'Take it and eat well.'

I froze then, not knowing what to do or to think, and although there were plenty of people about that day, it seemed as if there were only us two there at that moment. Cowardly, through the crowds, I moved away, expecting that she would begin to scream at any moment, but she never did. As I blended in with the refuse of the nearest alley, I sat in the slop, dazzling my eyes with the stones and gems of my booty so cowardly obtained.

How can a thief be successful if their victims do not mourn their loss? How can one have dominating power when the prey shows more strength at the very moment when fear should be in control? I had taken it by force, had I not? Did I not stalk and plot, reach in, then snatch it with every intent to shoot her, if need be, or at the very least club her with the barrel of my gun if she resisted?

Had I not been given a tainted gift?

Even now, I find it so unbelievable what she had done, sending me away unchallenged to pawn what I had stolen so I could eat and drink for another few days. As I sat there twisting with confusion, I beat my head against that alley wall until consciousness almost left me. For the first time in my vulgar existence, I had felt the pangs of guilt borne in the clear blue eyes of the girl with no name, and in my shortcomings of understanding this new sensation, all I knew was it had to be returned to her.

I followed her home without her knowledge until there, in the darkness, I listened to her play her violin. Within silken cloths I had stolen from a seamstress along the way, I wrapped her pretty brooch so crafty and fine. She played the melodious piece continuously as twilight became night; all the while I listened to her music, I begged the questions to which I got no answers.

Would I leave it wrapped on her doorstep proper for it to be found the following morning, or would it not be seen by careful eyes and trampled upon unknowingly as she departed for another day at the market?

Would someone like me be out and about before then, scurrying the darkness like a rat in search and happen upon it, soiling it with their filthy hands?

Should I rap on her cellar window low, leaving it like an abandoned babe, or wait until she answered, handing it to her with my musty hat in my hand, begging her for her forgiveness?

To suffer all the tortures that I put myself through on that cold October night—stamping my feet in place in hopes of keeping them warm—all the while, my heart ached with what I had done and always has since been unbearable.

Damn the Heavens for giving me a cowardly soul!

I felt a tap on my shoulder and my skin tightened cold, loosening my bowels with bile. The voice of a beat cop came just as clearly as the music flowed, demanding to know what I was doing lurking in the shadows, black.

I insisted that I had something that belonged to the young woman who made the very angels weep with her violin, just there down through the nearby cellar window-low. That if he allowed me, I would be no trouble to anyone if he allowed me to complete my quest. He would have nothing of what I said as I backed away from his probing eyes and jabbing baton, poking about my tattered jacket, seeking hidden pockets and what may lie within.

What did I have here? What did I have there? Who was I, and what did I have for the distant woman fair?

I sought answers for him but found none; he advanced, and I cowered away, praying for a moment to escape and leave that foul misery that drew me there on a wind of guilt. I begged him for understanding, and if he gave me a moment to ring the bell of the dwelling behind me, all things would be settled. I even attempted to assure him what a fool he would find himself to be when the violinist recognized me and the something I had wrapped so well in silk.

It was then that he noticed the wrapped brooch and demanded to see it, which I refused to do, knowing how these men of the law truly worked. If I dared come by morning, the same clip I was returning would end up at the neckline of his wife or mistress instead of where it belonged. He demanded my obedience loudly, shouting it. So, I cursed him with my refusal, spittle flying from my cracked lips with mixed obscenities, and when he no longer felt his baton gave me fear, he drew upon his sidearm, which I countered with my own.

"What is all this?" I heard that angelic voice which had whispered to me earlier that day speak firmly from behind, and as I turned to address her—perhaps to learn her name—that skilled officer of the law laid his sights in her direction. In such panicked haste, he then fired once, felling her lifelessly.

I screamed so loud that my throat shattered that very night, and in my rage, I emptied the four rusting rounds in my gun into the beat cop's chest, avenging his murderous act of the sweet girl and her music.

In the cold silence which followed, I slowly went to her, clutching the brooch in its wrappings so fair, my eyes finding hers; open, clear, and blue, yet now void of the music as they stared at the moonless sky.

Alarms called into the night, and I fled.

—

Now, as I write this on the very day in October so many years later, I listen to Canon play on the record player in my study, but the music is not the same.

I am forever haunted but now at peace because I know what I stole from her that day became a gracious gift, one from pure of heart in which a gentle soul saw something in me more than the filthy rat in the market. I beg for only her forgiveness because neither Man nor God can provide me any solace for what I have done.

If I genuinely plead to the shadows for one simple wish, I may get to see her once again after I close my eyes for the final time this very night. I pray that I do with everything I have, and if I do, I will present her with her brooch, and upon that moment, I will assuredly ask her for her name.

Adieu.

REFLECTIONS
IN A PLACE CALLED
NIHILITY

Dark Interlude III
Reflections in a Place Called Nihility

From whence are the outcasts and meek ones now led?
From the dark hallowed city where life is now dead.

Where are now the gay songbirds, that fly merry-sing?
All turning black as soot, on bladed perches they cling.

Was that not the sky spied earlier, so heavenly blue?
It turned dark from the fires, with a reddish blood hue.

And what of the rivers, and the streams and the bountiful lakes?
They became foul and stagnant, full of frogs and vile snakes.

O', the children! The children! Where do they now play?
Nowhere, Your Highness; a witch's stomach, I'd say.

And what of my husband, the King, where is he?
Hanging taught from the gallows, not so fancy, but free.
Did you spot my meat butcher, or the maid, or the cook?
To my best, they're all gone (if I had bothered to look).

So, then I'm alone, by myself, in this horrible land?
To a degree, that you are, but I'll give you a hand.

And what can you do that will assist me so dear?
Protect you from harm and from whatever you fear.

These calamities hurt my head; my attention has gone!
   'Tis because the hour is late… it is nearing the dawn.

Shall I sleep a long sleep now, as the day has passed waned?
   Why, of course, my dear lady, I can tell you are strained.

Quite right I shall rest until the coming of morn,
   By then, my Regina, your last breath shall be torn.

Why is this, my dear mirror, do you jest in such ways?
   'Tis just a quip before bedtime; a comical phrase.

I bother your expression; your eyes have grown bleak!
   Nonsense, Your Grace, only night's blessing I speak.

So, there is no need to worry; in calmness shall rest?
   Of course, my dear child; soft heartbeats under breast.

I believe you, I trust, over me, you shall stand?
   For an eternity plus a day, I swear by my hand.

Then goodnight my dear mirror, calm slumbers to you.
   Sweet dreams my own reflection, I bid you adieu.

Victor McSneed

Victor McSneed

Our Final Amusing Gasp

In a pub, on the corner,
of St. Nichols and Meade,
sat plotting and drinking,
a one Victor McSneed.

Through eyes of pure rage
which bulged from his head
he watched all of the patrons
while wishing them dead.

For Charlie, the beat cop,
who was drunk from the swill
with his own police club
Victor would kill.

Those girls on the dance floor
with their clothes O' so tight?
He will slash them and stab them;
their demise, his delight!

The snob little banker,
a one Trevor McDew,

he would chop with an axe
splitting his body in two!

The barmaid, a wench,
with a gleam in her eye
Oh, how many ways possible
can he make this one die?

By fire, by poison,
or a club or a knife?
Would she beg for his mercy?
Will she beg for her life?

"Care for round two?"
she asked with a grin.
"Yes, another full pint,
and a tall order of gin!"

The moment had come,
holding firm to his creed,
"Not even God can save you!"
screamed Victor McSneed.

With hands in his pockets
under the patron's shocked stare,
he fumbled with nothing
for his pockets were bare!

Empty without blades,
or poison or guns!
No clubs to do clubbing with!
Oh, what had he done?

Bedtime Stories

He had come empty-handed
his plan ill-equipped.
"I think he's gone bonkers!"
someone present had quipped.

They laughed and they pointed
they joked, and they jest,
so Victor left slowly,
his chin to his chest.

He stood all alone
on the walk in the rain.
He achieved nothing at all
there was no giving of pain.

So, he headed towards home
happy not in the least.
No joy for the humbled,
like Victor, the priest.

A good plan is essential.

Bringing the plan with you is generally helpful as well.

When Madness Calls

When Madness Calls

PART ONE
JoJo & the Bear

-1-

I tried to be a hero… once…

I really tried to save someone, but despite all my efforts, I let her fall and fail in ways far worse than the predicament she was in, and the greatest tragedy was that she took my soul with her. Not just the essence of it, no… the very fiber of it; the part which your shadow is adhered to now forever fleeing me like I am Pan without my Wendy to sew it back on and to give me a thimble kiss. She is gone, and I am lost, forever seeing her in the same place I once saw her so many times before.

I used to watch her on the Lake Express bus, sitting in the far back corner as she chewed on her fingernails, her eyes out the windows watching the city pass us by while her oversized shoulder bag sat in the seat next to her. She never moved it for anyone, not even when the bus was packed to the seams, standing room only, but then again, I never saw anyone asking her to do so. I am not saying she was the type who wouldn't have moved it, but it was her look that prevented inquests; a punkish-Goth appeal which, until recent education from a friend's daughter, that her look was probably emo, perhaps even 'scene.'

Whatever the look was, she was adorable wearing it: black bouffant hair with white and pink frosted feathered tips held perfectly with a shocking blue headband with dead kittens patterned on it; the double-layered shirts, one long, one short… the short one displaying a picture of a band I didn't know and lettering I could never read.

Although I never imagined myself hooked on someone who dressed as she did, there was something about her wearing that black and gray tartan skirt over black leggings finished off by heavy-looking boots on tiny feet. That certainly added to my attraction for her, this radical dresser who seemed to beam nonconformity, but it wasn't just that, no; it was her eyes. They were wonderfully large and blazing green, perfectly almond-shaped anime eyes painted with black and frosted grays. Then again, I think it may have been her lips; naturally full and perfectly shaped, sometimes painted, other times not, but either way, the thought of kissing them truly made my pulse quicken.

To me, she was simply breathtaking.

Yes, at times, I stared but not in the lustful way that one might think; it was the admiration of her bold independence that she displayed without an apology and her pure bravery of being who she was and not yielding to any conformity. This young woman almost seemed to roll into her clothes in the morning, but with purposefulness in her effort, albeit she had no one to answer to. That is why I stared at her so.

All she had to be for me to adore her was to 'Be.'

She never focused on anyone who rode our bus, perhaps a quick glimpse up from time to time if someone was speaking loudly into their cellphone, and then she would narrow her eyes to cat-like slits to burn holes through their souls; finalizing it always by mouthing the word *Fucker*' to herself. I would chuckle whenever I saw this, and I would consider the rude one a fucker even if I hadn't thought so before.

It was always during the morning commute when I saw her, and she would exit the bus two stops before mine right in front of the art school doors where she attended. Occasionally, she totted a large, black art portfolio with various stickers proclaiming anarchy. One, in particular, was just a fist with the center digit up with large letters beaming: *'STFU!'*

I often thought about her during my workday, daydreaming as I configured yet another piece of equipment so it could go out into the world to make people happy as they browsed the internet. I had gotten into the field thinking I could make a global impact on how people used the cornucopia of technology Mankind had to offer, only to be a cog in the machine providing online gaming, endless chatrooms, and pornography by the terabyte. That's when I thought about my mysterious Goth-girl the most because she had what I didn't have and that was freedom, or at least what appeared as such.

One afternoon during lunch, I purposefully walked along the towering buildings south to where her school stood. I didn't think I would see her, but I hoped I would; just a settling vision to clear all the white noise of humming equipment from my mind. It was mid-spring and very bright, cloudless, and the weather was warm enough that you didn't have to think about lugging a jacket along with you.

The large patio area in front of the school was crowded with students hanging around in small groups, smoking cigarettes and shooting the shit to pass the time before their next classes began. Amongst the masses, I couldn't see her nor felt too particularly disappointed either because the only expectation was my own, and there were no guarantees she would ever come out, save for her trip home.

Some of the young women out in front dressed like her, but none were her; their styles seemed forced and stereotypical, whereas my little Goth-emo-scene-whatever girl seemed completely natural.

I sat at the bus stop on a worn wooden bench and pretended to fit in amongst the crowds as I sipped stale coffee from that morning, looking for her. It wasn't until I had all but given up hope of seeing her that my eyes found her small shape far off to the side from everyone else, sitting alone with her back pressed against the building, knees drawn up and dark hair hanging forward as she mouthed words into her lap.

I felt my heart thud heavily with how she looked: sad and alone in her own world amongst so many, and no one other than me even giving her a sideways glance like so many forgotten souls tucked along an alley's run.

Before I had even realized it, my legs had a mission of their own, and I was standing in front of her, looking at her, watching her small mouth whisper towards her lap with an occasional nod and inspired giggle. She seemed so out of reach of anything in my world, and yet I wanted to touch her, to feel her pale skin and ask her for her name, and that's when I saw the welts on her calf; angry red and swollen as if she had been struck with something hard and unforgiving.

I had just convinced my body to get into motion to leave when those green eyes shifted upwards and found mine, locking, and for that moment, I wished I was invisible.

"Hey!" she chirped in a surprisingly youthful tone, and I mouthed a hello back with an airy rasp borne from disobedient vocal cords.

I could feel the sweat dancing on my forehead comically, a cruel betrayal by my own body which seemed determined to embarrass me further as her eyes slowly followed my darting gaze to her calf where the welts glowed. Calmly, she leaned forward, crossing her legs and removing the sight just as naturally as one might shift their weight from a tired hip. She was holding a small panda bear with a chain around its neck connected to a mass of keys on rings. All this time, when I had suspected that maybe she was speaking into a phone, she had been talking to it… to the bear.

"Hey," I managed back and nodded and started my retreat towards the office, only to be stopped by her voice.

"You're my rider," she said flatly.

"*What?*" I ridiculously asked for I had heard her clearly.

"My bus… in the mornings… the Lake Express?"

"*Oh!* Yes, I do," I breathed and relaxed a bit, returning my posture toward her. "So, this is your school, huh?"

"Yep, this is my day-dungeon, but it's not so bad, is it Bamboo?" she spoke, and I blinked twice, realizing that she had just redirected the conversation to the bear, to Bamboo as it was named.

She giggled and nodded towards it, and I could feel my feet shifting underneath me, daring to race me away. I took a sip of the coffee and attempted a smile which I knew she didn't buy for a second. She slowly cocked her head to one side, and I could see her lids flex as she probed my eyes.

"You think I am weird, don't you?"

"No, no, not weird," I lied and took a step closer to her so she would believe that her actions were about as right as rain. "You're just kind of different, that's all."

"*Hmm?*" she sounded, her eyes peering up into mine and following them downward as I squatted so as to seem more comfortable. "Okay, I will believe you… this time!"

We rolled into a giggle fit that I found absolutely adorable. The kind that tickled your insides just hearing it. She ended the fit with a pleasant smile, head cocked sideways as she studied my face.

"But most people think I am weird, but I am not; they are the weird ones, and most of them smell bad."

I choked coffee as her words rolled out and broke into a genuine laughing fit as I nodded in agreement.

"Well, *they* do!" she exclaimed with a pointing finger over the masses behind me, her face and actions completely animated. "Well, most of them do, especially *that* one; that's why I stay away from them. I don't smell, though."

"Well, that's good," I chuckled as I felt the tension in my back settle.

"See?" she quickly spat out and leaned forward, thrusting her multi-rubber-band-encircled wrist under my nose, filling my nostrils with the tartness of old, aged, mass-produced rubber, winter mint and vanilla with lilacs.

The scent was amazing.

I took another breath with closed eyes, only to open them to find lined scars peeking in between the rubber bands and then trailed to her eyes which tightened and fell. She knew I had seen the wounds, and she was ashamed of them, quickly hiding her wrist in her lap.

I dug deep and produced the best smile I could muster.

"You're right…you don't smell," I nodded, feeling the smile broaden with the truth. "As a matter of fact, you smell quite nice."

"Thank you," she replied as she blushed, her voice as soft as a whisper trembling on the edge of tears, and her lip quivered rapidly in place, daring the sobbing to rise.

"I'm Richard," I said quickly to change the moment's mood and thrust my hand out towards her.

With the edge of her long black shirt with her thumbs poked through purposefully torn holes, she wiped at the corners of her eyes and took my hand back. Her skin felt like cool, liquid silk.

"Hi, Richard, I'm JoJo," she smiled brightly; all recent worries dissipated. "Or Josephine if you want to be overtly proper, but I like the quick and easy if you'd please."

"Oh, that's fine… JoJo, that's cute." I smiled and nodded, listening to that soft voice echoing the name throughout my mind. "Well, I am glad to meet you… officially."

"Me too," she beamed. "You know, you could have asked me my name any of those days you were staring at me?"

I swallowed hard and felt my scrotum tighten in my crotch, daring to make my *'outies'* into *'inies'* as I squatted there. She had me dead to rights, and I had nothing to say to that.

"Don't worry," she giggled, and her eyes twinkled. "I am the only one who noticed when you did, but I am glad you do."

"You are?" I almost coughed it out as I rode along this roller coaster conversation which had more surprises than an amusement park would to a child.

"Well, yeah. I mean, you don't stare at me like I am a freak or something, and it's not every day that a good-looking guy looks at me as though he wants me, ya know?"

"Th-they duh-don't?" I tried, but I was a complete mess, the compliment was not missed. "I do?"

"Bamboo thinks you do, don't you, Bamboo?" she spoke to the bear and held it close to her ear, nodding.

A sharp giggle escaped her throat then she covered her mouth quickly with her hand as her eyes moved back and forth between the little bear and me. After a moment, she popped the bear on its little cloth snout and shook her head.

"Dirty bear."

"Oh, yeah, dirty bear." I chuckled, pretending, wondering if I should run back to the office without looking back and, in the future, find an alternate route into the city for good measures.

"Bamboo says you watch my butt when I get off the bus." She smiled, and despite the makeup on her face, I could see her cheeks grow flush. "Is this true, Richard? Do you watch my butt as I leave the bus?"

"Well, umm, I uh…if that's what Bamboo said," I stammered with a red face as sweat crawled along the spot where my scrotum had been; testicles now ovaries. "I mean, I do watch you go, yes, but—"

"Do you like my butt?" she inquired earnestly with her soft voice and large, pleading eyes.

She needed honesty, and she needed me to give it to her.

"Yes, JoJo… You have a very nice butt," I nodded with my voice low, and in a blink, she propelled herself forward and wrapped her arms around my neck, squeezing me.

She felt wonderful.

"Oh, thank you, Richard!" she squeaked, and as she moved away, I could see the light dancing in her eyes.

"You-you are welcome." I smiled, surprised and blinking, then chuckled honestly. I was confused as hell but enjoying the ride all the same.

"That is the nicest thing someone has said to me in a long time."

I nodded, welcoming her, and I stood, checking my watch briefly, and looked back toward where I needed, and wanted, to go. I looked back towards her only to find her standing before me with her bag over her shoulder and her eyes wide.

"Are you leaving?" her voice came in a rush.

"Yes… lunch break is about over, and I need to get back."

"Can I walk you?" she begged, hopeful, and as I stood there looking into those eyes, I could only nod.

Smiling, I extended my hand to the side, and we began to walk towards State Street at a slow enough pace that lazy turtles could pass us by.

-2-

We got plenty of odd looks as we walked; me a man in a shirt and tie and here a young woman all Emo'd out, a mismatched pair of socks amongst the high and tidies of the corporate elite, but neither of us paid them no mind.

She was an animated chatterbox that used tiny muscles I didn't even know the face possessed to enunciate every detail in pure dimensional form. I felt her oddity move further away from me with every word she spoke. At that moment, I started to truly fall in love with her. Not her look per se, but the woman beneath it all and with honesty beyond my previous hormonal infatuations.

"So yeah, I turn twenty-one in November," she paused and shoved the bear dangling from her waist belt into her shoulder bag and removed a pack of cigarettes. "Sorry, Bamboo hates it when I smoke, and I don't feel like hearing his shit right now.

"Want one?"

I nodded, taking one, and although I am a social smoker who usually only partakes when I am drinking, I never needed a cigarette as badly as I did then. The brand wasn't one I ordinarily smoked—Winston's straight with no 'Lights' insight, unlike the ultra-pansy ones I typically sought when I *did* smoke—but the flavor was thick and rich, and it helped to ease my senses as the heavier nicotine raced through my body.

"Anyways, I should be a junior, but I started college late."

"Oh, is it because of your late birthday?" I asked, lightheaded from the nicotine.

"You are pretty smart, Richard." Josephine smiled up at me, the top of her head barely cresting my shoulder at me being five-ten myself. "No, let's say I started *late*-late. Late, because my b-day is late in the year, but I was held back one year because I missed a lot of school my sophomore year in high school."

"Oh, were you sick a lot?" I puffed through my questions, but she didn't answer me for a moment; her eyes shifted amongst those past us on the busy street.

I didn't push it regardless of my wanting to know.

"Yeah… I was sick, I suppose," she said quietly, and I felt her draw close to my side, much like my young niece would do whenever we were in unfamiliar territory with questionable people.

We slowly stopped at the crosswalk, waiting for the light to change in our favor.

"I kept getting hurt."

"Oh, I see," I nodded and pretended to be carefree with it as if all she said was as commonplace as the day is to night and dragged so hard on the cigarette that I thought my chest would explode.

"You look a bit green." JoJo narrowed her eyes up to me with general concern, then took my arm and pulled me off to the curb. "You don't smoke much, do you?"

"No!" I laughed through intermittent coughs, giving the remainder of the cigarette a sideways glance just before tossing it into the street.

"I am so sorry, Richard!" she begged, squeezing my hand. "Please don't be angry with me, okay?"

"Whu-why…" I tried, then cleared my throat and looked into those desperate eyes. "Why would I be angry with you?"

"I dunno!" she said so quickly and nervously that I began to feel the hairs on the back of my neck stand up. "People get angry with me so quickly, and then they…."

"They what?" I said in a whisper, and she locked her eyes onto mine. That's when I knew she was somehow in trouble, but at the time, all I could do was have every empathetic fiber in my soul melt into those eyes. They were dancing before me, and I could see the tears rising along their edges until she blinked them out of view.

"So, how far away are you?" She looked about the streets, questioning, avoiding everything as if nothing was there.

"I am right there." I pointed at the pale-faced building which climbed eighty stories towards the sky across the street. "JoJo, I am a bit confused about people getting angry at—"

"What time do you get off?" She hushed me quickly.

"Six, why?"

"I will see you at six," she said quickly and popped up on her toes and kissed me softly on the lips.

I stood blinking, dumbstruck by the suddenness of it all, only to feel my wrist turn over in her small hand, and I heard the perfume spraying twice before I smelled it.

"There, so you can think of me today."

With a giggle and a smile, she was gone, and I stood there watching her little Doc Martens digging at the pavement with a forward angle as she hefted her bag up to a more comforting position on her shoulder. I stared blankly as she pulled at the chain tethering the little bear to her belt, and out it popped, only for her to pull the bear up to her ear as she walked. Occasionally, she would move it before her lips to speak to it, then back to her ear it would go. I watched as she moved against the flow of people, and how they all parted to give the little Goth-girl who was talking to her bear a wide berth.

Three light changes later, and long after she was out of sight, I eventually turned and crossed the street to my building; the whole time, I had my lips pressed together, holding on to that feeling of her lips. For the remainder of the day, my cubical smelled of vanilla-laden lilacs, of her, this JoJo-Josephine, and occasionally I would hold a rubber band close to where she sprayed so that I could smell her completely.

Six o'clock seemed so very far away.

-3-

I left a quarter to six that late afternoon, dashing from my desk before any last-minute trouble tickets found their way to me. As I stood by the elevator waiting for the car, I had every expectation that someone would approach me with something, trapping me. No one had, thankfully, and I was surprised that there wasn't the usual crowd waiting at the end of the workday. That didn't matter; I was about to see my little Goth-girl, my Josephine, my JoJo in all her wonderful weirdness and exotic beauty.

As I rode the car the twenty floors to the lobby, I felt my heart beating in a way that I had not felt since my early high school days when the probability of that first kiss was quite evident, but both parties were too nervous about making the first move. I was a giddy little fool who was greedy for more. I mean, she had already kissed me once, didn't she? I knew she had, for I could still feel her lips on mine, and I still tasted the flavor of her soft violet lipstick in my mouth as if it had just happened, yet again, it seemed so far away.

"Coming off or going back up?" a male's voice spoke to me pleasantly, and I looked about myself, confused, not having realized that I had reached the ground floor and was standing there like an idiot with my fingers to my lips.

Damn it, JoJo…what did you do to me?

"Oh, yeah, sorry," I replied nervously as I stepped from the elevator and turned to hold the sliding doors open for the gentleman. He chuckled for me as I chuckled nervously, shaking my head at the whole ordeal. "Long day."

"At least it's Friday, my friend." He smiled and pressed a button out of sight and towards Destination Unknown. I stood in the small hallway of banked elevators shaking my wits back into myself. It was Friday all along, and I had never even considered it.

Quickly, I crossed the lobby to the small convenience shop tucked in the side where you could get anything from a newspaper to a piece of fruit on any given workday. I collected up a pack of *Big Red* gum (just in case) and two bottles of water from the small cooler off to the side and then stood looking about the racks of cigarettes like an indecisive child in a candy store.

"Hi, yeah, let me get a pack of Winston regulars, box," I pointed out, thinking I would be a gentleman and get her a pack so that she would have more. I scanned the various types to find one suitable for me. "Also, a pack of Marlboro Ultra-Lights."

The small man behind the counter started to fetch my order without a word, and a pang of humility shot through my gut.

She's going to think you are a pussy, my mind told me, and my shoulders fell because of it.

"Can you make that last one a pack of Winston Lights," I braved up, going a bit stronger to show my manhood, but not to the level of choking to death. The man nodded and switched my request, and I paid him without counting out my change, then I headed out through the revolving door with my purchases in a small plastic bag.

It was six o'clock, and she wasn't there.

Nor was she at 6:30.

She didn't even show up at 7:00 when I finally gave up.

Chest-fallen and broken like a sixteen-year-old kid who got his hopes up about dating the most popular girl in school only to have those hopes stomped on, I slowly headed for my bus stop at the corner, cursing the world while wanting to curl up into a ball and roll away.

-4-

I rode alone on the Lake Express bus, the last run before the express stopped running for the week. It didn't matter if I was the sole rider anyway; I was hurting terribly inside and was conflicted with this by being angry simultaneously. Here I was, a grown man in his early thirties with an idiotic idea that a woman—a young woman—had found me attractive, and I bought into this belief blindly. For all I knew, I was simply a time passer she tolerated to talk to while waiting for her next class. I was pissed, but then again, she kissed me… I knew she had, because I was there, and at my lip's edges, I could still feel it.

I shifted the bag of purchases and retrieved one of the water bottles, spinning off the top, and then drank, wishing it was bourbon. After a while, I stared at the second bottle in the bag, the one I had gotten for her, and the cigarettes she would smoke. There was the gum I intended to chew so that my mouth would taste fresh after a day's worth of coffee, sitting in the bag unused. I huffed at it shaking my head because of the ridiculous idea that I needed that in case she kissed me again.

Oh yes, I had felt like I was a fool.

For the better of the thirty-minute ride, I stared at her empty spot in the rear corner of the bus and pictured her as I always saw her; fresh, young, and hip, with attitude to spare that she reserved for herself. I saw her large green eyes sensually narrow just before she kissed me, that damn perfect kiss with cool, relaxed lips that tasted like soft wax and mint. The thought made me shudder physically, but not in an overwhelming way, no.

I wanted her out of my thoughts, this haunting JoJo, this Josephine, who filled my entire world for twenty minutes of my life earlier.

I turned in my seat to watch the world go by just as she always did and wondered how she saw it all. Maybe this was her escape from whatever turmoil she had in her life, and I, who had little of it, could never catch a glimpse of what she saw there. My mind went back to the welts on her small calf, and it settled there, taunted by her words which came cryptic and short of adding to the possibilities of how they got there in the first place.

Did she do that to herself? I asked myself as my head began to shake slowly in dismal unknown. The lash marks were lateral and not vertical for her to have struck herself with something, or at least the Sherlock side of my brain concluded, so that means someone did that to her.

'People get angry with *me so quickly, and then they…'* her voice went through my mind, and I cringed at a sudden vision of this little Goth-girl standing in a room, palms up and pleading, those bright green eyes filled with terror as the tears poured from them as someone advanced on her with something terrible.

I turned away from the windows and pinched my arm to help erase the thoughts as the lash fell in my vision and that overtly animated face of hers twisted into an expression of white-hot pain. I didn't want to picture her like that despite my anger for being stood up, and for the remainder of the trip, all I could do was be worried about her well-being.

-5-

I almost missed my stop despite the robotic voice coming through the P.A. speakers alerting me that Winchester, my street, was coming up next. In a hurried rush, I left the transport from the center doors and stood on the sidewalk, watching it go. It would be two days before I would have to ride it again, and I wondered if she would be on it. Shrugging, I moved towards the corner to hang a right past the Common-Oath Bank building and then to the center of the block where my apartment sat, and then I froze; JoJo was there, waiting for me.

She was sitting on the edge of one of the stone, waist-high square potteries housing a thin maple tree that surrounded the bank building's proper with her feet crossed at the ankles. I stood motionless, staring at her as my heart began to race in a maelstrom of joy and anger, the latter of which was losing the fight quickly and getting the crap stomped out of it by pure elation.

She was smoking a cigarette and bopping her head to some music playing through her headphones which had been mended several times with tape, bandages, and a mass that looked like old chewing gum. I blinked twice, realizing that she had changed clothes: the black and gray tartan had been replaced by one of deep purple and black checkers; long thigh-high knitted stockings replaced the black leggings which gave just a peek of skin right below the hem of the pleated skirt. Most adorably, she wore a black and purple hooded shirt in a colorful panda spot pattern, and yes, it had ears.

To me, she was adorably stunning.

I was trying to be coy and quiet in my approach so that maybe I would surprise her, but then the oddest thing happened; suddenly, she paused in mid-head bop, brought that silly panda on the waist chain to one ear as a shocked expression crawled her face and then looked my way. In a blink, she was barreling down on me with a broad expression of glee; if I didn't have my wits, she would have tackled me flat.

"Richard!" she screamed gaily, drawing eyes from the passing herds heading off to unknown destinations, and at the last second, she leaped into my arms. "You are here!"

"Yes!" I laughed, surprised, taking her weight, which wasn't a burden, just a calm wind against my body, and through all those layered clothes, I could feel nothing but womanhood, which felt wonderful. I stood with her legs wrapped around my waist gently swaying her back and forth before realizing I was holding her by the small of her back with one hand and the other cupped firmly under one of her buttocks. Shamefully, I attempted to move the questionable hand only to have her rotate her hip against it suggestively.

"It's ok, Richard, you can hold my butt." She smiled, her eyes darting over mine with our noses almost touching, kissing distance. "You said you like it, right?"

"Yes—yes, I do," I nodded, and I was praying that she could not feel the erection growing in my khakis.

"I was worried you wouldn't make it," she spoke quietly as her fingers played with the collar of my shirt. "I was hoping you wouldn't get lost."

"Lost? But I live near here!" I laughed aloud, shaking my head, and she paused with a pained expression as if I was making fun of her.

"HA! I figured that," she smiled widely, the expression vanishing as if someone had flicked a switch and then kissed me on my forehead; the second time those lips touched me, and the second time I felt my body go numb. She had two steel hoops going through each side of her bottom lip which sparkled above her purple lipstick, and a small black stud through her right nostril; jewelry she had not adorned earlier, but they accentuated her glow so well. Slowly she unhooked her legs and slid down my body until she was looking up at me. "I get silly and confused sometimes. I am so glad to see you."

"You changed your clothes," I said in almost a whisper as my eyes found those deep sparkling ones before me.

"I know! Do you like it?" she bounced in a circle, showing herself off, and with each bounce, I liked it more and more. "I went home to change… I wanted to be pretty for you."

"Yeah, but…" I licked my lips and tried to find some piece of the resentment left for being stood up and found nothing more than a cooling ember dying in the rage spot. "Josephine, I—"

"JoJo!" she interjected quickly, clapping her hands with a bright smile.

"Yes, JoJo…you said you were—"

"Or Josephine! Whichever you like!" she quickly corrected, and I took a deep breath and tried once more without either naming attempt. "But JoJo is still preferred."

"I waited an hour for you," I said flatly as I sighed, and my heart ached as her small hands balled around my shirt. As she pressed her face into my chest, whatever agitation had been was no longer.

"Richard, I am so sorry," she said in almost a whisper, and when she looked up, her eyes were wet. I was confused... so damned confused. "Please don't be angry. I-I wanted to surprise you and to be pretty for you. I wouldn't have made a round trip in enough time, so I came here."

"How did you know I lived here?" I asked unthinkingly.

"Hmm, you are silly too," she smiled, her saddened expression quickly shifting to a gleeful smile as her internal switch threw again. "I see you every morning when you get on the bus right over there."

I followed her finger to the bus stop cattycorner from where we stood and felt stupid. Yes, she was always already on the bus when I got on. I smiled at her for a long time, taking in her beautiful face.

"I look for you every day," she continued. "You always have a V-Eight and a newspaper, but you never read it."

"No, I never do," I smiled, nodding.

"No, you are always watching me!" she beamed up at me, and a long 'E' sound in her throat escaped past her perfect teeth. I know I was blushing terribly; my cheeks were burning with it. She was adorable and animated just for me, her dimples perfect little smiles within the edges of the smile, and briefly, that glee turned into misery. "Two weeks ago, you didn't come for two whole days... I cried."

"Oh, I am sorry, Josephine, I was sick... had to take a couple of days off. I didn't mean to make you cry."

"It's okay; I'm stupid. I cry a lot sometimes," she mumbled as she played with the lanyard to her hood, and then the switch threw her spirit again into a broad happy expression full of gleeful hope. "You all betters?"

"I am perfect, I promise," I chuckled, nodding. I so badly wanted to pick her up and hug her tightly right then. She was too adorable to be out and about in this city, and for all her troubles, whatever they were, I wanted to protect her from them all.

"Oh, I brought us something!" she snapped her fingers, then stooped, allowing her shoulder bag to drop, and then rummaged through it, making *'doobie-doobie-doo'* sounds as she searched. In a minute, she bounced up as if attached to a spring, holding two bottles, one of plum wine and the other vodka. She was glowing with such proud brilliance. "Ta-Da!"

"Josephine!" I whispered sharply, pulling the bottles in close and then stooped to return them to her bag. "You are not supposed to be carrying alcohol; you are not of age yet."

"So what?" She blinked down at me, genuinely perplexed. "I am almost twenty-one."

"Yeah, but what if a cop sees you?" I said harshly, and she flinched away, hurt, and although it hurt my heart speaking to her like that, I was not about to tangle with the law because of her. "To anyone passing by, I look like a grown man messing around with a minor."

"You think I look like a kid?" her voice came dry and monotone as her eyes narrowed on mine.

"No, I don't, but you could pass for a teenager in a heartbeat."

Quietly she bent for her bag, lifted it, then set it on the edge of a planter and rummaged in it. Her lips were racing, but I could not make out what she was saying, and the more she searched, the more she got frustrated.

"…think I look like a child…" her voice grumbled up to me, and I swallowed hard with a wince as the beginning flavor sensations of my foot tantalized my taste buds. "Do I look like a fucking kid?"

"Josephine, please, it's okay," I begged, but she wouldn't hear it.

"Bamboo! Shut the fuck up!" she suddenly screamed towards her hip and smacked the little bear, which spun on its chain to the other side of her hip. I jumped, startled by the suddenness and her physical reaction to hit what annoyed her.

I didn't want to be there any longer, and at the same time, I did not want to leave her like that either; frustrated, confused and now overtly crying. I glanced around and found eyes on us from every place I looked, staring and wondering what all the commotion was and why this young girl was so upset in this grown man's presence. I swallowed hard, not liking their convicting eyes, and as I stood there with the plastic bag in my hand, new fears passed over me.

What if one of these onlookers made their conclusions and called the police? How long before a blue and white pull up to the curb?

'Messin' around with minors, aren't *ya, ya sick fuck?'* I could hear the imaginary burly cop's voice just before slamming the police car door shut in my face. *'They fuck up guys like you in prison!'*

"Here!" her voice ripped me from the brutal vision, and I focused on a driver's license thrust in my face. "Read the date of birth!"

"Jose—" I tried.

"Read it!" she commanded me with a shaking hand, making it difficult to read. I nodded to her quietly, feeling ashamed.

"It says that you are almost twenty-one."

"I am not some dumb kid, Richard!" she spat out and threw her license against me, snatching away her bag and began storming off. I blinked, astounded and without words. "And I really liked you too! Bamboo was wrong about you!"

"Josephine, stop!" I called after her, retrieving the grounded ID, and made several quick steps after her, taking her by her arm and rounding the bank's corner. I pulled her slowly in front of me while her head turned away, and her eyes narrowed down the block.

"Josephine?" I spoke but got no answer. "JoJo, please listen to me."

"What?" she mumbled. Slowly, I pulled down her hood, placed the tips of my fingers gently under her chin, and raised her eyes to mine. There were tears there, genuine hurt tears.

"I am sorry," I spoke quietly and directly, enunciating each word, so she knew I was telling the truth. "I really like you, JoJo; never get that wrong, and the last thing I ever want is for someone to give you trouble, especially me. I did not mean to insult you, I swear."

She studied my eyes for quite some time, judging them intently for any lies that may be lurking there, but found none. She nodded once without a word, and then she rose, taking my cheeks in her small hands, and moved in, slowly cocking her head to one side. I knew this would be a real kiss, which I had fantasized about since the one she had given me earlier. A part of me wanted to fight it despite my urges, but as my nose filled with the scents of her open mouth and vanilla with lilacs on her skin, I pressed in, returning it without regret.

Her tongue was softer than any words I could find then or now to explain, and as I pulled her body against mine, my groin ultimately betrayed me, and I no longer cared. I wanted her to feel it, and everything about me, and the soft moan that trailed up her throat to my open mouth assured me that she had done just that. For an eternal moment, we held and rolled our necks from one side to the next until she pushed away enough so that the tips of our noses touched.

"Wow," she whispered, her eyes slowly blinking and dazed, and I could feel her trembling under my hands.

"Double wow," I responded and slowly took one of her hands and brought us into a step towards my apartment where there were no presumptions or intentions. Her small hand cupped mine perfectly, and with a natural twist and a soft roll, her fingers expanded and intertwined mine, perfectly fitting between mine. I could do nothing but feel the glow of her race through me with each passing step, and at the moment, I did not want anything else.

We paused before the alley to allow a car to move through, and I glanced down at her dancing eyes, which had been watching me for untold time. I smiled, she smiled, the car moved on, and so did we.

Soon she was wrapped around my arm with the side of her face pressed against it as if she was fearful that I would suddenly sprint away. I had no intention of it, but if she needed comfort in the moment, I would not stop her.

She smiled when we arrived at the two-flat brownstone where I lived, and I pointed to the large bay window on the second floor and told her that one was mine.

I fumbled with my keys to open the outer door when I heard her whisper.

"Did you say something?" I asked as I shifted the plastic bag to the other hand.

"Oh, I was telling Bamboo that you are a really good kisser," she giggled behind me.

"Oh, thank you," I chuckled and blushed, dismissing her oddness for yet another time.

"You're welcome," she said, stepping up as I pushed open the door, stepping to the side so she could enter, and she paused just inside it with a wicked smile. "I also told him I think you have a really big cock."

Everything in my world, as well as time itself, stopped cold.

She entered the foyer and waited by the internal door for me, but all I could do was stand there frozen with a numbing twang inside my head. I had heard what she said, although my brain didn't believe it. At least her comment bolstered my ego enough to finally ejected my testicles which had crawled up into my belly earlier that day.

The manhood was back, and he was proud.

Swallowing hard, I moved to the internal door, hand shaking as I fumbled with the lock and missing the keyhole every time. I cursed twice, pressed it through where tumblers fell like marbles and then opened the door for her. She popped up and kissed my cheek, thanking me, and I stood watching as she took the stairs one at a time, her skirt swishing sensually with each step.

"You coming up?" she inquired with raised eyebrows from the landing.

Nodding, I stepped in on rubbery legs and started up after her with my head shaking away the numbness, allowing the door to close behind me without any thought.

PART TWO

Madness Pays a Visit

*

If I knew then what I know now, I would have run away that night from my very own home, leaving this young Goth-girl standing on my landing with her checker patterned skirt, round ass, luscious lips, and dazzling green anime eyes.

Yes, I would have run until my feet couldn't carry me any longer, and although my hindsight is twenty-twenty and 3-D clear, I think even then I was already ensnared in what was to follow, and no matter what I might have done, I was already lost.

God help me now.

As I sit here typing this all out, I have found my face damp with tears and perspiration, and I suppose there is nothing I can do about that. My eyes bleed for my JoJo, whom I can no longer touch or feel her warm body close to mine, and my skin cries, frightened and ashamed of knowing where these pages will take me.

I am haunted to never ride a bus again for fear of seeing her ghost sitting in the back corner seat with her eyes out the window or passing by a perfume aisle just in case a hint of lilac or vanilla should arise. I believe I would lose what little sanity I have left if either were to happen. I would implode where I stood while people gawked and pointed at the grown man who uncontrollably fell into sobbing tears, repeating a name repeatedly until my vocal cords bled.

This is my own hell where the Devil is my heartbeat, torturing me endlessly without mercy or an apology. Each night as I lay in my bed, it whacks inside my body as my eyes gaze fixed on the bar of light coming in from under the door, waiting for me to see the shadows of feet. I will be right there in that situation tonight once these pages are done; wide awake and sweating between the sheets, watching and waiting for it to come, all the while terrified despite having little Bamboo standing guard over me as he had her for so many years. Perhaps that magic was gone now as well because, in the end, it did not save my Josephine—my JoJo—from The Darkness.

Yes, I will finish this story tonight.

-1-

JoJo called me a slow-poke from where she stood outside my front door, the only entry on the second floor, which she playfully knocked on its wood surface twice and called out my name to see if I was home. I could do nothing but laugh. She was adorable in every way, and the thing I had already known about her was that none of it was forced.

"I'm coming," I smiled and snapped my head to clear it.

Yes, I was lagging, but not because the small plastic bag burdened me with water, gum, and cigarettes or because my early thirties were catching up to me. No, my heart needed to slow from watching her perfect heart-shaped bottom gently flexing with each movement under that skirt as she climbed the stairs. I finally knew what it meant to walk on three legs.

"Aww! You have a Calvin and Hobbes doormat!" she softened and kissed the tips of her fingers and gracefully squatted and pressed the detachable kiss to the stamped cartoon figures on the right and the left side of the mat, softly saying each character's names as she delivered the touch to their faces.

"So, you like them, huh?" I smiled, adjusting the key ring in my hand for the right one.

"I love them!" she beamed up to me with a Cheshire smile and then boosted up towards me with cat-claw-like extended fingers. *"RAWR!"*

"You have Hobbes down pat!" I matched her excitement and flinched a bit from my unpredictable minx. She giggled and started nodding enthusiastically, rocking forward and back with a glint in her eye. "What?"

"Nothing!" she spoke so rapidly it sounded as if she had said *'nutting.'* I pushed the door open slowly while holding her with my eyes, and as her little balled-up hands moved up to cover her wicked grin, I knew that it was not 'nutting.'

"You are up to something, aren't you?" I asked with a worried tone, only to get her rapidly shaking head as an answer. Twice I heard the squeal kept at bay in her throat crack through a bit, just a puff of it escaping. Trusting, I entered the apartment ahead of her. "Okay, well, this is me and—"

"RAWR!" she roared, and suddenly I felt her pounce on my back with her legs wrapping around me. I laughed, startled, and had to shift my balance just a bit from the suddenness of it, and all the while, she bit at my neck playfully, making chomping sounds. I fell in love. *"Nom, nom, nom!"*

"Shit, you scared me!" I laughed and twisted around, holding her ankles as leverage, and she loosened just enough so that she could spin around and face me. I stood holding her from under her buttocks while her mouth relentlessly chomped and kissed at my neck and throat, her eyes closed to thin slits with fanlike eyelashes until she reached my chin. I was admiring her with gentle eyes as she slowly drew her hands up to the sides of her mouth, slightly cupped, and then whispered to me;

"I pounced you!" she roared with an adorable tiger's voice.

I couldn't take any more of her cuteness, and I could feel my eyes grow misty in her presence. At that moment, it was my turn to be the kisser which I did slowly and long. She squirmed in my arms and against me with soft squeaks and moans that rose in her throat, and I thought I was going to unload into my undies right then and there.

Slowly, my hand slid along her lower back, feeling her perfect skin until my fingers grazed over a standing welt hot to the touch. Suddenly she arched her back away from my hand with a sharp painful hiss, and I had to use all my strength to catch her from tumbling backward to the floor below.

"Josephine, relax!" I begged her as I lowered her down, and she backed away from me quickly until her bottom met the back of the sofa. She was breathing heavily with a hand behind her, her eyes wide and terrified as they darted about the apartment as if she hadn't a clue where she was. I swallowed roughly, trying to find my voice as my pulse thudded in my ears. "Baby, I am sorry, I didn't—"

"Richard? Is that you up there?" Called a distant voice.

Shit! It was the voice of Mrs. Dawson, my downstairs neighbor and I glanced to find that in all the playing, I had left the door open. I growled with a heavy sigh, moved quickly out into the hallway, and peered over to wave to her.

"Yes, Mrs. Dawson, it's me."

"Is everything alright up there?" she pursued, looking up at me with concerned eyes. "I thought I heard roaring."

Giggles erupted behind me and then stopped.

"Oh, that, yeah," I smiled as I waved it off, producing a chuckle for her to know everything was all right. "That was us upstairs, umm, playing around."

"You have a visitor with you?" the nosy continued prying.

"Yes, yes, Mrs. Dawson," I licked my lips, searching, knowing that my neighbor was nosy enough as it was and giving her any information beyond the basics could lead to further inquests. "My little sister is visiting for the weekend—"

"So, I am your little sister?" JoJo's voice whispered from behind me laced with a giggle, and I felt a small hand squeeze my left buttock. "Kinky."

"—and she was pretending to be a tiger." I finished with the last words escaping my throat with a rising inflection.

"Oh, that's nice, Richard… I never see you with company," the old woman continued as she aired my hermit-like existence to the hallway while admitting unknowingly that she was a nosy old bat.

"Oh yeah, she's a handful!" I laughed, nodding, and then felt another handful of my ass disappearing into another squeezing hand.

She knew what she was doing, and I could picture her wicked smile stretching her face, daring to burst into laughter. I felt a small hand glide between my legs where my erection was returning, and I felt a flexing squeeze, followed by a soft whispering, *Wow!*

"Will she be staying the weekend?" Mrs. Dawson pushed on, and without a rational thought, I answered as small paws kneaded my rear end.

"Yes, she will, Mrs. Dawson," I attempted to sound casual, but I am sure my voice cracked through like a teen hitting puberty. The small hand was exploring from behind, and I was growing, and a sudden fear struck me that Mrs. Dawson could see the whole show. "Sorry for the noise!"

She nodded and returned to her apartment, closing the door behind her. I stood for a moment with my hands on the railing, my head low, and turned back towards JoJo, who was staring at me while she played with her fingers at her lips with an innocent look.

"You are evil," I smiled, but then I felt confused by her begging eyes, which danced with hope.

"I can stay?" she spoke so quietly that it seemed her voice came to me moments after her lips stopped moving. I stood upright, stepped close to her, and gently took her hands into mine. She was trembling again and wouldn't look at me, so I gently used both hands to raise her chin.

"If you'd like to stay with me, you can, JoJo."

"Really?" she squeaked from the back of her throat.

"Really, really," I smiled and kissed her hands in mine. She went from fear to elation in an emotional flow of expressions, rounded the edge of jubilation, and exploded into a gleeful squeal of relief. She bounced up, and rapid-fire kissed my lips and gave me a tight hug, then dashed into the apartment, leaping on the sofa as she sounded a long *Weeee!*

In a blink, she had pulled up her tethered bear and began jabbering the news to it with such celerity that I could barely see her lips move.

Slowly I entered my apartment, sighing, having made yet another rash decision without knowing whether I was following my heart or the thing that dangled between my legs.

<h1 style="text-align:center">-2-</h1>

I flash-chilled the plum wine she brought using a trick I picked up in college using ice, salt, and water, and once I felt the chill was taking well to it, I let it be.

I had been alone with my thoughts as JoJo explored my apartment, and I chuckled as her child-like cries of joy erupted as she jumped up and down on my bed for a minute. Mrs. Dawson downstairs could likely hear it, but I didn't care; to hear a soft female's voice in my place was a welcomed change since I had been single for a long time.

"I am sleeping in the bed with you, right?" she suddenly asked, landing on her knees as she looked up at me with hopeful eyes.

"I was assuming you were going to," I replied as I smiled as I watched her from the door with my back against the jam. *You're damn right!* It had been the words my mind wanted me to say, but I didn't want to sound *that* presumptuous. Although I always tried not to assume too much—in the end, this could have been just a fling for her— I pushed those thoughts away quickly and enjoyed her presence.

"Yay!" she exclaimed and sped from the bed, popping to her toes and kissing me briefly, then moving back into the apartment's heart, clapping her hands rapidly under her chin.

I know I have said it before, but she was just adorable.

"Can I smoke in here?" she asked, sliding on her socked feet from around the corner of the kitchen on my wooden floors.

"Of course, you can," I lied, living in a non-smoking apartment building with a nosy neighbor to boot. Quickly she moved to her bag in the living room and rummaged for her pack, which reminded me of the one I had bought her. I collected it and moved to her with a smile, toting my pack so we could smoke together. She was in the process of tapping out a half-smoked 'short' and was seeking out her lighter when I moved in close next to her.

"Maybe a fresh one would suit you?" I said, lowering the pack to her.

It was that look she gave me that shocked me to the bone, a pure expression of disbelief as her eyes locked onto the box, then rapidly shifted back and forth between it and me. She took it reluctantly and marveled at it as if I had just handed her a priceless artifact. She stood slowly, daintily holding it in her palm, cuddling its rectangle frailty.

A tear landed and burst apart on the cellophane covering, and she looked at me with soft eyes.

"You bought this for me?" she whispered as another tear fell.

"Well, yeah, earlier, no biggie," I blinked, surprised at her reaction. Yes, cigarettes in the city are expensive, especially buying them downtown, but it was not like I had gone jewelry shopping.

"No one has ever given me anything before," she spoke softly and then looked into my hand. "And you got some for yourself… my brand too?"

"Well, thought I would join you," I laughed, and she joined me with it, then squeezed me tight and kissed my neck.

"Thank you so much, baby," she smiled and started packing them with sudden ferocity.

Baby… she just called me: 'Baby.'

She made short work of her pack, slapping the top edge rapidly and firmly against palm heel and then tucked it between her knees and took my pack and did the same. The unexpected actions were warming, if not erotic. Once my box was beaten to her satisfaction, she opened both, removed one cigarette from each, and tucked both filters into the corner of her mouth. She retrieved her lighter and sparked them, and I watched how her cheeks caved as the two heads of the cigarettes glowed to life.

Maybe, just maybe, erotic was not the correct word.

She blew smoke, handed me mine, and then looked about the furniture for an ashtray. I thanked her as I moved quickly to the windows, opened them all, and kicked on the ceiling fan for good measure.

"Where's your ashtray?" she asked, searching.

"Oh, it broke," I lied again as I fumbled with the pull cord to regulate the fan speed. "Grab a saucer from the kitchen… the wine should be done too; glasses are in the same cabinet over the sink."

She snapped her fingers on both hands, ending with pointing her index fingers at me, curling them in, and giving me a double 'thumbs up' gesture before darting into the kitchen.

"I am going to make you a drink I call 'Sweet Fire'!" she called back to me as I moved towards her, dragging on the cigarette lightly as a precaution from earlier that day, giving the white smoking cylinder a nod for the flavor wasn't bad at all. "One ounce of vodka to five ounces of plum wine! You are going to love it!"

"That sounds… interesting," I said as I moved up behind her, placing my hand on her hip, which she instinctively pressed back against my crotch and giggled. She had the two bottles open, two large wine glasses on the table, and a shot glass I stole from Barnaby's Bar & Grill several months before. She poured a shot worth of the vodka into each wine glass, filled the shot again, knocked it back, shivered, and held it up over her shoulder to me. I took it and made it disappear, feeling the rawness of the distilled liquid melting down my throat.

"You are *really* going to love it," she said again, pouring the glasses the remainder with wine, then licked her fingers where some had run. She took her cigarette from the edge of the sink, dragged it heavily, and then returned it to finish her preparations. "It's a sweet-sharp drink which gets you totally zoned out, but not freaking-out-high, ya know?"

I sounded an agreeing noise as I dropped my spent cigarette into the sink, three-quarters done.

"Aww, you waste it like that," she whined and glanced back at me with a playful expression. "That's where Big Tobacco hides all the good stuff! They put it right near the filter."

"I will remember that next time," I smiled, smelling her hair as my hands held her hips.

I glanced down to see the edge of the shirt at her waist and a glimpse of skin. I had to see her injury despite knowing she would fight me. Slowly I began moving up her shirt as I leaned back for a better view, and immediately her body responded in an attempt to spin around to hide it. I was too fast and too strong, and my quick hands gripped tight, too tight, maybe because she squealed slightly.

"No, Josephine, I am going to see," I said firmly, and she attempted to pull away twice more, then finally submitted. I slowly moved the shirt away from her as she covered her eyes with her fists, and I knew she started crying as soon as she heard me whisper, *Jesus Christ!'*

Three long welts were moving up her back, just rounding the rear of her ribcage; each one was the width of my index finger and glowing up at me. Even worse, they looked very fresh.

I lowered her shirt slowly, returning her humility, and then dropped my forehead to the back of her head.

"Josephine? Who did this to you?"

Her tears exploded into sharp sobs, and I turned her around into my chest and held her as she gently struck my chest with her fists as her head rocked back and forth with a continual *No.'*

"Tell me please, and I will see to it that whomever it is pays for it!" I spoke directly but softly, although I wanted to scream it as I felt the rage build up through my midsection.

"It was my fault, Richard…please, don't make me!" she cried, trying to hug and silence me, but I would hear none of it. I took her wrists in my hands and held her, insisting that she speak. "Richard, please just let me hug you!"

"No, Josephine, I need you to tell me what happened. This was not your fault! No one should have hit you, no matter what you did!"

"But I fucked up!" she begged for my reasoning, and none of it I could give her. "Please let me go so I can hold you. It was just a simple punishment! It didn't even hurt that bad, I swear—"

"Punished for what?" I barked at her, startling her, feeling my cool leave me despite how hard I tried to maintain it. I didn't want to add any more fear to her life, but I could not stand idle while someone had been hurting her, my Josephine, my little JoJo.

"For loving you, Richard!" she screamed it so powerfully that I felt it on my face.

My hands relaxed, and she fell into my chest, sobbing. I stood motionless as my eyes locked onto nothing above her head, and my hands slowly held her back as I allowed her to cry. She said the *'L'* word and my name were included in the sentence just as clearly as a July morning. I no longer felt anger or anything for that matter, and for a long while, I don't think I even breathed.

"You love me?" I felt my mouth move and heard the words escape, but I hadn't given my brain the command to do so. I could feel her head nod repeatedly and sternly against my chest, making my toes go numb.

"I have for a very long time, Richard," she sniffed, looking up. "You are my savior, my destiny, my life... Bamboo even thinks so."

I studied her eyes and found nothing but truth despite the oddness of the titles she declared me to have, all the while picturing that little bear hanging down from her hip, giving a thumbs-up gesture with its paw if it could do so.

Her and her bear, I thought to myself, and I shook my head slowly, cracking a thin smile. *My silly little Goth-girl.*

"Your makeup has run everywhere, JoJo," I smiled at her, changing the focus of the conversation, and I wiped away the running tar from whence the makeup ran. I showed her the tips of my fingers, and she burst forth a ballad of giggles and wiped at them too.

"I must look horrid to you right now," she giggled away the last of her tears and sniffed away the painful moment.

"You can never look horrid, JoJo," I smiled, and I meant it; she never could. "You are so beautiful."

"Thank you, baby," she smiled, wiping at her eyes and nose, and once again, I felt that warming numbness run through me as she called me a name I had not heard in a long time addressed to me: *Baby.* "I am a complete mess, though."

"Why don't you go get cleaned up," I smiled at her. "If you'd like, you could take a shower. I have excellent water pressure, and the shower head is one to die for. After your day, you need to relax."

She giggled, blushing, and then kissed me warmly. The affection refreshed my soul with how a cool glass of water bathes the senses on a hot summer day, and I loved it. Quickly, she turned and grabbed the glasses, handing me one, and clinked mine with hers and raised it.

"To my savior," she beamed a smile, and I clanked her glass in return with mine with a nod. We drank, and she was right; it tasted magnificent. "And yes, a shower sounds wonderful! Wait, I don't have any of my makeup! Are you still going to like me without it?"

I laughed at her, almost comically… *Was she serious?*

"Of course, I am going to like you without it. I am attracted to you, not the makeup, JoJo."

"Mmmm!" she bounced on her toes and kissed me again. "You called me JoJo; I love it when you do. Okay, I will take a shower; that sounds great!"

"Alright," I smiled, taking another sip and liking the drink while my mind faded away from the welts on her back. I knew I should have pushed it, maybe just a little more, but the one thing I knew already about this young woman was that she had some instabilities that I did not want to tilt too far. "I will get you a clean towel then."

"Shit!" she whispered sharply over her bag.

"What's wrong?"

"I have no clothes for tomorrow," she mused and twisted her mouth to one side in a pondering look. I stepped close, bringing her glass with me, and I licked my lips which had gone dry from her loving assumptions, to come prepared to stay at least the night with me. "I am so stupid. I get forgetful at times."

"No, it's okay, JoJo; I have plenty of shirts and some sweats or boxers if you'd like to wear my clothes?"

"Like?" she looked up at me and sprung up and planted a kiss on me. "I would love to wear your things, Richard."

I wish I had a camera to capture her look, but then again, looking back now, such a picture would be my albatross to torture me with. She had her hands clasped in front of her mouth, which peeked out on both sides with her dimpled smile, and despite the running mascara and liner, her eyes sparkled with pure adoration.

I handed over her glass, went to my room, and got what I had said: choosing a black T-shirt since she evidentially loved the color and some gray sweats, which were comfortable on me but would probably be drowning on her, but at least she would be comfortable. I stepped back into my narrow hallway and paused to bring them to her. She was halfway inside the bathroom, resting on her haunches and leaning forward towards Bamboo, which she had sat on its bottom on the floor just outside. She was pointing toward him and whispering, quietly giving instructions in a childish voice.

"Listen now, Bamboo, I am going to take a nice shower and get into some of Richard's lovely clothes. I want you to stay right here, okay?"

From what I could see, the bear said nothing in its reply, but she paused, tilting her head just ever so, and leaned in close, gently raising it until ear level.

"I cannot hear you when you mumble, Bamboo," she shook her head at the bear as she gently scolded. "And yes, I know you protect me, but if I take you in there with me, you will get all fluffed, and you hate that."

She listened to the bear again and giggled, then quieted her whisper.

"No, silly bear," she continued, kissing the bear on its snout and returning him to the floor. "You cannot eat Richard if he tries to come in, but he's a gentleman, and I don't think he would do that."

I am not THAT much of a gentleman, I thought to myself and waited, rudely eavesdropping on a conversation that should have me quite concerned. To me, then, this was just her way, and perhaps she confided in the little bear for it could never do her any harm as someone apparently had.

"I am going to shower now," she smiled and turned the bear around so that its back was at the door. "Stand guard, Mr. Panda, and if 'It' comes, you must protect Richard too."

She patted the bear between its ears and disappeared into the bathroom, shutting the door behind her. Slowly, I crept up the hallway with clean clothes in hand and stopped before the little bear whose alternating colored glass-like eyes stared out towards the adjoining living room on guard as promised. It didn't move nor address my presence in any way; it just sat there with its little bear arms out to its sides and a little of her lipstick on its cloth nose.

'If 'It' comes, protect Richard too,' her voice echoed in my mind, and I shivered. She didn't say 'He' or 'She' or 'They'; she said 'It': a sexless something that she feared, a name given to something which normally dripped blood from its claws and teeth.

Regardless of what this 'It' was, she feared it, that was certain.

I squatted down slowly and set the folded sweatpants and T-shirt outside the door, my eyes never leaving the little bear, which didn't seem to care about my presence. There was a whisper somewhere close, quiet and soft without a sensible word spoken, and I slowly leaned towards the bear with abated breath and idiotic belief that maybe—just maybe—it was speaking.

Josephine suddenly broke into song in the shower, singing words to a melody that I didn't know, snapping me out of my ridiculous actions.

I stood, shaking my head, and moved back into the kitchen where the bottles sat and took two shots of vodka straight to the head, lit another cigarette, and grabbed a saucer. Quietly, I moved into the living room, waiting for her to finish her shower while I thought heavily about some things and worried.

-3-

The time that I waited in my black leather recliner passed unrecognized as I sat and thought while smoking cigarettes and drinking another glass of her 'Sweet Fire' concoction. My mind wasn't focused on my watch or the round-faced wall clock above the mantle. All I could think about was Josephine and the multitude of secrets she kept from me. They are her secrets to keep mind you, but as my eyes stayed focused on the little bear holding guard outside the bathroom door down the hall, I wondered if I would ever breach the surface of them.

I could have asked Bamboo. I could go over and collect him up, then present my questions to him directly. I would then move him up to my ear so he could whisper all her darkest secrets if the little bear were so inclined to tell me. Could he tell me who had been beating my little Goth-girl with enough ferocity that standing welts were left on her perfect pale skin? Perhaps the little bear might riddle me an answer to why she was so damned afraid and why my forgiveness for the slightest of things was so unbearably desperate for her to have.

'Is she hurting herself?' I would ask Mr. Panda, who would snicker distantly as the overhead fan whirled on.

Well, of course, she is, Silly-Richard, the little black and white panda-Pooh would answer, shaking its little panda head at me in complete bewilderment.

'Is she half-cocked out of her mind due to some chemical imbalance, and now she's here, in my life, for me to deal with?' I would follow up with only to have the little thing sigh and tell me flatly:

This is your problem now, son… you opened the door to this, so what did you expect? For her not to walk in?

Bamboo would have been right on all accounts; I was being silly, and this was my own doing. I didn't have to bring her home, just like I didn't have to start falling in love with her when she was a nameless young woman on a crowded bus, chewing her fingernails in the back corner seat.

I swallowed hard and focused intently on the bear from across the room on my next question. That was simple enough since her haunting words still echoed in my intoxicated mind,

'What happens if this It comes, Mr. Bear?' I would coyly smile. *'Would you, all full of fluff-n-stuff, protect us?'*

I would have laughed then, mocking the poor little thing, only to see Bamboo grow dark before me as it gazed at me with its glass-like eyes, one red and one green.

I would protect her, Mr. Pompous Pompadour of the Fast-To-Erections Kingdom. You, I'm afraid, will be on your own.

I blinked awake to find Josephine standing before me, her green eyes locked onto me and a thin smile on her face. Her hair was damp, leaving darker spots on the already dark shirt, and it was the first time I saw her without any makeup. I had fallen asleep during my thinking quest only to have been awoken by an angel.

She was just radiant.

"Hey," I said with a soft sigh and sat upright and straight. "Sorry, I dozed off a bit."

"That's okay, baby," she smiled and looked down at herself, setting Bamboo on the coffee table in the center of the room. "Your sweatpants were too big on me, so I decided just to wear the shirt if that's okay?"

"It's perfectly fine, JoJo," I nodded as my eyes scanned her from the toes up, eyeing those beautiful legs that disappeared under my T-shirt mid-thigh. "You look wonderful."

"I do?" she asked with begging eyes, and I nodded. "Thank you so much, Richard… I-I believed you that I didn't need my makeup, but— *Are you sure?*"

I nodded once again and extended my hand towards her. She stepped over slowly and took it as she looked over her shoulder towards the bathroom, then found my eyes again with an ashamed expression.

"I had to put my panties in your sink to soak a bit," she said in a whisper. "They got sticky from earlier."

I cleared my thought and prayed that it didn't squeak when I spoke.

"That's-that's fine, JoJo," I gave it my best and was happy that I sounded convincing as I reached for my wine glass and took a sip. "So, you have nothing on under the shirt, then?"

"No, just me, see?" she replied, as shamelessly as a child she showed me, lifting the shirt above her navel. She caught me; I was in mid-drink again and almost choked on it.

"Yu-yes… beau-beautiful," I nodded, my eyes affixed on the perfect V that covered her womanhood.

I saw alright, and if the Sirens of yore could see what I saw, they would breathe their voices to the heavens until the angels wept. I had all I could stand and set my glass to the end table while pulling her towards me.

"Come here."

She didn't fight me in the slightest way, giving her body to me as I took it, having at times to slow myself from being driven by every past image of my Josephine since the day I first saw her.

She tore at my clothes with sharp groans and grunts as I explored her body, silently trying to avoid touching the welts on her back. The heat from the shower had abated them to small, long rises along her skin, but I knew they still had to hurt, so I took care, but Josephine wouldn't have it. She gripped my hands at her waist and forced me to hold her by them. She wanted them to hurt her, to feel them, yet through my gripping hands, she wanted my presence as if I had the healing power to make them all go away. Maybe I did have such magic in me, for she winced only once, and then she looked into my eyes with such an expression of satisfactory release that the mere sight of them made me want to hold her indefinitely.

I loved her, I knew it, there was no doubt; I could taste it just as I could taste my hot breath as she squirmed in my lap, removing my clothes, and she told me that she loved me repeatedly as she moved. I so badly wanted to return her words then, having felt that so often, but for the moment, I said nothing, fearing that my expression would come out as an unbelievable returning gesture… maybe because I would probably cry once the words left me.

I had that truth inside of me, that was for sure, and I was doing all I could to show her in my actions and tolerating her teeth as they dug against my chest and neck viciously.

I loved every minute of it.

"Wait!" she spat out, her eyes full of concern as she boosted off my lap and dashed towards the front door, snatching up Bamboo. She quickly reached the door, scooted back at an arm's length, took an additional step, and then squatted, rapidly speaking into its ear and then sat it down facing the door. In a dash, she was standing before me again with an odd smile, biting the corner of her lip. "I'm sorry… I didn't want him watching us."

"It's okay," I smiled as I stood, giving tw- shits less about the bear or her sudden pause, and I advanced on her with every vein in my body pulsing blood furiously. She was embarrassed by her recent actions, and it was difficult for her to keep her eyes on mine as they constantly sought something to look at, but I was drawing near.

"Richard," she whispered to me as slow tears began to run down her cheeks. "Do you—?"

"Shhh," I sounded and pressed a finger to her lips while I wiped away the tears with my other hand, locking my eyes onto hers, into them, and probing as deeply as possible. She was shaking, which I still couldn't understand because of her previous displays of passionate aggression, but perhaps she trembled because I was now the aggressor. I rolled my fingers under her chin, pulled her bottom lip down with my thumb, and moved in.

"Yes, Josephine. I do love you."

We kissed for minutes for what it seemed, and when I pulled away, her face was lined with tears, and for once, I did not try to stop them, for these were joyous, and I knew that they would just come regardless. She was panting softly and disorientated, looking up to me at quivering lips and saying three words I will never forget.

"Richard… I'm dripping."

-4-

The nightstand clock told me it was midnight, but it didn't feel like it. I was mentally awake while my body was drained of every ounce of energy, all of which I put into the little angel sleeping on my chest. She was younger and more vital, but I was more experienced and mature, taking my time and conserving my strength to be the man she needed for me to be, the great lover.

I did my best.

I found a new affection for smoking that night with her, and I was on my third as I lay propped up against some pillows at the headboard while in thought. We had been at it for almost two hours while she cried while we made love. It threw me at first, but then I quickly understood that the tears came in her relief at the love, being loved, and being wanted for exactly who she was and not some perpetual idealistic idea of what she should be.

She was crying because I wasn't hurting her as someone else had been, and although her small body did resist me at times, causing her to flinch and call out in pain, those tears had nothing to do with these instances. I found it odd while I was sitting there smoking how when the tables were turned, she rode me and intentionally made our lovemaking hurt her by grinding down when I knew I was already stretching her past her limits. She would grit her teeth and continually moan in pain from deep within, only to call out my name and then relax once the pain threshold was reached. I said nothing of this, nor had I ever in our little time together, for I understood that she wanted to feel the pain and the life that had been so dead in her for so long.

It was in that position that I also noticed the bite scar and the sight of which burned into my memory like a searing hot branding iron.

It was just beneath the cup of her armpit, old, having healed unattended without proper medical care. It was a large bite and was human, an impossible feat for even the best contortionist to perform, so I knew that that was *not* self-inflicted. I said nothing about it, but it almost killed the moment for me, and the only thing that ripped my mind from it was her sudden explosive rocking on me as she rushed into yet another orgasm, her ninth thus far if I was a counting man. I wasn't one… for the most part.

I stroked her long hair as she made little baby snores on my chest, and I softly giggled whenever her hand made little gripping motions on my skin. Twice, she gently whispered *'I love you'* unconsciously, and I felt my chest grow damp each time as silent loving tears ran from her closed eyes. I would return her words of affection each time, whispering them as I gently ran my fingers along the length of her back.

I avoided the welts there, but I explored the edges of older wounds, some of which left permanent crisscrossing lines in her flesh. I knew these, unlike the scars on her wrists, were not self-inflicted. These were the signatures of a belt or a whip that came arcing through the air setting it a fire by muscled arms. Someone had been beating this girl for a long time, and here I was, her protector from something she only called 'It'; that nameless, faceless thing she was so afraid of.

I physically shuddered at the thought of it.

"You think I am crazy, don't you, Richard?" she said softly from my chest, unmoving. I gripped her shoulder for comfort and told her that I did not. "I believe you."

Slowly she sat up, and her eyes seemed so brilliant and clear in the dim light. She took the cigarette from between my fingers and drew heavily on it, holding it, and allowed it to exit on its own as she spoke.

"It's called The Madness, Richard," she began as simply as if she was talking about a walk in the park. "The thing that hurts me... I know you have been wondering, so there you have it."

"Is that what you call him? *The Madness*?"

"No, it's not a *He*, or *She*; it's a *Them*... all in one place," she turned towards the bedroom doorway and then broke into a giggling fit. "Bamboo! Did you watch me and Richard make love?"

In a dash, she was off the bed and across the room, retrieving the little bear which should not have been there. It had been by the front door; I was there when she put it there, and neither of the time we made love from the living to the bedroom had either of us claimed him. Perhaps I dozed off, and she had gone to get him, but no... she just asked the bear if he had been watching us.

"Such a silly little bear," she smiled, jumped on the bed on her knees, and knelt there. I lit two cigarettes and handed her one and then placed the saucer I had been using between us. "Thanks, I was just going to ask you for one."

"Bamboo seems like he's always on guard," I said with a fake smile as my eyes held its glassy ones. As ridiculous as this may sound, that thing frightened me.

"He's my buddy!" she chirped and then nuzzled its nose with her own. "I have had him since I was a little girl."

"So, he's had to protect you for a long time then, huh?"

"Yeah, not at first, though," she smiled as her eyes went dreamingly away. "No, at first, he was just a bear I used to cuddle at night when I was sad."

"Or hurting," I cut in with my mental grenade in hand with the pin pulled, but my hand was still holding the hammer.

"Yeah… that too." Josephine fell quiet as her eyes fell to the sheets,

"I need you to tell me about it, JoJo," I said softly, but you could hear the desperation in my voice.

"Why?" she sniffed, and I saw tears fall from under her bangs. "Can't you just love me now? Do I have to talk about it?"

"I know it hurts you to talk about it, baby, but I need to know what has happened to you."

"Because you love me?" she asked, her face snapping up towards mine with the most desperate begging eyes I had ever seen.

"Yes, because I love you," I nodded and produced a genuine, trusting smile.

"If I tell you, you have to promise me that you won't send me away!" she was crying soundly, and I was afraid for her. "I trusted someone once, and when I told them, they put me in a place without Bamboo! I almost died there!"

"Josephine, breathe for me," I moved towards her kissing her forehead, and wiped away the tears as best I could, but they were never yielding. "I love you and would never send you away; I promise you that."

"Never?" she sniffed with begging eyes, and I shook my head slowly, so she knew I meant business. "If I tell you I can never go back home. I would have betrayed the secrets and will be punished… *badly*."

I decided while she slept that I would never let her go back to whatever home she had, and I explained that to her then. She dove in on me with hugs and kisses, thanking me repeatedly and almost getting both of us burned by the cigarettes.

After what might have been the twentieth time telling me that she loved me, she pulled up Bamboo and hugged him as well.

"This is our new home, Bamboo!" she giggled childlike, and I prayed that all my decisions up until then were correct.

After a moment, she gave me one last look of uncertainty and asked if I was sure.

"One hundred percent sure, JoJo," I smiled, nodding. "This is your and Bamboo's new home."

"Okay… I will tell you now about The Madness," she whispered, holding the bear tightly between her breasts, and quietly began to speak.

I learned then that sometimes knowing is truly not half the battle.

-5-

The Madness came to Josephine when she was five, but at the time, it had a physical form called Mom and Dad. She also had a three-year-old brother who was always getting into her things like little brothers did, but she loved him very much.

Her mom was an alcoholic who smoked whatever powder she could get her hands on and sometimes took on a 'John' when the mortgage was running behind. She would service these men in the same house she and her little brother played in, once giving a blow job to a customer as her little brother played with his *Matchbox* cars on the living room floor less than five feet away.

Dad was also a boozer who did odd jobs around the neighborhood to make ends meet, having been injured on a construction site and bled his disability for every cent he could while blowing it mostly on betting on boxing or the ponies. He was also a beater, whether drunk or sober (the title was always present), and the latter was a rarity. He loved hearing a woman scream; it was his kink, but sometimes her mom was too drunk or stoned to scream, but a five-year-old girl would always scream.

"He used to use a wiffleball bat on me," she spoke slowly as her dazed eyes guided her back to the darkness, a place I asked her to go, and I hated myself with every spoken word. "He would beat my little legs until they glowed red, but then I started kindergarten, so he used a section of garden hose on me so he wouldn't leave standing marks."

"Dear God," I whispered without knowing I had spoken.

"I never saw God around, so I didn't think he cared," she said dryly, shrugging, and then continued. "He would never beat my little brother because he said only the little whores of the world deserved it, and one day I would grow up and be a big whore like my mother."

"Did she try to help you?" I begged for the possibility.

"No," she killed it flatly, eyes narrowing out of reflex at the mere thought of her mother. "She was usually passed out or watching him beat me, sometimes putting in her two cents shouting: *Hey Bill! That right ass-cheek doesn't look so tanned to me!'*

"For someone who called her a 'worthless dumb bitch' all the time, he sure would listen to her then."

The intermission she gave me was welcomed as she stretched across my body to retrieve another cigarette from the nightstand. I could feel the rage swelling inside me, my veins pulsing.

She looked blankly towards the shadows in the room, but I knew she had already traveled back to another horror trapped in time which I would soon learn about.

"When I turned nine is when it really got bad," she whispered and dragged half her cigarette into her lungs.

"Did he ever abuse you, umm—?" I asked, but I didn't want to know.

"Sexually? No, he never did because he couldn't," she gave me the answer I was praying for. "The accident, on the job… there was a chemical spill that burned his thing off. He never did, but it made him bitter because of it, and I was his anger release."

She continued filling my ears with horrible words and painting vivid pictures in my mind for me to envision in crystal clarity. He was a talented abuser who rarely left questioning marks and never broke bones. Still, the actual effect was the fear of insanity, which prevented her from telling a single soul that she was in trouble.

At nine, the garden hose began to bore the son of a bitch, so he moved on to more creative tools. His favorite became the adjusting rod from the old horizontal blinds which hung over the window in her living room. He liked how it felt in his hand and how the air would hiss when you swung it, and most of all, it never broke.

"It was spring break from school when he first laid into me with it," she spoke as long, hot tears streamed down her face. "He discovered it the week before when my little brother, Jacob, pulled it down while playing. I saw in his eyes how much he liked how it felt in his hands when he was trying to put the blinds back up, and he swung it a couple of times in the air, looking at me.

"'Ya see this JoJo? This here is the tool of an ass-whooper!'

"That whole week before the break, he would count everything I did wrong: Spill my juice at supper? *That's ten, JoJo!*

"Forget to cover my mouth when I coughed? *That's now twenty, JoJo!*

"Yelled at my brother for doing something? *Oh, you just doubled up there, little bitch! That brings it to thirty-two, JoJo!*

"That Saturday morning of spring break, he woke me up beating me with that rod, and I could barely walk by that night. Apparently, I had accrued a hundred and twenty, but he threw in twenty more when I tried to reach for it, you know, to stop him?"

I sat there with my eyes in my lap, staring at balled fists. I wanted blood.

The more she spoke, the more I felt the pressure build, and my mind filled with self-repulsed nausea because just hours before, I was throwing her all over the bed with my cock stabbing away into her; this broken young woman who had seen every level of hell and then some and I as a pig just poured my lust into.

I felt sick. I wanted to scream. I wished to pull my teeth out.

"Then my mother got sick," she blew out smoke, extinguishing the cigarette, and asked for another, which I gave her without question. "Like, really sick. It was her liver from drinking straight rye from morning 'til night every day."

She drew heavily, filling her lungs, and she began to speak as she exhaled,

"I was there when he killed her."

"What?" I snapped my head up only to find her nodding.

"The only halfway decent thing she did was mind my little brother, but then she was so sick she barely left the bed. He came home to find that Jacob had gotten into his tools, so he took it out on her. He kicked her in the guts so hard that it ruptured her already swollen liver.

"Docs said that she must have fallen in her condition and landed wrong. They said it wouldn't have taken much to rupture it. They didn't care either way; she was a white-trash-alchy-drug-head who reeked of cock and gin when they brought her into the hospital."

"No one investigated then?" I asked, but I knew the answer.

"No, no one," she shrugged. "He was worried that The People might come to talk to Jacob or me, and he told us we would be so sorry if we ever spoke a word about it. No one ever came, and we never spoke a word."

"When did Bamboo start protecting you?" I whispered, hoping that this tale of terror was nearing its end, and I would find a way to get to the last chapter as quickly as possible.

Those bright green eyes turned cold and dark, that of a shade of kale with no reflection in them. The syrup-like tears hung on her face and dripped ever so slowly as her mouth uttered silent words long before she spoke.

"When he killed Jacob," she finally squeaked the words that hit me like a hammer fall, and my breath caught in my throat, preventing me from speaking a word. Slowly she brought up her knees before her and held the little bear there, looking into its eyes. "Yes, that's when you saved me, but you couldn't save Jacob, could you, Mr. Bear?"

"You-you don't have to talk anymore, Josephine," I said, begging, but she only shrugged.

"I gotta get it out, Richard," she sounded, her voice that of a child. "It's the only way I can be free of it."

I nodded and told her that it was okay when all I wanted to do was scream.

"Jacob had broken one of daddy's tools, but he never punished Jacob for doing things. It was my fault because I wasn't watching him close enough, so he tore my clothes off and started to whip me with the rod.

"He kept yelling at me that I was getting a *'real whuppin'* and that he wasn't gonna stop 'til he was tired and had just woken up from a nap. Jacob had had enough of watching his big sister getting the shit beat out of her, so he took one of daddy's hammers and hit him.

"That's when he killed Jacob," it came as a whisper, and then her face twisted.

"*'Siding with the whores are ya, boy?'* WHAM! WHAM! WHAM! Daddy did with his fists. *'Going to beat the Man back into ya, ya little fucker!'* WHAM! KICK! STOMP!

"And then Jacob… died."

"Di-did yu-you run away?" I was trembling, and I think she could see it.

Slowly she glanced between the bear and me on her knees and leaned in once to listen. Her eyes came back to me and narrowed.

"No, they sent me away… the doctors." She exhaled smoke, unblinking.

"So, a neighbor called the police, then?" I begged.

"Yes, they had to because…" she trailed smoke as her eyes involuntarily dilated. "…I then killed daddy."

Time stopped… the air hung stale and poisonous, and my heart skipped.

"You did what?" I begged, unbelieving.

"I killed him, silly," she smiled at me and giggled. "He took my Jacob, so I killed him for it."

"But you were just a kid," I licked my lips, trying to find the reason. "And he had just killed your little brother! I mean, they didn't try to place you with family? I mean, that was self-defense!"

"I know, Richard, I know," she giggled again and then kissed the bear's nose. "But that's when The Madness came calling, and no one wanted this broken little girl with The Madness calling."

"I don't understand what The Madness is, baby," I pleaded because, at the time, I did not. "What are you talking about?"

"The Madness is *them*, don't you see?" She smiled and gave me an expression that read *'Duh!'* "Plus, it's a mixture of all they have ever done and those they did it with. The Madness always follows me, but you and Bamboo are my protectors now, and you put a lot of your protective fluids into me, so it cannot harm me anymore."

"Josephine, you are starting to scare me a little, baby," I whispered faintly, for she was scaring me a lot.

"Why? It can't get in here now that we have shown each other our love, Richard."

"Huh? Wait… you sound as if it's near?"

"Yeah, silly, Bamboo said it was just outside the front door."

I leaped from the bed, driven by fear and adrenalin, and raced to the front door, my rational mindset aside from the horrors of her story, and I snatched it open.

There was no one there and no 'thing' either, just an empty hallway of shadows and cool air.

I damned myself for being a childish fool who believed too deeply in the campfire stories, like when I was a child who would sit up all night with a flashlight before my face jumping at the noises made by the night bugs.

I swallowed, turned to shut the door, and found Josephine standing in the hallway behind me with the bear between her breasts. She was pointing in my direction, and as I looked about myself, I saw the claw marks on the wood panels; deep, jagged, and all too real.

"See?" she whispered, pulling Bamboo up between her breasts tighter. "Told ya."

Michael Frost

I shut the door, locking all the locks.
I did not sleep the whole night.

PART THREE
Unnatural Selection

-1-

At some point, just as the robins in their nests began to chirp their welcome to the new day and as the sky took on that soft blue hue of the morning, I slept. It was a hard sleep broken with a mixture of pleasant and terrible dreams, and all of them had Josephine in them. Twice I woke with my fist jammed into my mouth to prevent the screams which dared to race out into the darkness, confirming that I was frightened and perhaps teetering on madness; afflicted by the innocence of the little one who slept in the crook of my arm.

I kicked my feet off the bed to clear my thoughts and smoke, a feat seemingly easy to most unless you had a young woman clinging to your every move without even waking.

In the dim light, I stared at the bear sitting in the doorway where JoJo had placed him before we turned in to look over us, his glass-like eyes constantly peering out and on unyielding guard. Seeing his form in the dimness disturbed me because as my eyes attempted to adjust for clarity, I could have sworn I saw the little thing breathing. I was being silly, it was early morning, and my body still chugged along stale 'Sweet-Fire' in my veins. It was simply a toy bear full of old fluff 'n' stuff and about as intimidating as a mouse would be to a gorilla, but to her, it was powerful, and she believed it kept her safe.

Who was I to argue such things?

'When did Bamboo start protecting you?' I heard my own words from earlier that night haunting me.

'When he killed Jacob,' she replied without blinking, and I sat on the edge of the bed thinking. Of course, the bear protected her; she saw her brother in it after her mind had finally snapped that horrible day when she had witnessed her brother's death and wondered what kind

of sounds her sanity made all those years before when it shattered into a billion pieces in her mind.

The sound must have been deafening.

I shuddered as I rested back down, only to feel my little femme-constrictor wrap her tight little body around mine. She felt wonderful and smelled fantastically of a mixture of sex, plum wine, and cigarettes. I kissed the top of her head as her small hand kneaded at my chest, and I told her everything would be all right.

"I know it will, baby," she whispered softly and then turned her eyes up to mine with a smile.

I apologized softly while rubbing her back, insisting that she return to Slumberland because she needed the rest.

"I will," her smile widened and became dimples in the darkness. "After I have you back inside me."

I didn't argue or fight it. She had me.

-2-

The following day I made three essential phone calls: the first to my landlord, the next to my boss, and finally, most importantly, to my lifelong friend, Steven.

These were the most important calls I ever made, and by definition of the statement 'life and death,' it was all too real. Although I never used those words during my conversations, I was not going to take anything but complete compliance as an answer from any of them. These were to be three declarations of JoJo's independence from the dictatorship of the black veil that hung over her soul daily; without them, I knew that this person she called The Madness would surely kill her.

"Yes, Ms. Leavitt, I know this is just a one-bedroom," I spoke calmly into the phone with a cigarette hanging from my mouth. I was down to four remaining in the pack and was already anxious about running out. Social smoker no more; I was hooked. "And no, we are not married—"

I wasn't listening to the tight-wadded bitch. She was a good enough landlord as landlords came, but she, like her widowed sister who lived beneath me, had her nose so far up the ass of people's business you would have sworn she was Pinocchio.

"Look, Ms. Leavitt, if this is going to be a problem, we can discuss terminating my lease then," I was blunt, yes, but worse; I was getting angry. "Two-hundred extra a month? No, that would not be a problem.

"Thank you. It will show on the next check, and I will come by to sign off on that lease showing that my—" I choked for a second…*What do I call her?* "—girlfriend living here as well.

"Thank you." I hung up, whispered bitch twice, cunt once, and peered down the hallway. JoJo was showering off the night of sex and tears while Bamboo stood guard outside the door.

Quickly, I dialed my boss's private cell and waited, knowing he was always up early on the weekends to work on his boat, which he never took to water. He called it his hobby, although I knew after meeting his overbearing wife once, it was his weekend escape where he could dream of a life on the seas without anyone telling him that it was time to clean the gutters or to run to the store for another bottle of extra-dry vermouth.

"Hey John, it's me, Richard," I smiled into the phone, praying he was in good spirits, and then lowered my tone so I could perpetuate the lie which formulated in my mind with each passing moment. "No, there's nothing wrong at the office. I have a bit of an emergency here. No, no, nothing like that; I need to take some of my vacation time starting Monday."

I listened as he talked, his tone coming distantly to know what was up without seeming like he was prying. He deserved the truth—my Un-truth—and I was going to give it to him despite feeling the pre-chills of remorse for lying crawling my skin. We got along great both in and outside the workplace, and I had never lied to him until then.

"My sister is here—" *Shit! Which one?* "—Gloria. Yeah. She had a pretty big fallout with her husband and—No, he didn't hit her or anything; I would be in jail right now if he had."

Does Gloria ever call the office? I asked myself; a little bit too late in the game for me to ensure all the players were present and in their proper positions, but I was committed; I would wing it.

"She really needs me right now… up all night crying. Yeah, I know, gotta look after the baby sisters.

"What? No, I have three weeks' worth of vacation time built up, but I figured I would clear it with you before sending in the official letter.

"Yeah, I know; we have that new office turn up in a week."

Fuck! I thought, feeling the edge of unwanted possibilities creeping in. If he fought me, I would fight back, and if he insisted that this was not the right time, I had only one choice: was I ready to walk away from a job I have had for nine years? I heard JoJo's singing and giggles crawl up the hallway, soft, distant, and full of comfort.

You're goddamn right! I decided. I would quit in a heartbeat.

"No, everything on my side of the table is done and ready for the install engineers, and I could be available at a moment's notice if one needed to reach me." Yes… sort of… most of that was true, but oh well. "Great, John, and thank you, really; you have no idea how relieved I am.

"Yes, I was thinking about letting her get it all out during the weekend and then take her up to our aunts for a few days so she can ride the horses or something to clear her mind.

"No, I will take good care of her. Thank you again and give my regards to your wife."

I hung up, panting and slick with sweat.

Two hurdles down, and now the final piece: Steve.

*

"Where are you going?" Josephine whispered past trembling lips as she stood in the living room damp from her shower in a pair of my boxer shorts and a fresh T from my dresser while holding Bamboo to her chest. She hadn't started crying yet, but I knew the tears were close, and I tried my best to assuage her fears, although I failed miserably.

"Baby, I just have to pick up some things from the store and get some more smokes," I spoke softly as I rubbed her shoulders.

"But I have plenty of them left," she begged with a cracking voice as she pointed to her pack sitting on the kitchenette table. "And we don't need anything."

"I will be gone for only a little bit, baby, I promise," I insisted, kissing her forehead, and as I saw the first long tear run her cheek and then rounded her chin until gravity claimed it, my heart fell with it. She was terrified, and I was leaving her alone with it.

"Please don't go!" her voice was as airy as a dry breeze and very strained as the words rolled up from her toes. I moved in and held her, feeling her body tremble as she death-gripped my shirt. I had to convince her that I would be back.

"Josephine, listen… to… me—" I stressed it, taking her by her hands which intertwined my fingers tightly.

"JoJo!" she expressed, demanding it. She was making small bouncing motions to match the broken moans from her throat as if she had to use the bathroom, but she was dying inside, and I was stabbing the life out of her heart. "When you say 'Josephine,' it means that you are gonna say something serious!"

"JoJo, sorry, no, this is not something serious, baby," I attempted to show her that my leaving was just as carefree as breathing. She wasn't buying any of it.

"Don't leave me, Richard!" she begged, and I swallowed back my promises that I wouldn't go out right then. "I have been alone so long!"

"I am not leaving you, JoJo. I love you too much to leave you. I am just running to the store, and I will make you pancakes when I get back, okay?"

"Really?" she attempted a smile which the sobbing fought to subdue. "What kind?"

"Chocolate chip like my aunt makes them," I promised her as I repeatedly kissed her cheeks. "And I will bring you back a present. I promise."

"But—but what if The Madness comes?" she found one last stake to tether me to, and I froze, wondering that very same thing. I would have to lie.

"Baby, listen to me," I licked my lips, searching for something convincing, and hated myself for it. "No one caused those scratches on the door —"

"They're by *It*!" she cut in desperately.

"—I accidentally made those scratches a few days ago," I closed my eyes briefly to her words and pushed the lie in deep like a jagged syringe full of deception. "My… Our landlady is going to have a fit when she sees them."

"You said 'Our'!" she beamed up at me briefly, having found the right emotional switch and throwing it wide open.

"Yes, I did, baby, 'Our,'" I sighed with a smile, seeing the light coming quickly out of the darkness of the moment. "This is 'Our' place; you, me, and Bamboo's."

"Did you hear him say it again?" she spoke to the bear that had nothing at all to say in return. "Yup! Bamboo heard you!"

"I am sure he did," I smiled and walked her toward the table. Quickly I flipped over a utility bill envelope and wrote down my cell number. "Here, if you get scared, you can call me, but you shouldn't be because Bamboo is here."

"Can I call you a kabillion times?" her voice squeaked like a child, and her eyes were with anticipated hope.

"Of course, if you feel you need to," I nodded, gathering my keys.

She resisted my departure, holding my hand and dragging her feet stubbornly. I opened the door and dismissed the scratches with a wayward hand, a *'Pfft!'* sound towards them.

"Stupid bike."

I wanted to shudder at seeing them, but I fought it well. She ignored what I said as she lunged into my arms and shot her tongue down my throat. I stood there kissing her back until she was good and ready to let it end.

Several minutes later, she smiled into my eyes and nodded.

"So, you are coming back, right?"

"Of course I am, baby," I smiled as I lowered her to the floor. "It won't take long, I promise."

"Okay," she nodded once, nervously.

"I want you to lock all the locks, including the chain," I smiled as my eyes did their best not to look at the scratches on the door, which seemed to call out to me so that they could show themselves off. I ignored their calls by locking my eyes on hers. "I will call you when I am just outside the door, so you will know it is me."

"But you didn't take the phone number with you!" she panicked, and clarity washed over her face in a moment. She bopped herself on the forehead with the palm of her hand and giggled. *"Duh!* It's your home phone number. I get stupid-silly at times."

"No, it's *'Our'* home phone number," I reassured her. I needed to go, which meant I also needed to shut up because everything I said she found romantic, and another long kiss ensued. "Okay, I am going now. You have my number, right?"

"Right!" she beamed, clapping her hands together.

I stood outside the door until I heard every lock close and the chain jingling as it was run along its guide, and the whole time, I avoided looking down at those deep scratches never caused by a bicycle. Once convinced she was soundly inside, I left, passing Mrs. Dawson on the way out, who was standing at her door pretending she was doing something.

"Good morning Mrs. Dawson," I smiled as I pulled out one of my remaining smokes and popped it into my mouth, and the sudden expression of surprise to see me with one made my smile grow even wider.

"Richard… I heard all these ungodly sounds coming from your place last night!" she gasped as her eyes jittered between me and up the stairs. "Moaning and screaming… I was so worried!"

"Oh, nothing to worry about, Mrs. Dawson," I winked at her as I pulled open the door. "Those were the sounds of sex. You should try it!"

I left Mrs. Dawson standing in her doorway on the verge of apoplexy, and I didn't care. Surely she was dashing to the phone to call her sister and tell her all about that sinful man who had a cigarette in his mouth spouting foul language about fornication with his sister, no doubt. Fuck her, and I didn't care; I was alive for once, and it was that little Goth-girl who brought me to the light, and nothing was going to snatch me back.

I had gotten as far as the sidewalk when my phone rang.

It was JoJo. I told her I was right as rain.

-3-

"You know, when you told me what you needed, I thought you were pranking me." Steve sighed as he looked at me, eyes studying. I could lie to my boss and even manage a loving white lie to Josephine, but Steve knew me all too well.

"Did you bring it?" I cleared my throat, keeping my voice down so no other diners in the hole-in-the-wall restaurant could hear us.

I was only three blocks from home. Before meeting Steve, I had already collected what I needed along the way: a carton of smokes, a bag of chocolate chips for the pancakes, a bottle of Merlot to go with our dinner that night, and a little bear I bought only for its Snap-on police uniform which looked like it could fit Bamboo. I would get rid of the little bear though. Hopefully, there was a child I could gift it to on the way home, but I figured JoJo would like to dress-up her panda just a little bit.

"Yeah, I got it," he nodded, sipping at his coffee. "But I am just curious why do you need it? Someone bugging you?"

"There's been a lot of break-ins lately," I attempted my lie, stabbing at the possibility that it would fly.

"Break-ins? Up here? In Poshville?" he laughed, not buying a single word of it. "Brah, do you see the kind of people around here? Money, all of them, including you. What's the average rental up here? Fifteen hundred a month for a tiny box studio? You got the bulk of the city's police force cruisin' these streets, keeping them all safe.

"Break-ins? *Bah!*"

He had me dead to rights.

"Listen, Steve; the fact is that no, I do not feel quite safe now, and yes, someone is after someone whom I care a whole deal about and—"

"A girl?" he asked, surprised with both brows rising.

"No, a boy, smart ass!" I hissed at him and playfully moved to hit him. "Yes, a girl, and she's sorta in trouble with—"

"An ex?" Steve was good at 'helping' a story along.

"You can say that." I nodded, sipping coffee. "He was quite physical with her in the past, and I think he knows where she's living now."

"Where's she living?"

"With me," I said and coughed, and for the second time that day, I was the cause of near-apoplexy in someone. He sat across from me with a slack jaw so wide I could have put my coffee cup in there without grazing the teeth, top or bottom. I nodded and shrugged, hoping that I as a sideshow attraction would quickly lose its notoriety. "What?"

"Nothing!" He raised his hands innocently and began to laugh, clapping them together with applause, which I couldn't find the sincerity out of the sarcasm. "About fucking time, man! Please tell me that you're hitting it!"

"Dude, the piece?" I pressed, having never been a 'kiss-n-tell' person, and I was not about to start by airing what Josephine and I had together now.

"Fine, fine. You gave me my answer anyways," he smiled and shrugged, reaching into his jacket pocket, and then leaned forward towards the table with both hands hidden. "Here… take it."

I looked about the diner to ensure no one was looking and leaned in. He had put the handgun in one of those old, purple *Crown Royal* bags with the yellow-gold drawstrings on top, and through the velvet-like fabric, all I could feel was cold hard steel. I nodded to him when I had a proper hold of it, and we made the exchange, and then I nonchalantly sat up, concealing it in the inside pocket of my jacket.

"No worries, it's clean," Steve spoke quietly, and for the first time that day, he sounded serious. "That's a compact forty-five, A-C-P, with hollows… guaranteed one-shot-stop."

"How much does it hold?" I whispered back, feeling the dead weight of it in my jacket.

"Five in the mag, one in the pipe," he shrugged. "But you don't have to worry about capacity 'cause you will only need one."

"Yeah," I whispered, and we fell silent over our cups. After a long silence, he broke in, "Is she worth it?"

"Absolutely," I responded, and he didn't find a lie in my face that time.

"Good," he smiled, raising his cup, which I returned with my salutation by clicking his edge. "As long as that is settled, let's have a piece of pie."

-4-

I had agreed to have one slice, but then I would have to go. Steve didn't fuss about it even though that had been the first time we had seen each other in months. I allowed myself to describe Josephine in every little detail outside of the bedroom, and the whole while, he stared starry-eyed as I spoke as if I was speaking about the most angelic woman on Earth. Once I finished talking, he let out a long, genuine sigh of awe.

"Well, my good sir," he shuddered playfully as if he had the tingles, and for all I knew, he had them. "A woman like that you are damn tooting you protect her. If that fucker comes around, pop him an extra one in the *culo* for me."

We laughed, and suddenly I felt odd as a heat wave took over me, and my stomach turned. Coffee, just like anything acidic after a night of drinking, is never a good policy, and I began drinking at the glass of ice water the waitress set before us when we first sat down.

"You okay, buddy?" Steve asked, concerned as I wiped at my forehead.

"Oh, yeah, yeah, just suddenly felt hot," I nodded and fanned myself by my shirt collar. "Kind of nauseous."

"All that talk about your hot mamma did it!" he squawked, breaking into a laughing fit with which I attempted to join.

"Yeah, something like that."

My phone began to ring. It was Josephine.

"Hey, baby, what's up?" I started only to hear soft whimpering through the phone.

"Richard!" she whispered sharply. *"Where are you?"*

"I'm chatting with an old friend," I said, standing, wiping at my forehead, and then looking about myself for a vent that might be accidentally blowing hot air. "I will be heading home in just a minute—"

"Did you suddenly get hot?" her words came, and I heard them, but they seemed very far away.

I locked up, my lungs froze, and I could feel the air growing stale.

"Yes, how did—"

"Look around you," she squeaked. "Do you see anything?"

Slowly my eyes moved from side to side in their sockets, scanning, but I saw nothing that I should not be there in the dinner: tables, booths, fattening foods, patrons eating the fattening foods, and waitresses; all normal.

"JoJo, please," I attempted feeling a flare of anger toward her for the first time. I didn't believe in monsters anymore, I was a grown man, but in her eyes and words, they were very real things. It frightened me. "I don't see anyth—!"

"Blur your eyes, baby!" she begged, and I knew she was crying in sheets. "Make everything look fuzzy!

"Do you see it?"

I swallowed hard, believing nothing I heard, but my fear had taken control over rationalization, and I flexed my eyes until everything became a double vision and blurry.

Slowly, I looked about myself, feeling the heat coming down on me heavily while my mind filled with the fuzzy shadows of diners, staff, furniture, and—something moved. It was right there, back by the folding countertop, so the waitresses could get back and forth easily from behind the business side of the diner, it moved. The darkened mass of a hundred horrid faces with a hundred reaching hands it moved, and it was watching me.

Air rushed from my lungs, bringing a startled moan with it, and automatically my eyes returned to focus, and I saw nothing; just a display case of three-day-old cake slices and apple pies.

"The Madness is there, Bamboo told me!" she vomited the words into the phone, and I could hear the sharp panic blazing on top of my thudding pulse. "Do you see it?"

"Yes!" I whispered back to her just as sharply, nodding before I spoke.

"Richard, run!" she screamed, and I did what she said without saying a single word to Steve, whom I left there sitting wide-eyed and blank without a clue in the world.

I ran the whole way back to the apartment without looking back.

PART FOUR

The Madness and Bamboo the Bear

*

There is no way to consider my own madness in these words as I sit and watch the characters appear line after line before me as I type them. I mean, I do see them appear magically with each clicking keystroke, but I am not seeing them either if that makes any sense. All I am observing is the reflection of a horror that left Josephine that night for good, only to become my cross to bear, growing heavier by the day while burning my senses away to such a degree that the collected ash would not fill a thimble, let alone a sliver of the emptiness I have in my life now.

It is well past being late here as I write the final pages of this story, my psychotic narrative which, after completing—entering that last letter of the final word—I wonder if I will truly tumble down that darkened rabbit hole where only madness will find me, or I it.

I am going to smoke another cigarette and drink down a quart's worth of 'Sweet Fire' and then tell the rest of this story…

I am almost done with this.

-1-

I don't remember the race home; that vision is left to any who may have witnessed a grown man running to catch something fleeting or fleeing something in the chase. Honestly, I think I was running for both of them because rationality and reality apparently no longer had a bearing in my life.

I remember Steve's voice following after me as I dashed blindly into traffic outside the diner and Mrs. Dawson calling out concerned as I sharply turned up the walkway of my building just as she was entering a *Lyft*. All the in-between parts of this history are gone from me now; just a blurred, fuzzy haze like a drunken false-memory. I knew my body ached from the punishment I was giving it, and the day-

and-a-half of heavy smoking wasn't helping in the least. Josephine somehow knew I was coming long before I reached my apartment door, which opened before my fist drew back for the first pounding fall.

"Richard!" she screamed with a face twisted with both terror and relief, but I was to have none of it. She thrust forward to embrace me, but my hand was faster, pressing the open palm against her chest, pushing her out of my way. I was wrong for doing it; I know that now as I knew that then, but I was frightened, and fear always drudged up anger within me.

"Richard?"

I ignored her as I moved quickly to the kitchen sink, yanking the cold water to ON, and then bent my face to it. I was not drinking as much as sucking the cool liquid down my throat while twisting my face into its refreshing downpour. I could hear her slowly shut the door behind me, locking it, and then move into the dinette area.

I stood, panting, while waves of nausea washed over me as the sudden chill of the water met the hot adrenalin swirling in my stomach. I didn't want to puke, not then nor at all, because that would show my weakness, and I could not allow it. I had to maintain my wits and anger for the situation; the latter felt good because I felt powerful with it.

Behind me, I could hear her pull out a chair slowly to sit on, and I nodded in agreement with my anger as so many things began to make sense, or at least the idea of sensibility.

"I am not the first one, am I?" I spoke flatly as possible as I wiped my face with a paper towel from the spool over the sink, dotting the edges of my eyes where the sweat found places to sting. I heard no answer, not even a whimper, and the lack of it got me chuckling while, on the inside, I was screaming. "I am not talking about the first lover, JoJo, because I know that I am not... no virgin screws like that—"

"Don't be cruel," she whispered behind me, but I was not done, so I raised a waving hand over my shoulder, wanting her silence.

"I am thinking that I am not the first of your lovers to find themselves in this fucked up predicament that I am in right now, am I?"

Calmly I turned, twisting the towel in my hands as I leaned against the edge of the sink and stared at her. She had her head down towards her lap where both her hands were hidden, but I knew what she was doing; she was stroking that silly bear and wishing the world was right as rain still.

"Are you going to answer me?" I asked, fighting against the mounting anger her silence was fueling. She peeked up at me from under two streamers of hair along her bangs, blinked, and then shook her head rapidly. "No? As in, *no,* I am not the first one, or *no,* you are not going to answer me?"

There was a mumble somewhere from under that bowed head of hair, and I felt my valves blow.

"Speak to me, damn it!" I roared, boosting from the edge of the sink and slammed two fists onto the table, which sent her recoiling into a ball on the chair, her legs retracting upwards in a blink, and her fists shot up to one side of her tucked head; defending against an expected blow with Bamboo clutched in between them. The sobbing rushed out loud and sharp from her small throat as her body shook uncontrollably.

Yes, I felt guilty for doing all of this to her, but I had had enough. I needed some solid answers without being led astray by her cuteness, love, or fears, and above all else, not by Bamboo, which I snatched from her grip, tossing it blindly behind me.

"Am... I... the... first?"

"No!" she bawled against her trembling legs.

"How many have there been, JoJo?" I spoke quickly to retain the upper hand in the confession circle. "How many have you led to this very spot?"

"Please give me back Bamboo, Richard!" she sobbed, reaching out towards me with pleading hands. "I need him!"

"You said I was your protector now," I shrugged, the asshole I was, and then countered. "Isn't that what you told me?"

"Yes, but—"

"Did you ever tell any of 'Them' that too?" I stabbed with it, cutting her deeply, and it showed as her face twisted with horrid disbelief at my accusations.

"No! Bamboo chooses my protector," she begged, reaching, but I wouldn't let her touch me as my hands waved to her to remain seated. "Baby, please, I have only loved you, Richard! I thought they could love me, but they didn't! They just wanted my body! Can't you see that we love each other? Can't you see I need you?"

"Why should I believe anything you say, JoJo?" I parried then thrust deeply, expecting no counter to my words only for her to cry sharply,

"Because you love me too!" she screamed it, silencing me for a moment. I had assumed that that was going to be her answer, but until I heard it, I didn't know what my reaction was going to be, and what I got was calm numbness that sucked the strength from my limbs.

Slowly, I straightened with blank eyes locked onto this frightened pale leaf, trembling in a ball on our chair. I had nothing to say to her to ease her fear; at the time, I did not feel one ounce of guilt for it. I turned to the counter, claimed the carton of cigarettes, and removed a pack. Smartly, I thumped it on the counter, top-down, packing them. I pulled out a cigarette, leaving the top open, and moved back to the table, sliding the pack across its top, followed by the lighter.

"We need to talk," I said flatly using *THOSE* words—the favorite words that all my past ex's when they had reached their end with me; the words which always sent a dreadful, pain-filled spike throughout my body—and for once, I wielded them with the same level of purposefulness.

I felt empowered for once, and it felt wonderful, but only for the moment.

-2-

"Why are you doing this to me, Richard?" she bawled, leaning forward wholly on the edge of the sofa while I sat on the edge of the coffee table, attempting to be strong with every ounce of my being. She knew as soon as I said *THOSE* words while we were in the kitchen where our bond was about to go, and she initially attempted to charge me with begging arms and pleads, but I was strong.

Strong? Fuck that, I was being a prick, and I think I knew that then, but my mind was frustrated, and my body still pulsed with terrified adrenalin of what I saw in the diner. Right then, I couldn't see anything other than my overall goal.

What goal? That of having my life back, that same old day-to-day boring life, stuck in a mundane job that hadn't gone anywhere in nine years, to being nice to the nosy-assed old lady beneath me and having friends like Steve, believing that for me to be single for as long as I had been, that I was perhaps a virgin all over again.

Yes, *that* life! That's what I wanted back, but oh no! Since I followed my curiosities a day before here, I was overwhelmed and overrun in every possible way! Home, common sense, stability, safety, EVERYTHING, gone in a blink!

How does that Dinah Washington song go? '*What a difference a day makes… Just twenty-four little hours…*'? You had better fucking believe it!

"Don't you love me?" I heard her begging from a distance, intruding on my mental strokes of the sledgehammer falls as they pounded in the spikes to hold my logical railroad to keep chugging along.

GRR!

Damn her for those words which punctured deep into my soul like steely knives, slicing up my free will and determination! How dare this young one attempt such futile efforts when I had already walked a dozen country miles before she had given up eating mud pies as a kid? Me, the thirty-four-year-old tech-geek who was looking forward to a weekend of streaming some childhood classics and eating take-out.

Had I not only spoken with the mysterious girl on the bus, my life would have remained simple, but here she was, in my life and my home; sharing my bed while passing fluids back and forth between our bodies without a shred of protection.

Sigh.

What did I get for opening my mouth wanting to know her name? Here I was sitting there in front of this abused, unstable girl who talks to a stuffed animal with a fucking gun tucked into my jacket while smoking yet another cancer stick, listening to her sobbing while occasionally blurring my eyes so to see if I could spot that of what I saw at the diner and feeling myself a damn fool!

That's what I got out of it!

I was a terrified little boy who was too afraid to kick his feet off the edge of the bed at night for fear that claws would reach out and grab hold, leaving me to tremble under the sheets just like this woman before me was until I wet the bed!

A damn fool! A fucking damn fool!

I had…

I had had…Damn it!

I had had enough of being used—

"I have not been using you," she whispered so softly I almost didn't hear her. Quietly she sniffed at the mucus running through her nostrils, glistening on her upper lip; all the while, I tried desperately to blink away my thoughts. "That's what you are thinking about me, isn't it?"

"Yes, I suppose I am," I sighed, uncomfortable with myself, for that had been yet another time in my life when someone else spoke the obvious statement I should have been saying myself.

"You are breaking up with me?" she begged, and with each crack of her squeaking voice, I wanted to take her up and hold her, to scream that I loved her and that that had all been just a horrible mean joke, but all I did was nod.

She pinched the agonizing moan back with vise-like invisible lips, pinching them so tightly that I couldn't see their pink edges as she looked away. She began nodding to herself with running-river eyes, but she said nothing.

Quietly I glanced at my watch and then straightened.

"I cannot do this anymore, Josephine," I whispered, hurting inside. "Whoever is after you is probably after me now too… I can't deal with this."

"It's not a *'who'*!" she whispered sharply, her eyes flexing and narrowing on me with utter disbelief. "You saw it! I know you saw it!"

"I saw nervous panic created by you, JoJo, that's all," I replied with false logic and attempted to stand my ground, but then my eyes exploded with stars as a small open hand blasted against my cheek. I caught the offending wrist and squeezed tightly in a startled reflex action, but she did not flinch against my grip. She merely narrowed her eyes tight as her head shook back and forth.

"You lied to me!" she growled.

"JoJo, what the fuck do you think you are—?"

"You said you didn't think I was crazy!" she bawled as I took up her free hand just in case she wanted my other cheek. "You are no better than the others!"

"JoJo, stop it!" I growled back as quietly as I could so as to control the situation, which was spiraling downward. I jerked her once with her wrists angrily, feeling the small joints pop, but she didn't care. "You have no right to—!"

"Fuck you, Richard!" she screamed, yanking against my grip. "I shouldn't have listened to Bamboo! I can see it in your eyes! You want to beat me, too, don't you? You want to whip me and make me beg for your forgiveness? Go ahead, take off your belt, and beat the living shit out of me then!"

"What the fuck are you talking about?" I whispered sharply with my nose within touching distance of hers, my mind a blown mess towards understanding the switch-flip, which seemed without restraint in her mind.

"Everything was fine until you got a little spooked!" she condemned me with pure rage in her eyes as she fought against my grip. "It's ok to fuck the crazy girl but not believe her, right?"

"Stop it, JoJo!"

"Pound her little guts all night, then kick her out the next day, huh?" she continued, and before I could utter another word, she spat, catching me open-face with it. I shoved her away onto the couch and made my retreat, enraged and disgusted, but more so because I wanted to hit a woman for the first time in my life.

"Fuck this, JoJo; you need to leave now!" I shouted as I backed towards the front door with her saliva on my face.

I couldn't think; my anger and preservation-driven fear from earlier at the diner had returned. I didn't know what was happening; the situation had gone beyond the realms of sanity, and I started to feel very warm. I thumbed the deadbolt and twisted, jerked the chain off its runner, and then spun the safety latch, snatching the door open as my final action. Clarity appeared before her eyes, which grew wide with complete and horrible understanding: I was putting her out.

"I will die out there," she whispered, the trembling returning. "You promised you would not send me away."

"JoJo, you have to go; sorry," I shook my head to confirm my words then I winced, feeling the waves of heat roll over me.

Her eyes grew wide, and as if her head was connected to a ball joint, she slowly turned back towards the bear, which had landed face down with a little tail rump up on the counter. After a brief moment, her face turned back towards mine as white as a sheet.

"Richard, please close the door," she whispered, taking several steps back, her body shrinking as she slowly crouched with each backpedal.

"No more talk, JoJo, it's over!" I demanded with an airy breath as sweat balls formed on my forehead.

"Richard! Shut the fucking door!" she screeched it, stabbing my eardrums with her voice, but I shook my head like a fool.

"No… out… now, Josephine!"

"Richard!" she squeaked, pushing underneath the kitchenette table, her little index finger pointing. *"It's The Madness!"*

"Huh—?" I sounded as I wiped at my forehead and directed my attention outside the apartment, just past the door jam. There it was, bearing down on me with its translucent oily shimmer of a hundred faces, twisting, biting, and contorting ghoulishly with a hundred reaching hands amongst a form I could not outline, but it was there, advancing.

I remember having enough time to thrust my hand inside my jacket for the gun only to find it still wrapped inside the *Crown Royal* bag, and then the sudden acknowledgment that this thing was now on top of me, blazing my veins with scorching fire. I felt teeth accompanied by searing pain, and then I was flying backward into my apartment, briefly admiring how lovely my molding looked along the ceiling and that I should dust up there someday.

Darkness flowed in as I heard my little JoJo screaming, and just as the unconsciousness took me, I could have sworn I heard the roars of a bear.

-3-

My eyes slowly focused back into the realms of consciousness, and I lunged upwards in a panic only to have my thudding head snatch me back down again. I fluttered my eyes rapidly, blinking them into clear understanding that I was lying on my back on the bed, and based on the use of lamps, night had come. I began to breathe heavily; my mind stirred and mixed like thick gumbo with heavy andouille sausages and about as clear as mud.

"Josephine?" I whispered into the room and got no answer. The room was quiet, just as the apartment was, without even the slightest sound stirring other than my rising pulse.

I attempted to sit up, feeling the raw grinding of my chewed chest flesh which my hand shot to as a sharp hiss escaped my throat. There was a bloody square bandage just off-center to the left above the main pump, and I could make out the faint pattern of a horrendous bite wound in the dim light.

Every nerve ending screamed at me as I leaned to my side and dared to push my feet off the edge. I called her name several times and got the same answer: nothing. I winced at the pain screaming in my head and chest and then shook away the wave of pain-filled tears that dared to fall. I managed to corral them at the socket's edge and then blinked the gloss out of my eyes.

I was alone in the apartment; there was no doubt about it, or was I?

On the floor just inside the door sat bamboo, his little stubby arms facing outward in a continual hug, his alternating colored, glass-like eyes staring forward and always on alert. I blinked heavily as I studied him in the soft light and noticed he was slightly different. Josephine had found the little police bear I had bought earlier and stripped it only to dress up Bamboo as I had hoped she would.

"Josephine!" I called out loud enough that she would have heard me if she had been downstairs jawing it up with Mrs. Dawson, but still, no reply came. I reached over to the lamp and tapped its base twice, increasing the intensity with its nifty buttonless, built-in feature. The new brightness stung at my eyes, but I needed to see everything and what I saw was a folded note waiting for me just under a pack of cigarettes. My heart skipped because I didn't want to read it; any note left after an argument was never good.

Slowly I took up the pack, removed a cigarette, lit it, and waited, my eyes never leaving the note, which read my name in large letters on its backside. I swallowed hard and opened it, and began to read:

My loving Richard,

Before you read another word, I want you to know that I love you above all else... more so than Bamboo, as well as my own life. You are a wonderful man and do not deserve what I have brought to you, but you have given me the one thing I have never known: true love and bravery. You may not think this as you read on, but you have.

I softened from earlier and found my hands intertwined between my knees, ashamed of my thoughts and anger as I sat watching you rest. I didn't know what to do or think, so I listened. I listened to your heart beating inside your wonderful chest and felt warmth there, hoping to find just one flame of anger towards me, but I found none.

Do I truly love you? That's a silly question... one that a silly girl like me might ask but let me tell you that I do love you. I knew this for a very long time since you used to watch me on the bus. Whenever we went under an overpass, I could clearly see your reflection off the glass. You never once looked at me as a piece of meat or that I was a freak because of how I dressed. You would smile a lot when I did something cute, which I would try to do so that you could watch me, which also made me feel good about myself.

I know none of this makes any real sense, but what <u>does</u> make sense is that I must leave you tonight, and I will not be returning.

That hurt me writing that as bad as it hurts you reading it but let me explain. I know why you were going to send me away. I was mean to you, hit you, cursed you, fouled you with my spit, and even worse, I never truly explained The Madness. Here it goes, my love, and I hope you understand what I am telling you because understanding me is really the only strength I have left...

The Madness is <u>ME</u>, my father, my mother, the neglect, the abuse, the pain, the blood, the tears, <u>EVERYTHING</u>! I absorbed it all over those years and made it mine to torture me for all the wrongs ever done. I could not, and would never escape it until I met you, and you gave me the power to kill it, to rid everything of it. I couldn't save my little brother, but you have saved me from me.

Does this make sense?

I have to go soon, and my hand is already hurting from writing. You are probably wondering how little Me got big You into bed. Well, as I told you, Bamboo protects us, and he hurt The Madness when it hurt you. You should have seen it! I am talking, HE HURT IT BAD!!!! LOL! Bamboo was quite upset when you wouldn't wake up, but I assured him that you would sleep a little while and be back up in no time. He didn't want you on that hard floor, so he put you in bed, and that's when I mended you.

I so love you.

I am going now, my baby-my love-my Richard, and I am taking your gun with me. I know you brought it to kill The Madness, but that is not how you can kill it, and if I told you how you could, you wouldn't have done it. I tried to kill it twice before, but the pain of slicing my wrists again was too much to bear, so here I have the best option, you know?

This way, it will be painless.

I am not going to do anything close to our home, so no worries. I know where The Madness enters our world, and that's back where I used to live, so I am going to go there and wait for it, and just as it is about to take me, I will take us both.

You have probably noticed I left Bamboo with you, and I LOVE the outfit you got for him!! That was SOOOOO cute of you!! He's a 'Police-Protector-Panda' now and says he loves it.

Ask him! He will tell you!

I told Bamboo to watch over you always, and although he was quite sad about my decision, he understands now (although I think now he has always known). He will be there whenever you are unhappy, Richard, and more so, he will be there if I fail tonight.

Do NOT go anywhere without him, Richard, that is key; NEVER FORGET HIM ANYWHERE!!!!

Please do this for me. I will love you for always, my love,

Yours always,

JoJo

** **

I have been watching the cursor blink repeatedly at the beginning of this sentence for almost an hour now as I drip tears on the handwritten note she had left me more than a year ago.

No, I never heard from her again, but I do have a pretty good idea that she died that night at the end of the handgun I had gotten with the intent to protect her. Two days following that day, they found the body of a young local college student in an abandoned house in the far Westside of the city. Police think there was foul play involved because she appeared to have been severely beaten, although she did die from an apparent self-inflicted gunshot wound to the chest.

Like all news stories involving unimportant people in this world, that story was a small blurb hidden deep within the newspaper print amongst an article about the growing health conditions of family pets and a buy-one-get-one-free cutout coupon for insulated windows. Police were still investigating, and after that one blurb in the paper, her death was never mentioned again.

There wasn't even a small picture so I could be sure.

A year is gone now, and my life went with it, leaving me with the shadows of our time together, damp and growing cobwebs in my mind because I refuse to think of the sinister events outside of me writing this.

I have kept one solitary promise to my Josephine—my JoJo—and that Bamboo goes wherever I go without fail. As I write this, he is sitting on guard in front of my home office door in the little lounge chair I bought for him from a hobby shop intended for dollhouse use.

I know he likes it… he whispers it to me sometimes.

I will end this in a minute, and he and I will venture into the bedroom, where he will go on guard once again; just inside the closed bedroom door in his little chair. I will lie down to rest these haunting dreams away while my eyes grow tired as I watch the thin slit of light coming in from under the door. It is just a narrow strip and never bothers me when I sleep, but it is there with a purpose: it will show me the shadows of The Madness swarming if she did fail that night.

Yes, it's getting later (or earlier, depending on how you look at it), and it is getting warmer in here even though the windows are up and the screens are down. This has been happening a lot lately. These heat flare frequencies have increasing by the day, but I am not going to worry; I have Bamboo here to protect me as it had that night… the same night I failed to protect my little Josephine, my Goth-girl, my love.

That is my one true worry, however, that one night, he might remember that I failed her, and he might 'accidentally' fall asleep while on duty and let The Madness have me. I don't know, I kind of like that idea sometimes because then my own madness would be over with, but in the end, no, he wouldn't do that… something tells me there's a lot of my Josephine in that little bear as well.

I sometimes hear her whispering in there too.

Goodnight.

— Richard M. Shelton

DENOUEMENT

Denouement

a Malice From this

To know him is to know me…
So often is the ruse so easily distracted,
torn away from the ideals from which they all began:
The steadfast dream of a child to weave the words
which He, She or I amongst the masses wander aimlessly to
understand.

I beg to ask at times is it all lost,
carried asunder by winds of ill-virtue and timing;
pursued continuously by the demanding of the saints and souls
where even he—the one who writes—can no longer see the
dream?

To speak of this; as I do now,
cryptic and misleading for those who attempt to understand,
Do I really speak so uncaring to the reader?
Should I tell the *'All'* as my mortal horn keeps blowing?

How many close calls must one have?
How many ill fates must ride the winds and travel to the throat
—clawing away at it in attempts to get in—
only to be deflected by some unknown will and want?

Am I to accept fame and fortune,
or fail and falter like so many broken dreams;

murdered or sacrificed so that the masses can feel equal?
Shall I be just a burdensome claw in the side of society?

Are these my real questions to answers I will never know...
Is this just my own trepidation to what comes next?
That glorified reasoning that perhaps I have come full circle,
to that place where I should begin again?

Most importantly, will this riddle of my own enigma ever be
understood?
Should it stand the test of time for others, and if so—
can it, should it, could it, would it ever explain the Me behind it
all?
The real enigma in my name, as well as the title to this piece
entirely?

a Malice From thIs...

Don't you see? Can you not read? Is it not clear?
Does it not speak in volumes what the ultimate riddle tells?
Can you not read the words before your very eyes?

Read once more,
that I beg of you,
read it carefully for you then might see,
my anagram listed before you as it is written before all-seeing!

a Malice From thIs..

Riddled once,
twisted twice,
it reads exactly as it should:

I am Michael Frost, and I am a riddle no longer.

A Word from Michael Frost

Well, there you all have it…

A collection of some of my short stories that have spanned the years, and I thank you all for taking the time, albeit that tea nor cake was served along journey. I do appreciate it, I sincerely do, and even though not all the tales above were that of ghost and goblins, they were dark ones, nonetheless. I hope you enjoyed the quirky ones as well.

In the end, I pray that this collection finds you well, and of course, instills in you a pause.

Yes, just a short pause. Just as the adrenaline spikes and the hairs stand up on your body moments before you open the cellar door, or peek under the bed to find that missing shoe.

Why?

Oh, for no reason at all, but are you sure—*absolutely sure*—that as you reach in or under, feeling about in those shadows, that there is not something there also reaching out for you?

Consider the possibilities and choose wisely.

You have my heart,

Michael Frost

About the Author

Michael Frost is an American author, engineer, math and science nut, who lives with his wife and a growing collection of green things thriving both inside and outside his home.

He is a proud father of three grown daughters, and the loved Papa to their playful grand-pittie, Moana.

Oh! He's VERY fond of cheesecake, like on a whol'nuther level of fondness, just a FYI if you have some handy.

(Flavor of which notwithstanding).

Also, by the Author

Available everywhere in eBook, Paperback, and Hardcover

www.belenbookspublishing.com